A BRIGHT PARTICULAR STAR

A BRIGHT PARTICULAR STAR

From India, a story of love, passion and betrayal

By Dr. Sarala Barnabas, The American Biographical Institute's Woman of the Year for 2002.

Writers Club Press
San Jose New York Lincoln Shanghai

A Bright Particular Star
From India, a story of love, passion and betrayal

Writers Club Press
an imprint of iUniverse, Inc.

For information address:
iUniverse, Inc.
5220 S. 16th St., Suite 200
Lincoln, NE 68512
www.iuniverse.com

Any resemblance to actual people and events is purely coincidental.
This is a work of fiction.

ISBN: 0-595-23921-8

Printed in the United States of America

It were all one
That I should love a particular bright star
And think to wed it, he is so above me.

All's Well That Ends Well
I. i. (97)

Dedicated to

the 'little people'

JOSHUA and CYRUS RAO

Author's Note

Bombay-born, I am the product of three universities-Bombay, Yale and Pune, with a Ph.D. in American Literature. I have loved college teaching, but nothing has brought me more pleasure and satisfaction than creative writing. I have always loved to tell stories. My children, Nandita and Tarun, refused to eat supper unless I told them tales. I started out with a novel about a family, the Khans, and then when readers asked what happened next, I wrote a sequel. The saga ends with THE RAINBOW AND THE COVENANT, just published by Minerva Press (London, Miami, Sydney, New Delhi).

My next venture was to begin a series of novels, each focusing on a woman character. To my delight, Professor Lal, the Director of the famed Writers Workshop, Calcutta, himself a scholar-poet, published three of my novels in a single year-SAKSHI, NAYANTARA and ANJOLIE. Subsequently, WW brought out INCIDENT AT WAVERLEY. I have found women readers in particular, identifying with the central characters in these stories. Since some novels have been translated, readers unable to read the original English version, have reacted in the same way. I happen to be a hopeless romantic at heart, and it shows in my writing!

A PARTICULAR BRIGHT STAR has found a special niche with readers. Some of the personae reappear in DREAM SEQUENCE. In fact, Cyrus Samartha has been so well liked, that I wrote SONG OF INNOCENCE where he is the protagonist. One more novel about the same family, A BRIEF MADNESS, is nearing completion. The threads of NAYANTARA were picked up in DARK PASSION, stories about two princesses who rebel against tradition.

I hope readers will enjoy A PARTICULAR BRIGHT STAR. Certainly, I derived immense pleasure in writing it.

My grateful thanks as always to my husband, the Reverend Professor Joseph Barnabas, whose encouragement and positive vision have always sustained my writing; to Benjamin Rao for his tireless efforts.

Sarala Barnabas

PART I

Know how sublime a thing it is
To suffer and be strong.

—Henry Wadsworth Longfellow
The Light of the Stars

SAKSHI

Where and how does one begin a story, I wonder. With what breathless anticipation did I read the opening lines of the much-beloved stories of my childhood. 'Once upon a time', they would say, or 'Long, long ago and far, far away'. I can see myself now, a small green-eyed sprite with a mop of dark red curls, sitting tucked away in the window of my little room, lost in delight as the tales unfolded of princes and princesses, fire-breathing dragons and wicked stepmothers. But this is not a fairy story at all, nor did it take place long, long ago, or far, far away. It is my story, and it happened here and now. Nor am I a princess, not even born to riches. Wicked stepmothers, dragons? None. And the prince? Well, a kind of prince. At least they call him that. Still, a story must begin somewhere. Perhaps it is best to start mine with my dearest Mumsie and Daddy.

CHAPTER 1

My father's name was Adrian Jerome. He came from a long line of men who had served with pride in the Army. From his forebears who had served their country with such distinction had come, among many other sterling qualities, an inherent love of horses. Such an affinity sprang up between him and any horse he came into contact with that they seemed actually to communicate with each other. As he stroked and patted them, spoke softly, apparently they listened and understood, ears flicking, liquid eyes fixed on him intelligently. It was almost uncanny, the rapport he shared with them. It was a family joke that when he was very young, Adrian had declared when he grew up, he was going to be a horse. What he did grow up into was a Cavalry officer.

How can I do justice to Daddy, describe him as he was? He was very tall, easily six feet two, with a physique to match his height, a deep rich voice. Extremely fair-skinned, he had a golden tan, the result of being outdoors so much. He was a man of his word who never compromised on his principles, and utterly trustworthy. His courteous manners were beautiful to watch, as was his gentleness with children and animals. Children came running to him, to perch on his knee, or sit on his lap. Dogs came bounding out to welcome him, put their paws on his shoulders if they were big enough, tails wagging furiously. He loved to laugh, had a rare sense of humor, and loved nothing so much as to spin yarns to listen to which an appreciative audience gathered in no time.

Young Adrian had been an only child, brought up single-handedly by his officer father. He had lost his mother early—and thereby stands a tale. Visiting an ailing friend at the Scottish Presbyterian Hospital in Bombay, young Major Dominic Jerome's attention was arrested by an intriguing figure. A European, she wore the starched white uniform and distinctive cap of a Sister. When she came into that particular ward later, Dominic noted she had green eyes and auburn hair. With the courtesy that was second nature to him, he stood up when she passed. At which point, his friend asked her a question, which perforce she halted to answer. Dominic had some questions of his own which she answered and went away. It did not take him long to discover her name was Fiona Cameron, that she had come from Scotland to learn about tropical diseases and their treatment, that she was here for one year. It is not known whether Dominic's friend wondered at the devotion with which the Major visited him.And if it so happened that a certain young lady passed through the ward at visiting time, it went unremarked, for she was there in the line of duty.

Dominic was enchanted by this pretty Highland lass who spoke with a delightful Scots burr. So did the handsome Major, so dashing in his uniform, charm Fiona. Inevitably, they fell in love. It was no easy matter for Fiona. All kinds of problems loomed large. Apart from the differences in race and nationality, startling enough in themselves, there was the troubling question of religious backgrounds. Dominic was a staunch Roman Catholic, while Fiona came from a long line of stern Calvinist forefathers who surely would turn over in their graves at the thought of her marrying a man they would call a Papist. It was, however, from the living that the greatest dissension came. Fiona was summoned, reprimanded, threatened, and when all failed to change her mind, there came pleading and coaxing.

They were married—and should have lived happily ever after. It did not work out that way. All Dominic's love and devotion could not compensate for the homesickness and ennui Fiona felt. Cut away from her family, which had virtually disowned her, she could never reconcile herself to moving from one military center to the next every three years. She found nothing in common with the other officers' wives, or with the life-style she was forced to adopt. Not even the birth of a son compensated for all she had lost. Had Dominic not been a soldier, perhaps the situation might have been different. A more settled life in a place more to her liking, perhaps where there were some Europeans with whom she could have made friends, might have helped her to accept a lifetime in India. Adrian was two years old when Fiona left him in the care of a friendly officer's wife while Dominic was away on an Exercise. In her note she said she was more sorry than she could express, but she could not take it any more. She was returning to Scotland. She begged Dominic to forgive her.

Dominic went through the full gamut of emotions. Stunned dis-belief, self-castigation for not realizing what Fiona was going through, and finally, anger coupled with bitterness. The immediate reality was Adrian. For a few years, the boy lived with his father's sis-ter. When he reached school age, his father put him in the best boarding school he could find. For father and son, the happiest times were when the boy came home for vacations. There was a special bond between them, which both cherished.

It was inevitable that Adrian would join the Army. That was the Jerome tradition, and he never contemplated doing anything differ-ent. Of his mother they had had no word in all these years. He had no memory of her at all; therefore the question of missing her did not arise. He accepted the fact that his father frequently pored over an old album of photographs, and that at such times, one did not disturb him. In Dominic's wallet was a photograph in color, a most precious possession. I have both album and photograph with me.

At a New Year's dance, Adrian met Rebekah Anton, daughter of a fellow officer. Pretty, petite, Rebekah's elfin charm was instantly appealing to Adrian. Interestingly, the Antons had a Dutch ancestor, last name unknown, referred to as Mynheer. The marriage of Rebekah and Adrian was one of the happiest alliances. Deeply in love, they shared the warmest, most caring relationship. The arrival of a daughter put the final seal on their happiness. Dominic lived long enough to know this small granddaughter who had gold-flecked green eyes and hair shot full of russet highlights. It was said he wept at the sight. He died in a freak accident when I was four. Attempting to repair a faulty electric connection, he failed to turn off the current while working, and received a fatal shock. He left behind an inconsolable son.

Daddy dreamt that some day when he left the Army, he would train horses, perhaps even own one of his own. It was a dream he was to realize, but at great personal cost.

Taking early retirement, he bought a small piece of land outside Pune, where he built an unpretentious but comfortable house. It did not take him long to find the kind of job he was looking for. The Dubash Stud Farm, situated not far from our home, was a highly reputed one. For one year, Sohrab Dubash observed Adrian keenly, and then put him in charge of training his prize stallion, Black Knight. Daddy was in his element. He spent even his off-duty hours at the Farm. Black Knight won the racing event of the year, thus vindicating all his trainer's efforts.

CHAPTER 2

I had a wonderful childhood. We made a happy trio. If Daddy had had a special bond with his father, he had another with his daughter. Between us was an unspoken understanding that Mumsie whom we both loved dearly needed our protective care. Never very strong, her health had suffered after she gave birth to a stillborn baby boy.

When I look back, the most blissful times were those when on weekends, I went with Daddy to the Farm. With Aftab Dubash, three years my senior, I had a merry time. Together we went riding to our hearts' content. Most exciting were the races we attended at the Poona Race Course, watching with heart in mouth if a Dubash horse was in the fray. I loved the color, noise, and throngs of people.

To me, Aunt Gulnar and Uncle Sohrab were kindness itself. Uncle Sohrab predicted that I was destined to be one of those rare creatures, a woman jockey. I would have liked nothing better!

Unfortunately, around the age of twelve, I began to shoot up at an alarming speed. I suppose, with my bloodlines, it was inevitable I would be tall. Mumsie watched apprehensively as my ever-increasing coltish legs forced her to keep lowering the hems on all my skirts. Her main worry was that if I grew too tall, I would never find a husband. Daddy found this terribly amusing, and said I would have to resign myself to towering over my future husband. Luckily for Mumsie's peace of mind, at five feet eight inches, I stopped growing. Gone were my dreams of becoming a jockey. But by now my talent for drawing and painting had been recognized by my teachers at school. I enjoyed doing quick pencil sketches of schoolmates, which they carried home to display with pride. I loved best to draw horses, and filled my sketchbook with likenesses of every horse on the Farm. I still have some of my early watercolors, amateurish of course, but which I now see captured the motion, tension and color of horses running at top speed.

We were hardly rich, but my parents always wanted me to have the best. Thus was I able to learn to play the piano, for which training was offered at school. I had always loved music, and enjoyed my lessons immensely. I acquired sufficient prowess to pass several grades of the Trinity College, London, examinations. If that achievement made my loved ones proud of me, then the prizes I won for painting were responsible for the decision to send me to the J.J. School of Arts in Bombay. It was a wrench to leave home, but I had the compensation of being able to go home twice a month, coming back refreshed. One day, I had to say goodbye to Aftab Dubash who was off to the U.K. to train as an architect. It is always sad when the close-knit circle of childhood breaks up. Nevertheless, I was very happy at J.J. Bombay too had its own charm. There was my jolly group of friends and classmates. One might well ask if there was anyone special in my life. The answer is that although I went out with the group for all kinds of pleasurable activities, I steered clear of any one really close relationship. I wasn't ready for one, I was having too good a time in my unencumbered state, and, most important, so far I hadn't met anyone to whom I felt especially drawn.

One of Daddy's dreams—to own a horse—had materialized. He bought Tammie as a foal from the Stud Farm, raising him with love. Tammie was hardly racehorse material, but made a grand mount. It was my pleasure to ride and exercise him whenever I came home. Affectionate, high-spirited as he was, Daddy and I loved him also because he was indisputably ours. One of the stable hands at the

Farm brought a young nephew to help look after Tammie. With Daddy away all day, and Mumsie alone in the house, Dinya pursued his lazy shiftless ways, neglecting to clean out the stall most of the time. Daddy was forced to reprimand him repeatedly when he would turn sullen, and complete the tasks with ill grace. Used to the discipline of the Army, such behavior irked Daddy. He made up his mind to replace the fellow as soon as the month was up. I was not aware of any of these happenings.

Final examinations were two months away at J.J., when I was called to the Office urgently. The Dubash estate car was waiting to take me as fast as possible to Pune. To my shocked questions, the driver only said my father had had a serious accident. I sat stunned, hideous thoughts whirling through my head.

We drove straight to the Hospital.

Mumsie was sitting outside the Intensive Care Unit. Uncle Sohrab was conferring with two men in a corner. When I burst in, Mumsie looked at me with bewildered dazed eyes like a child who does not know why it is being punished. I took her small frame into my arms, and looked at Uncle Sohrab in mute query.

He shook his head, indicating he would talk to me later. When I slipped out after some time, he followed me and told me the story.

Daddy had asked Dinya to saddle Tammie. He had waved to Mumsie before taking off. She had watched him canter off, and then it had happened right in front of her unbelieving eyes. Daddy had lost control at the reins! He had fallen off Tammie's back! I could see the whole thing unreeling in my mind's eye in slow motion. Mumsie racing desperately all the way to her unconscious husband's aid, racing back to summon the neighbors, Dinya having disappeared. The nightmare ride in the ambulance, and the long wait. How could it have happened, I asked despairingly. Daddy's expertise on a horse was extraordinary. Tammie, though high-spirited, was always good-natured. The saddle girth had been cut, Uncle Sohrab told me gravely, almost all the way except for a tiny portion. When Tammie picked up speed, and with Daddy's weight, the girth had snapped. I knew very well that in such an unexpected event, the most experienced rider would not be able to save himself. There was no doubt it had been done deliberately. Dinya was nowhere to be found.

I could not take it in. My Daddy, so magnificent of physique, in such splendid health, was lying in deathly stillness after emergency brain surgery. My whole world had collapsed around me. And there was Mumsie. I had to be strong for her sake.

I will not linger over what happened next. Indeed, I cannot. Daddy never recovered consciousness, all of his strength notwithstanding. He lingered for a week, and then slipped away from us forever.

Concealing my own bitter grief, I did my utmost to comfort Mumsie. Uncle Sohrab was a tower of strength. It was he who insisted that I return to Bombay for my final examinations. Aunt Gulnar would look after Rebekah in their home, he said. I learnt later that Mumsie stayed only a few days before returning home. All her memories were there, and she could not bear to be away. Friends were very kind to her.

Particularly attentive was the lady I called Binty. Matron of one of Pune's biggest hospitals, she was Mumsie's friend. Her first name was Bina, and my childish tongue had combined that with "aunty" into Binty. It was she who arranged for a woman to sleep in the house at night till I was free to come home.

I still do not know how I managed to pass through those days, to study and get good grades. I kept telling myself fiercely that I had to do it for Daddy's sake. He had sacrificed so much to send me to J.J. In fact, studying became a form of escape. My friends and teachers were wonderfully helpful, their kindness sustaining me through the most terrible period of my life. There was no breathing spell after the examinations. I had to return to Pune at once. Mumsie needed me.

With Uncle Sohrab's help, I sorted out Daddy's financial affairs. It was an alarming picture. There were substantial loans to be paid off on land and house. Mumsie would have a small income, hardly adequate for her needs. To be considered were taxes, repairs to the house. One of the first possessions to he sold was Tammie. There was simply no way we could afford to keep him. Uncle Sohrab had settled the enormous hospital bill, but I was determined to repay him in due course. What it boiled down to was that I had to get a job at once, and that too in Pune, so that I could stay with Mumsie. I would get one certainly, but would it be the kind of position I wanted? Bombay would have been really ideal for one with my qualifications.

I have not mentioned yet that Mumsie had become very quiet. The only time she had roused herself from wherever it was she had mentally retreated was to refuse flatly to follow up Daddy's accident. With her husband gone, she saw no sense in further investigation. Always frail, now she had become a shadow of her former self. Binty shook her head over it. We all hoped that Time the great healer would be able to help her so that eventually she would accept the inevitable. We were terribly wrong.

One evening, I took Mumsie to the Deccan Gymkhana for a few important purchases. I stopped to buy some fruit from a handcart, assuming Mumsie was right behind me. She wasn't. A commotion erupted, there were shouts, people running. That was when I saw the double-decker bus at a standstill, and the crumpled small figure lying on the ground. Mumsie had stepped off the curb, straight into the path of the oncoming bus.

I shall not linger over that time. I did not dare let myself conjecture why it happened—whether she had tried to cross the road—or simply reached the point where she could no longer live without Daddy. In one fell swoop, I was left alone in the world, an orphan in every sense of the word. The only branches of the Jeromes and Antons had migrated decades ago, the first to Australia, the second to Canada. Sakshi Alexa Jerome was bereft of all family. Father

Sebastian, the nuns who had known me all through school, Binty, the Dubashes, and many more, stood by me in those pain-filled days, which I moved through like an automaton.

Even if there had not been so many loans to repay, I am sure I would not have kept the house. The bitter-sweet memories it held were too much to bear. Still, the decision to sell was hardly in my hands. Even after I took a job, I would not be in a position to pay the installments on Daddy's loans, the taxes and repair bills. Uncle Sohrab stepped in at this point, finding me a buyer willing to pay the highest amount possible.

In time, the property was sold, all debts paid, including the one owed to Uncle Sohrab in spite of his vehement protests. I was left with a couple of thousand rupees, some heirlooms, cartons of memorabilia, the last two to be stored for me in the Dubash attic. What I kept was a bronze horse of Daddy's. Now there was nothing to keep me in Pune.

It was the end of my childhood. It was the end of an era.

CHAPTER 3

Dame Fortune having destroyed my happiness now seemed to relent. One of my teachers at J.J. recommended that I try for a job with Orion. Unsure of myself as I was, I doubted very much if this prestigious advertising agency would select me. A shivering wreck inside, I did my best at the interview, trying to give the impression that I was poised and self-confident. I must have succeeded, for to my combined relief and astonishment, I was offered the position.

Orion was part of the Samartha Group, one of its many enterprises. As an advertising agency, Orion had achieved spectacular success, many of its efforts winning awards annually. Orion occupied the entire fifth floor of the imposing building, the rest divided among various other departments of the Group. During working hours, the whole complex hummed with activity, giving the impression of the highest efficiency. To the mind of such a novice as I was, wide-eyed and wondering, the place teemed with smart people, all intent on some vitally important task.

The top Boss of Orion, Naren Kaushik, was a martinet. Never indeed would he have won a popularity contest. Inefficiency, shirking, laziness were simply not to be tolerated in those who worked under him. To Naren, the word "deadline" had sacred connotations. All of which was partly responsible for the extraordinary reputation Orion had built up.

The rest of the credit had to go to my immediate boss, Prem Chandran, Executive Creative Director, and his bright young team. A man of about forty, not given to saying one word more than was necessary, Prem was marvelously talented and creative. Strict he might be, but as far as ideas were concerned, he kept an open mind. As a result, Orion came up with the most eye-catching advertisements, often daringly innovative, frequently responsible for the phenomenal success of a new product. I was assigned to be assistant to Prem himself.

Being the newest recruit, my services were often those of an errand girl. I did not mind at all. I loved being part of this lively set-up, and willingly performed all small tasks. At first, I did not venture to speak out at discussions, trying to blend into the woodwork—no easy task with my coloring! But I listened with all concentration to the ideas being thrown back and forth. I wished to learn the ropes, not to display my ignorance. In time, I realized that participation was expected of me. The first time I ventured to speak, I thought carefully before opening my mouth. All eyes were upon me, my point was seized, hurled from person to person till it was ragged, but deemed to have merit. What a relief it was to feel accepted! That was the starting point, for from then on, my confidence grew until I could project my own ideas boldly.

There came a time when I backed up a suggestion with my own artwork for the group's perusal. Prem looked at me as if discovering a hitherto unsuspected facet of his lowly assistant. After that, I was entrusted with more and more of the actual layouts. I was gratified. If that meant staying overtime once in a while, I did not grudge the extra hours of work.

An easy camaraderie existed among the younger members of the Department. Just as I was Sakshi to them, so also I called them Rohit, Purva, Kunal, Clemmie and so on. We worked together harmoniously. If sometimes we disagreed, it was all in good spirit, always keeping in mind the Orion name. I liked the recognition and appreciation of each one's special talents. Rohit, for example, was a master with words. He spun them out with such magic that they ensnared the unwary consumer, making the product irresistible. Certain slogans he had dreamed up had become part of everyone's daily routine nationwide.

The same held true of Kunal's delightful jingles which, set to lively music, caught the imagination of the TV and radio audiences. In my case, they loved the crayon sketches I had done of each one, telling me quite frankly that I was wasted here, and should be a full-time artist, perhaps specializing in portrait painting. On a different level, they banded together to protect me from the unwanted attentions of certain males in the complex, thus saving me many an embarrassment.

Through Clemmie, I had been able to find living accommodation in Bandra. It was part of a house, had its own entrance, and comprised a single, fairly large room, a pocket-sized kitchenette and bathroom.

The landlady, Mrs Fonseca, preferred to rent to foreign students, but was perfectly willing to take me on as a tenant. Her reasoning was quite simple. The students left when their visas expired, whereas other tenants might not be so easy to dislodge. Clemmie said laughing that one look at me had convinced the good lady that I too was a foreigner, an impression neither of us was going to dispel.

I spent a small amount of money on essentials. A divan, which converted into a bed at night, a table and chair, all from a second-hand furniture shop. Each month I added an item or two until my bed-sit became a pleasant place to come home to. At my request, Uncle Sohrab sent on the things I had stored with him.

Getting to the Orion Offices involved a bus journey of one hour's duration, which wasn't bad, considering distances in Bombay, but still it was less easy to be philosophical at the end of a long day, standing in a serpentine queue at the BEST bus stop. That is the life of a commuter, and I was one of the millions who traversed thus.

In describing my new life, I have deliberately avoided mentioning my ever-present grief, and the loneliness, which engulfed me when I was alone in my little dwelling place. I could never stop mourning my parents—not merely their absence, but the tragic waste of it all. In a certain sense, it was Mumsie's death that shocked me more, for it had happened when she was with me, within a few feet of where I had been standing. The memory of it was imprinted indelibly on my brain. But I dealt sternly with myself at these times. I had a wonderful exciting job, a decent salary, fine people to work with, and a roof over my head. I had health and youth, a fine heritage, the sweetest of memories. I must endeavor to emulate St Paul: "Forgetting the things which are behind, I press on." I could not forget, of course, but I could press on, to look forward to the morrow, not keep looking over my shoulder at yesterday. I succeeded in my resolve—most of the time.

I was tired at night so the lack of social life did not bother me. I had Daddy's tape recorder, and my collection of music to listen to. That was both my solace and my joy. There were times when listening to a piano concerto, my fingers itched for a keyboard. On weekends, I shopped with Teresa Fonseca, or went exploring on my own, picking up bargains as thriftily as my Scots forebears must have done. And on Sundays, I attended Mass, and came away renewed.

About one matter I had made up my mind very firmly. The Dubashes had been extraordinarily kind to me, but I must not cling to them. I had given them my promise to remember they were there if I ever needed them. I was grateful beyond words for that assurance, but I refused to become a millstone around their necks. So I wrote to them every few months, using Orion stationery with its distinctive logo of Orion the Hunter, bow poised as he fitted an arrow to it, filling my letters with heartening news. It was Aunt Gulnar who wrote back, for Uncle Sohrab was no letter writer. I missed riding so much, but it was one more thing I had put behind me.

I could look now at myself, and say in all truth that I had settled in.

When I arrived at work one morning, I found everyone looking disturbed. The news was that Prem's older son, a boy of eight, had been rushed to hospital the previous night, and was being operated upon this afternoon for an intestinal obstruction. With both parents by his side, the vexing problem was that of the younger boy left in charge of his grandmother, herself in poor health. How the old lady with her heart condition could cope with a lively child missing his mother was an added worry to the frantic couple. To me, that did not seem to be a problem. I told the group I would be glad to look after the boy, and stay overnight if necessary. They fell silent for a moment. Kunal said, "Good girl, Sakshi," and darted off to Naren Kaushik's office, only to return beaming. I was to take a taxi home to pack a bag for myself, and then go straight to the Chandran home. Initially, I was being given two days off after which the situation would dictate the next step. The entire Department escorted me downstairs in the elevator, waited till I was ensconced in a taxi, and then waved off with a cheer.

Shortly before noon, arriving at Prem's home, I found everything in a chaotic mess. Grandma had collapsed in an exhausted heap, and Ranjan was in the midst of a tantrum. I cannot claim I performed any miracles. The child greeted me with belligerence, for after all, I was a total stranger. But at least Prem's mother was pathetically grateful for my presence. It took hours for things to settle down. A telephone call from Prem brought reassuring news. The operation was over, the patient pronounced to be in a satisfactory condition. Prem himself would be in to pick up some things for his wife who would stay on at the Hospital. Ranjan had evidently grown tired of being a hooligan since the newcomer, unlike Grandma, had remained unimpressed by his tantrums. Since he had emptied his glass of water into his plate at lunchtime, no one had offered him anything more to eat all day, so he had consumed his dinner with gusto. Minutes after he had finished, he was drooping with fatigue, which was only natural, considering how much hell he had raised all day. He was fast asleep when his father arrived.

I could see Prem was immensely relieved to see me there. 'We shall have no worries about the home front,' he said tiredly. 'I think I'll stay with my wife at the Hospital. I haven't been happy to leave her, especially tonight.'

"Of course you must. We shall be absolutely fine," I told him.

A bath, some food and he was gone.

Ranjan went off to school till noon. I wish I could say he was a reformed character, He wasn't, but he did respond to firmness combined with fun when I played with him. I stayed on for an extra day, and then Prem's sister arrived to take over. Back at Orion, I was given a royal welcome, and accorded the status of a heroine. It was good to be back in the midst of my colleagues, to plunge into work. A little nervous, I answered a summons to Naren Kaushik's office where I gave a report on the child's condition, and was told my timely help had been greatly appreciated. I escaped, but with a glow in my heart. I hadn't done anything so remarkable, only lent a hand.

I did not realize that my little adventure would yield such a rich dividend. A few weeks later, I was invited to Prem's house for dinner. His mother welcomed me with affection, Ranjan with enthusiasm, but it was Prem's wife, Bhanumati, who overwhelmed me with thanks. I liked her so much. She was warm and loving, a South Indian beauty with knee-length hair, and large lustrous eyes. She reminded one of those beautiful sculptured figures in ancient temple carvings. In no time at all, I became part of the family. Often I spent a Sunday with them. An M.A. in Psychology from Madras University, Bhanumati was highly intelligent and articulate. It was a pleasure to converse with her.

Watching my Boss as a family man was a revelation. Firm with Ashok and Ranjan, he spent hours with them doing interesting things which were both instructive and entertaining. To his mother, he showed gentle love and concern. Without making it obvious through word and deed, the rapport and deep feeling husband and wife had for each other, were there for any discerning person to see. But at work, Prem was his usual self; driving himself and everyone else, stopping short of nothing less than perfection.

CHAPTER 4

Orion had its own prima donna in the person of Balaram, photographer extraordinaire. The man was temperamental to an extreme degree, issuing a never-ending stream of contradictory orders to his nervous minions so that they leaped about, sweating from every pore. His genius with a camera produced such brilliant results that he was the envy of other agencies. Our work was particularly involved with Balaram's since naturally it was an integral part of our layouts and visuals. Purva and I often tiptoed in when the lights were focused on the subject for the day, and the rest of the studio in darkness, for Balaram hated strangers there, and the sight of one could ruin an entire day's work. We drank in the sight of the live models, men or women, even children, wondering at their poise in spite of blazing lights, and the never-ending stream of instructions. When a series of shots was completed, or a sequence filmed for a television commercial, and normality was about to be restored, we dodged behind a convenient curtain, and slipped away before the great man spotted us.

Around Balaram's beautiful results, we would put in the finishing touches. Rohit waxed lyrical, words pouring out of his fertile imagination, trying out every manner of caption that would leap off the page to catch the attention. Whenever I saw one of these Orion ads adorning magazine pages, an audio-visual reality on the TV screen, appearing everywhere in public places on huge hoardings, I felt a tremendous sense of pride and satisfaction, for had I not been a part of the team that had created it?

Prem had assigned me a piece of work that day with instructions to have it ready by evening. When he gave an order, one obeyed. Although I had labored diligently for hours, there were still some finishing touches to be put in. It was not just my boss who was a stickler for perfection. I was my own worst critic, taking infinite pains, redoing anything that did not completely satisfy me. Consequently, when five o'clock came, I was deeply absorbed in my task. My colleagues stopped to commiserate before going off with a cheerful farewell in their various directions. Absentmindedly I told them I would need only a half hour or so. It had become very quiet after the offices emptied. A security guard popped in on his rounds to stand behind me and watch with interest. Since he was rather a pal of mine, I sensed he would have loved a chat, but I was unable to oblige him. Reluctantly he went away with the reassurance that he would return, and I was not to be afraid of being alone.

When I finished at last, a horrified glance at my watch showed me the time. I knew with a sinking heart that I had probably missed even the six-thirty bus, and had an hour's wait for the next one unless I took a taxi. I could ill afford an extravagance like that. At top speed, I locked away my things, grabbed my haversack and purse, flipped off electric switches, and yanked the door shut so that it gave a smooth satisfying click to tell me it had locked automatically, and then I was racing down the corridor. A humming sound indicated the elevator was coming up, so I put on more speed to catch it before it began its descent. I was nearly there when it happened I crashed head on into a solid wall. My purse flew out of my hand, and burst open. I went down on the floor in what must have been the most ungraceful sprawl. I became aware of two things simultaneously. First, of a dull but persistent ache in my hip on which I had landed, and second, of a pair of brilliantly polished elegant black shoes near me. Then strong hands were helping me to my feet. I winced as my hip gave an acute twinge.

"I'm so terribly sorry!" I gasped out to whoever the person was, realizing I owed an apology.

"My fault entirely," a deep voice said, and for the first time I looked up at my rescuer. I placed him instantly, of course. Without doubt, one of the male models for a suiting ad. And dressed already in an impeccably tailored dark suit and tie. He had the arrogant unsmiling look, which seemed to be an essential of such advertisements. Also the height, for I had to look up a considerable distance, But, I thought puzzled, there isn't a soul around. There's been none of that frenzied preparation that precedes one of Balaram's sessions. Oh well, perhaps he had come, as they say, to case the joint, see where he would have to report for the modeling assignment tomorrow, for surely it was his first time to work for Orion. In any case, it wasn't my business. And I was late!

The male model had stooped to collect my things scattered hither and yon. Hastily I began to scoop up the rest of them. When we straightened, he was holding out several articles balanced on the palm of his hand. Why do women accumulate so much trivia in their purses? I was embarrassed to see a dog-eared library card from J.J., a half-eaten chocolate still in its foil, my keys and a powder puff. I stuffed them somehow in my purse.

"Tha—thank you so much!" I stammered.

"Not at all. Especially since I'm the one responsible for the collision in the first place."

My eye fell on my watch, and I turned desperately to press the button for the elevator. Mercifully, it came up at once, naturally empty at this hour. To my surprise, the model followed me in. It was he who pressed the right button. I glanced at my watch and groaned to myself. I should have been at the bus stop at this very moment, for a bus was due now. It just isn't my day, or should I say night, I told myself.

"An urgent appointment?"

I was startled by the query. We hadn't exchanged a word so far.

"Yes. With a BEST bus."

"On your way home?"

"Yes."

The moment the elevator reached ground level, I was out calling a hasty thanks and goodbye over my shoulder, and was out of the complex into the twilit world outside.

Traffic was heavy on the streets. I hurried so fast, practically running, dodging the thronging crowds.

When the bus stop was in sight, I saw there were twenty people ahead of me in the queue. I could have wept. Oh well, there was no alternative. I took my place at the end of the line.

It must have been ten minutes later that the car slid in front of us, its long bonnet gleaming under the street lamps. I glanced at it without curiosity, and my eye passed on. A sharp toot brought my attention back with a vengeance. From the driver's side, the male model put his head out through the window.

"Come along," he called. "I'll drop you off home." He sounded impatient. Doubts whirled through my head. One simply did not accept lifts from strange men. Every girl could tell horrendous stories about foolish females who had yielded to such temptation. My hip gave a painful twinge. I realized suddenly that I was starving. I was dying to get home. Everyone in the queue was watching with avid interest. Other cars were piling up, and honking furiously. What choice did I have? I dashed around and clambered into the front passenger seat. The car slid into smooth motion.

I had subsided onto the cushioned comfort of the leather upholstery. To my untutored eye, the dashboard looked terribly complicated. Even the interior smelt expensive with its aroma of costly masculine cologne. My rescuer surely must earn fabulously as a model if he could own a car like this one.

"You took your time deciding whether to come with me." The statement was made with a pronounced American accent. I shot a sidelong glance at his profile, and was struck by the chiseled perfection of it.

"Did you think I had designs on you? Rest assured I don't."

"Oh, I didn't think that!" Which was blatantly untrue.

"But since I knocked you down, and made you miss your bus, the least I can do is to see you home. Where is home, by the way?"

I bit my lip. "I'm afraid—rather far out. Bandra."

He halted for a traffic light. "No problem."

"But don't you have a photography session? Won't you be late for it?" The sleek head turned to me.

"For the ad," I added helpfully.

Light seemed to dawn. "Oh, the photography session. No, not tonight."

"I wondered why no one else was making an appearance. Balaram is so temperamental. He has his entire team running. Spends so much time in preparation for these sequences. But you know that better than I do." A thought struck me. "But then you must be on your way to some function. A party?"

"A late dinner."

"Oh," I exclaimed in distress, "and I'm holding you up! Look, I can take a cab from here."

"And you'll go alone at this time of night?"

"I'll be all right. It's not so late."

He ignored that. "What did you have for lunch?"

"Lunch? A sandwich."

"What do you do for an evening meal?"

"Cook it."

"You won't have to tonight. We'll have a bite somewhere."

"But—you have a dinner engagement!"

"One of those buffet dinners where guests drift in and out." He swung into a quieter lane. "You must be hungry."

"Starving!" I said fervently, and went silent with embarrassment. "Look," after a moment, "you're being so kind about giving me a lift. You don't have to feed me too."

"Not even if I'm hungry too?"

"Oh." I mulled over that. "Then may we go to a fast foods place please?" I wasn't going to let him pay for an expensive meal.

"Why?"

"Because I love fast foods." I saw his eyes on my face, but he made no comment.

Twenty minutes later we were there, waiting at the counter for my order to be filled. For all that my companion claimed he was hungry, he settled for a lime soda. Suddenly I was glad to be here. The appetizing smells of food, the gay décor, an extraordinarily handsome escort—what more could one want for a pleasant interlude after a long hard day?

I really was ravenous, and attacked my food with gusto. The bun was freshly baked, and very soft, sprinkled with sesame seed, the chicken melted in the mouth. The salad in its little paper cup had a tasty dressing, while the French fries were a crisp golden brown. Sitting at the little table, I concentrated on the meal with single-minded zeal. When the first pangs of hunger were assuaged, I lifted my head to encounter an enigmatic gaze.

"I'm sorry," I said awkwardly. "I've been making a pig of myself."

"I'm glad you're enjoying it. Tell me, what were you doing so late at the Orion offices?"

I rolled my eyes heavenwards and told him. "My Boss would have had my head if I hadn't finished," I ended.

"That's Prem Chandran, I believe?"

"Yes." I speared a last French fry. A thought struck me. "He isn't a friend of yours, is he?"

"No. We've met."

"And the Boss—Naren Kaushik?"

"We've met too."

"They call him Idi Amin."

"Oh? How come?"

"Because he's a dictator. Drives everyone like a slave master. But," I added hastily, "he's very capable. And Prem Chandran—my immediate boss—is wonderful."

"Is that so?" I had pushed away my empty plate. "Time to choose your dessert. There's a delectable-looking ice cream cake in the pinup there. But the choice is yours."

"Do you think I should indulge?" looking longingly at the said poster, and then at the array in the glass cabinet. I caught his eye, and laughed shamefully. "It's too much to resist!" I dithered between a chocolate marvel and a layered strawberry and cream affair, finally settling for the latter.

A glint of amusement in his eyes, my host said, "Since it's such a tough decision to make, have both."

"Oh I couldn't! At this rate, I shall become a butterball!"

"I doubt that very much. You're slimmer than you should be. Why aren't you a model?"

I grinned and told him, "Nobody asked me, sir," she said. As I relished each mouthful of this rare treat, he asked me what I did for Orion. I told him briefly.

"You have rather unusual looks—exotic with that coloring."

"Blame Fiona for that! And Mynheer too!"

"Who are Fiona and Mynheer?"

When I looked back later, I could not believe how naïve I had been. Perhaps it was the fact that though I showed a cheerful façade, I was in truth extremely lonely. To be able to talk about my loved ones to an excellent listener who seemed genuinely interested, and made all the right responses, was so heartening, that I poured out my story. It was, of course, only in outline, but all pertinent details were covered. I doubt if I could keep out the anguish and loneliness from my voice as I spoke.

"Goodness," I said at last, "I've bored you to tears. You should have stopped me."

"You're a person of great courage," he said quietly, "I can't think of a single girl of my acquaintance who would have taken so much the way you have."

We fell silent. I hadn't tried to trade on his sympathy, but undeniably, I was completely without family. With determined effort, I changed the subject.

"What do you do, besides modeling for suitings? Surely that by itself can't bring you enough of an income? Do you work for Orion in other capacities perhaps?"

"You could say so," he agreed. "Jack of all trades. General factotum and dogsbody."

"Oh," I said sympathetically, "they make you do all the donkey labor."

"And how!" he said warmly. "Well, shall we be on our way?"

Traffic had thinned considerably. To my sorrow, it did not take as long as I would have liked to reach Bandra. And then we were drawing up in front of the Fonseca house, I was offering my profuse thanks, which he shook off, and then the sleek car was out of sight.

It had been the strangest encounter, I thought, as I went to bed. I realized suddenly I hadn't asked the stranger his name. I decided to say nothing to Purva and Clemmie, or any of the others about this evening. In fact, for me it took on the aura of a dream.

At Orion, there was a rather pleasant dining area set aside for lunch. I suppose there were similar ones on every floor of the complex. At the self-service counter, one could order snacks, which were served piping hot, or drinks. Most of us brought along our own sandwiches, and had a hot beverage or something cold. Supposedly, the hall was for everyone's use, but inevitably, a class barrier had set in. The lower orders—meaning us—did not venture into the farther section where the VIPs sat—top executives, departmental heads, and clients or guests. It did not matter that they had to go the counter like us, and order the same items that we did.

On the day after my adventure, we had adjourned there in the break. It was Clemmie's turn to bring our teacups. I was taking mine from her hand when she hissed, "Did you see him?"

"See who?" I asked blankly. Only now did I follow her gaze to see a group of men and one woman enter from the farthest door to settle at the largest table.

"The C.P., silly" And seeing my puzzlement, "The Crown Prince as they all call him. Son of the top, top Boss. In the gray suit. Jai Samartha." She sighed. "Isn't he stunningly gorgeous?"

Unerringly, I found the one she was describing. It wasn't difficult. In the suit she mentioned, with a toning shirt in deeper gray and an elegant striped tie, and with those looks, he stood out a mile. My blood ran cold. So now I knew who he was, the man who had masqueraded as a male model. No wonder he hadn't volunteered to tell me his name. Jai Samartha, son of the legendary magnate, Ketan Samartha. Orion was just one of the many enterprises of the parent organization, along with a chain of department stores, textile and paper mills, factories manufacturing the finest steel furniture, and who knew what else. How naive and stupid I had been! Fiercely, I castigated myself for crashing into him, accepting a lift, allowing him to give me a meal. What had possessed me to pour out my life history to a perfect stranger, no matter how sympathetic and receptive, to lean on a shoulder even temporarily? Suddenly; the tea tasted bitter, the sandwich like ashes in my mouth.

"U.S.-educated," Clemmie was whispering. "Acting Director. Runs the Samartha Group by himself now since his father is recouping from an accident. Was called back from the U.S. to take over." She cast another adoring glance over her shoulder. "You must have seen his photographs in all the society pages. Gossip columnists adore him. Women fall all over him." She giggled. "So would I. Not that I'd be allowed within a mile of him!" She drained her cup. "The woman's name is Ila Anjan. She's P.A. to the General Manager. Smart, wouldn't you say? Not pretty though. I can't understand why, when she's flat as a board, she gives the impression of being sexy. Is it bec—"

"Haven't you finished?"

"Mmmm." She swallowed the last bit of sandwich "But you haven't drunk your tea, Sakshi."

"Tastes like dishwater. Shall we go?"

That evening after five, we were all downstairs, passing through the glass revolving doors when we saw Jai Samartha again. He was walking across to the car park with two men. A uniformed chauffeur was holding open the car door. Of course, I thought, he would have a chauffeur, even though he wasn't in evidence yesterday. The men were put in the back seat, and the chauffeur climbed into the passenger seat in front. Clearly, the C.P. was driving. The car backed out of the space, and turned, coming our way. Clemmie and all the other girls had stopped walking, and were watching avidly, as people do for royalty. As the car passed us, the man at the wheel looked straight at me. I dropped my head, and looked steadfastly at my flat-heeled shoes. Anger, humiliation, self-disgust—these were new to me, but I was filled with all of them. No one likes to be deceived, or made a fool of. When I had prattled on and on about his being a model, why hadn't he corrected me? I squirmed to think of all my foolish candid comments on Kaushik, Balaram, and Orion in general. He had drawn me out, positively encouraged me, pretending an understanding that had acted like a spur.

We caught glimpses of Jai Samartha on his occasional visits to the complex. He never deigned to step into the Department, but Prem accompanied Naren to conferences of all Heads. Needless to say, decisions taken there guided our work. Every time, I saw the C.P., the same waves of humiliation overcame me. It would take me a long time to get over it.

CHAPTER 5

THE REPRESENTATIVE FROM COQUETTE HAD GONE ON HIS WAY, leaving behind a box of samples of its latest product. A maker of the finest quality cosmetics and toilet soaps, Coquette was a regular client of Orion. A new luxury toilet soap was to be launched now. The fact was that the market was already flooded with excellent soaps. To build up an advertising campaign that would project this offering of Coquette presented no small challenge to our team.

When we went into a huddle, and ideas flew back and forth, we sensed they lacked originality. We all approved of the name Rohit had found for the soap—*Komal.* As Coquette claimed, it promised to deep-cleanse the way cold creams do, and also to soften and pamper the skin, keep it youthful. Kunal seized upon that last word. The accent should be on it, he insisted. That would appeal to every age group—to the not so young who would like to acquire such a complexion—and to the young who would want to retain theirs. His words were met by approval. Prem said firmly, "One thing we shan't do is to use film stars. I'd like to use a really striking model."

Names were tossed out, the dossier of photographs studied. Prem dismissed them with a flick of his hand. "Nothing novel about them. Those faces pop up all the time," he said with uncharacteristic irritation.

"How about launching an unknown?" from Rohit.

I ventured, "Won't that entail a talent search? And if so, isn't it a very complicated time-consuming process?"

Prem grunted an assent. He was playing with a cake of Komal, turning it over and over in his hand, but obviously deep in thought.

"Luscious shade of green. Rather unusual for a soap," Purva observed idly. A frown creased her brow. She stared at me. "That's it! It's the exact shade of Sakshi's eyes! No wonder I had this feeling it was familiar—so different from the usual pastels!"

"Don't be silly!" I said as all eyes came to rest on me. I felt acutely embarrassed.

"Of course," Rohit said in growing excitement. "And she has this lovely clear translucent complexion!"

Kunal blurted, "You can't beat her for looks! With the right make-up, we can project her exactly as we want! Mysterious. Sexy. What-ever."

Prem had not uttered a word. But nor had he taken his eyes from me. Distinctly shaken, I stood up. "This is the most ridiculous conversation I've ever heard. I'll see what's delaying our coffee." As I stalked out, I saw all of them draw up their chairs closer, and a babel of voices assaulted my ears. I fled.

It didn't help. I was over-ruled completely. No arguments, protests or pleading made the slightest dent in their determination. To tell the truth, they were on the verge of bursting with prideful excitement. Not so myself. I was petrified. What was this that had come unbidden upon me and in such an unexpected way? Here I had been grateful beyond words to find a safe niche for myself, enjoying my work and the company of my office colleagues. I was content. Now an avalanche had come down so that forces undreamed of buffeted me. I who had helped to plan so many advertising campaigns was actually the center of a new one that had begun to take shape.

Naturally, every assignment Orion took on was shrouded in secrecy, so imperative in a highly competitive field. This one could have been labeled TOP, TOP SECRET. The Allies launching the Normandy landings could not have made every move with greater stealth as our team did. Since I was an employee, the matter had to be cleared first with Naren Kaushik. Far from raising any objections, he was quite elated. I felt like saying, "*Et tu, Brute.*"

Naren ordered Prem to have the whole thing ready before the highest authority was approached for permission. Before anything could be set in motion, the Coquette people had to approve of the girl who was to launch the new soap. If I had a faint hope they would reject me, I was doomed to disappointment. In particular, by a Parsi lady, so stylishly groomed that I felt like a country bumpkin in my skirt and blouse, and the flat-heeled shoes I always wore, since Rohit and Kunal said I gave them an inferiority complex when I towered above them in heels. The lady examined me very carefully through the designer glasses on her nose. I was sure it was a supercilious scrutiny. I was quite sure she would come out with an outright no. I was reduced to a quivering jelly when, quite unexpectedly, she smiled at me. I was not to be nervous, she exclaimed. I had a most delicate innocent look. How did I achieve the redness of my lips? It was natural? Amazing!

She swept her group off for a confabulation. The Orion team waited with bated breath. The final outcome was that Prem was given complete approval. We could all sense the unmistakable wave of excitement that emanated from them. Kunal winked at me and held up his thumb where only I could see it. I heard Prem explain the situation about my being an employee, and how clearance was yet to be obtained.

"Oh!" the Parsi lady exclaimed in dismay. "You mean there's a chance permission might be withheld? But that's ridiculous! Why, it's a feather in Orion's cap that they even provide beautiful models from their own staff!"

Prem said that in case permission was denied, they would scout around for another model.

"We don't want another model! We insist on this one!" Naren murmured something placatory, and promised to let them know within a specific period of time. They went away, talking volubly among themselves.

An amazing interlude began for me now. I had to submit to all kinds of make-up combinations. My hair was twisted, coiled, pinned, left loose until my scalp ached. I wriggled in and out of clothes, had fabrics held against me, wrapped around me. The teen-age look with jeans and T-shirt. The ethnic look with bright, colorful cottons. The glamorous look with gold-embroidered silks. All were vetoed.

My colleagues told the experts their approach was totally wrong. The very word *komal* had connotations of tenderness, softness, gentleness. The girl in the ad was to project the image of someone very young, very innocent. The look had to underline the freshness and clearness of her complexion. With that in mind, a whole new spectrum of experiments was launched. The final result was greeted with satisfaction by all. Rohit said that the sight made his brainwork overtime, and the words that poured out were sheer poetry. No catchy jingle for the Komal commercial. Only the softest most lilting music, and the most mellifluous male voice speaking the honeyed words.

It was decided to drop all jewelry for the Komal Girl. And to think of the endless pairs of earrings I had tortured my poor earlobes with! All the clothes I had tried on were rejected. A very beautiful and ruinously expensive fabric had been found. It was the exact shade of the soap—and of my eyes—and was not to be stitched into a garment at all. Extremely soft and clinging, it was neatly anchored at one shoulder, and draped across my breast, leaving both arms and the other shoulder bare, somewhat in the manner of a toga. When I stretched out an arm, glimpses of bare back were seen. My neck rose quite unadorned out of the lovely material. Around my upper arms were circlets made entirely of jasmine. They had given me a loose coiffure, softly curling to my shoulders, framing my face with tendrils, some of which had escaped to my brow. The lightest make-up, my mouth touched with rose.

I stared at myself in the mirror and saw a butterfly emerging in all glory out of the chrysalis.

"I can't pose wearing nothing more than this!" I protested vehemently! "I'm practically naked!"

"Rubbish!" Purva retorted. "You're covered perfectly adequately in all the right places. You'd wear a sleeveless blouse, wouldn't you? Then why the fuss over this? Especially when your skin is so lovely!"

"This isn't a sleeveless blouse! It's positively indecent! I feel—exposed. Think of the millions who'll see me like this! My modesty is being outraged!"

"Hardly that," Rohit observed dryly. "Dressed like that you're only emulating women's fashions from ancient times in India. Have you seen what models are wearing for some ads? A wisp of something, which leaves nothing to the imagination. Comparatively, you're well covered. And look exactly right!"

So were all my doubts systematically torn to bits. Finally, it was my sense of humor that came to the rescue—that I, Sakshi Jerome, horse lover, occupant of one of the lower rungs of the Orion hierarchy, was now the center of the entire staff's attention. At least, I could chuckle over the fact that Naren hovered around, and that the great Balaram was to preside behind the cameras.

In the studio where Purva and I had secretly watched countless sessions, I was subjected to long hours of posing. I'd never realized before what a model has to go through. I think what bothered me most was the dazzle of lights in my eyes, the unreality of all that brilliance. They made me hot and uncomfortable when I was to look my coolest. The entire team came with me. For once, Balaram permitted it. It was a great comfort to have everyone there, boosting my courage.

We ran into a problem now. Balaram explained it to me as if I was a slightly retarded child—which I was as far as modeling went. Prem added, "Sakshi, when you raise your eyes towards the male model, your expression must reflect shyness. You're a girl lifting your gaze to your lover. Can you do that?"

"I—I'll try," stammered.

"The thing to do is to imagine he is your lover," Rohit said encouragingly.

"Shouldn't be difficult. This chap is dreamy-looking enough." Clemmie glanced at the male model lounging at the other end of the studio. 1 followed her gaze. Yes, he certainly was a splendid specimen. The only trouble was he hadn't made the least impact on me. The face was very handsome, but to my eyes, it had no character.

"Or any man who has appeal for you," Purva put in. "Don't yon have a favorite movie or pop star?"

"You can think of me," Kunal suggested. "That should put stars in your eyes."

We laughed at him, but I was pondering over their words. It was true. If in my imagination, I could superimpose the right face on the model's, I could mime the: desired expression better. Unfortunately, I didn't have a favorite film star, and pop music wasn't to my taste. A face flashed in front of my eyes—an arrogant face, giving nothing away. Was it capable of softening, the dark eyes of looking with ardor into those of the beloved? What on earth was I thinking of, visualizing the C.P. in such terms? Why, I cordially disliked the man! Then why was my heart racing in this strange way?

"That's it! That's it!" Kunal was almost dancing. "You've got it, Sakshi."

Bewildered, I stared at him.

"The way you looked just now! You were thinking of someone, weren't you? Keep thinking, dear girl. Starry enough even for Balaram!"

It worked. This time, I kept Jai Samartha's face steadfastly in my mind. I no longer minded the dazzle of lights, or Balaram's steady stream of instructions.

"Cut!" he called.

"Think it was okay?" Prem asked.

Balaram grunted noncommittally, but patently he was quite pleased. We were summoned by him to see the results next day. The atmosphere was filled with excited anticipation. The room was plunged into darkness, and all eyes were riveted on the screen. The good-looking young man was gazing down at the down-bent head of girl. The bright head lifted and tilted up to him. The camera zoomed to close in on the girl's face with its sweetly adoring bashful expression, the green eyes softly melting. The man's eyes mirrored his admiration when he held out a flower, She hesitated until he inclined his head coaxingly. She took it and, then as if suddenly overcome with shyness again, dropped her eyes once more. The voice, the music, all contributed to the mood.

There was total silence for a few moments, then Kunal stammered, "Sakshi, good girl! it couldn't have been more perfect!" Everyone burst into speech, talking at top speed.

Prem was lost in thought. He roused himself. "It was excellent, Sakshi. Rohit, you can finalize the copy. We've requested an appointment this afternoon. Every VIP will be there."

"Will there be any trouble?" Clemmie asked anxiously. "I mean, will they refuse permission?"

"That remains to be seen."

That afternoon, none of us could concentrate on our work. In spirit, we were up on the top floor where the VIP offices were located. We had a long wait. Eventually, half an hour before closing time, Prem returned. We rushed to surround him to inundate him with eager questions.

Most of the VIPs were not only impressed, but also completely sold on the idea, he said. We sensed he was keeping something back. What about the C.P., Clemmie asked. Reluctantly, Prem reported that he had not seemed overly pleased. Of course, the C. P.'s expression was never readable. Did he object because Sakshi was an employee, Purva asked, because it might set a precedent? Prem said that point hadn't come up at all. The C.P. had asked a couple of questions. One, if this meant that the girl model was now leaving Orion to launch full-time into a modeling career. Hastily, Naren assured him she had no intention of doing anything like that, As it was, she had been extremely leery of accepting even this assignment. The C.P. had pounced on that. Had she by any change been pressurized into it? Naren had denied that vehemently. Two, the C.P. had pointed out that Orion was morally bound to see that the model who was not a professional received the full monetary benefits due to her from Coquette. Naren must ensure it was legal and water-tight. Receiving a fervent assurance there, the C. P. had asked a final question. Who was the male model? A pure professional, he was told, a frequent model for the suiting and shirting ads Orion created.

When Prem had finished, there was great jubilation. Naren hosted a celebration lunch the next day.

I was a caught in a blizzard of publicity for which I was ill prepared. The TV commercial was a fantastic success. Posters of the Komal Girl were seen everywhere. On the wrapper of the soap appeared a picture of the girl with the rosebud held to her cheek. Women's magazines featured Coquette's latest find. Coquette offered an exclusive contract. Offers from other companies poured in for all kinds of products from cold cream to cooking oil. Two film producers approached Naren. I refused all of them. My colleagues thought I was quite mad. How could they know that, lacking any family at all, and therefore any protection, I had no intention of going out into the wicked world, that it was at Orion that I had found a safe refuge, which I did not want to let go? The fact that Prem backed me fully was extremely heartening.

I was the cynosure of eyes wherever I went, whether in the complex, on shopping sprees, or commuting to and from Bandra. I took to wearing a scarf around my head, and dark glasses.

Out of the Komal incident came a windfall I had never anticipated. I put all of it into a fixed deposit account. With the small
amount I had set aside, I brought some badly needed replenishments
to my wardrobe, and a few small mementoes for my Orion friends.

CHAPTER 6

OCTOBER WAS HALF-GONE WHEN A LETTER WAS DELIV-
ERED FOR me via an office boy. It was in an expensive-looking
envelope matching the thick cream sheet. Written in a sloping hand,
it read:

My dear Miss Jerome,

*It has just come to my notice that the beautiful Komal Girl is none other
than the daughter of Adrian Jerome. My husband and I knew him well. We
were grieved at the untimely passing of such a fine person.*

*I understand Orion has a three-day break for Diwali. We would be happy to
have you come up to Pune to spend your holiday with us. If you do not have
other plans, I can arrange to have you picked up, and also to see you are
taken back to Bombay afterwards.*

*A message through Miss Kagal of the Samartha Group who has her office in
the same complex as Orion will reach me.*

Looking forward to meeting you.

Sincerely,

Firoza Samartha

To say I was flabbergasted would be a rank understatement. I mulled over that note for hours. What was I to do? Did I have a choice at all? Wasn't this tantamount to an order from the highest echelons? Was it at all possible for me to plead a previous engagement, and if so, would I not be giving much offence? In any case, how did one behave in a millionaire's home" What did one wear? The writer of the note seemed to be sincere and warm, but suppose, in reality, she was all haughty and condescending? I shivered at the thought of meeting Ketan Samartha. And worse, of facing the C.P. again. Perhaps he wouldn't be there at all. I'd heard he had a luxurious residence on Malabar Hill. No doubt he would be involved in an exciting social whirl in celebration of Diwali. One could devoutly hope so. In the end, I did what I had to. I contacted Miss Kagal, who promptly told me to be ready at 6 a.m. the first day of the break. A car would pick me up.

There it stood on a rise, elegant and gracious, its creamy white walls gleaming in the mid morning sunshine of a November day after the monsoon. Tall hedges screened it completely from the road, while a steel mesh fence protected it from intruders. The gates opened for us, no doubt by some electronic means, and we were driving through an avenue of silver oaks, the path curving until we came to a halt in front of a flight of broad marble steps. Immediately, a manservant came down to collect my overnight bag from the chauffeur. It was the best bag I owned, but suddenly it looked cheap and shabby. As I ascended the steps, I saw an enormous mural adorning the entrance. It showed a multitude of stars against the heavens, and the word KAHEKSHA. There was no time to ponder over that, for I was being ushered in.

A slim woman in glamorous silk pants and flower-printed silk shirt, one single streak of gray highlighting her short hair in a most striking manner, came forward with outstretched hands.

"My dear," she said, taking my hands in hers, "I can't tell you how happy I was to know you could come. I'm not going to call you any-thing so formal as Miss Jerome. You're young enough to be my daughter. I shall call you Sakshi, if I may? Let me show you your room first, and then we'll have coffee.

"There's just you and I for lunch, I'm afraid."

We went up a magnificent staircase to a large airy room, done in cream and peach tones. It had a pretty little bathroom. We stood for a moment looking at the view of the rolling countryside. And then it happened. Hooves. I heard the sound of galloping hooves. My ears pricked up. Sure enough, the horses came pounding along, tails streaming behind them. Four of them and a foal. Unconsciously, I had clasped my hands together in delight. I hadn't realized how much I missed riding till now. I must have made a sound of admira-tion. Madame Samartha laughed.

"But of course! I'd forgotten! You love horses, don't you?"

"I adore them!" I said, my eyes shining with the pleasure the sight afforded me.

"Then we're kindred souls. I adore them too. No need to ask Adrian's daughter if she rides."

I shook my head. "I rode before I walked."

"So did my sons. What could the poor things do with a horsy mother!" She laughed. I was struck by her natural manner. There was no trace of snobbery in her. For which I was profoundly grateful. But the greater ordeal when I would confront her husband was still ahead of me. "We'll go for a gallop after tea. Would you like that?" she was saying.

"Above all things," I said simply.

For someone who managed with a sandwich for lunch, I found myself tucking away a substantial portion of the delicious meal we were served. Through it, we chatted pleasantly in the small alcove where the table had been set for two. But I was careful about what I said. I had learnt a bitter lesson about pouring out my heart to strangers.

After lunch, my hostess suggested a rest. She knew I wasn't used to siestas, but it had been a tiring journey from Bombay, and I must have risen early. She told me merrily that for her, a nap was a must. We went our separate ways. Back in my room, the bed looked tempting. I thought I would stretch out for a moment—and fell asleep. It must have been the haven of the mattress, the complete quiet, and the cool air that poured in through the big windows that lulled me.

I awoke refreshed. Never dreaming I would be riding, I had nothing suitable to wear except a pair of slim-fitting pants, which I had tucked in at the last moment, and a blouse with a floppy bow at the throat. They would have to do.

It was sheer bliss to feel the movement on a horse, the rhythm of hooves, the wind in my hair. I laughed aloud in sheer exuberance. My lady companion laughed with me. When we slowed down at last to rest the horses, I was totally relaxed as I had not been for many months. My earlier reserve had melted away. We settled under the shade of a banyan tree, and let the horses crop the sweet grass.

"I was terrified when I received your invitation," I confessed.

"But, my dear child, why?"

"An invitation from such a VIP even though you'd known my father. I was sure you'd be snooty, look down on me."

Surprisingly, she chuckled. "I couldn't be snooty if I tried! My sister-in-law often takes me to task for not being more dignified—as my position demands."

"Oh," I said warmly, "I think you're wonderful. So approachable, so easy to talk to. But I'm terrified of meeting Mr. Samartha."

"I think you'll enjoy meeting him. He's not an ogre, I assure you." Her tone changed. "Did you know he'd had a very serious accident last year?"

"Yes, I'm so sorry."

"It's been a terrible time for us all. It happened on the Bombay-Pune highway. An oncoming truck trying to pass, crashed head-on with his car. Both drivers were killed on the spot." She fell silent. I touched her hand in quick sympathy.

"Ketan suffered multiple injuries. Underwent several operations. That was when our eldest son had to take over. Ketan's very much better, though still a convalescent. It's his leg that continues to plague him. Injury to a nerve. He can get around with a stick, having graduated from crutches, but keeps off it because it is very painful. Prefers a wheelchair. A physiotherapist comes in four times a week. But he has a full office set-up here—secretarial help. His P.A. puts in regular hours, and our son is in touch several times a day from Bombay."

"Can nothing be done about the leg?"

"At the moment, Ketan refuses to have any more surgery. Let's see. I haven't given up hope of getting him to the States before long."

I looked at her sweet face. Remembering Mumsie, I thought how much a wife has to suffer.

Impulsively I asked, "Forgive me for asking, but was yours a love marriage?"

Some of the sadness left her face. "It was indeed! And created a furor! We met in college—Ketan was my senior. Lost touch when he went to the States for higher studies, then ran into each other again. And it happened!"

"Did the Samarthas object?"

"Everyone objected—my people no less. My father was affluent, but nowhere in the same league as Ketan's family. I couldn't have cared less about that aspect. It was Ketan I loved—the only man I'd felt so much at ease with because we were so compatible. In a sense, I'm an odd sort of person. I don't enjoy noisy parties, though I love small groups of congenial friends. I dislike clubs—have my own activities, which I enjoy. Several charities I'm involved with. And horses! I get away with it because I have a husband who indulges me shamefully. He built this house in Pune so that we could keep horses.

We used to ride together so much. There's a Samartha House in Bombay—belonged to my father-in-law—where our son resides when he is there, which is most of the time. Except for a weekend here once in a while. Cyrus, our second son, is also in Bombay. He's still at college—but he steers clear of the House. Prefers to be in the center of everything."

"He has an unusual name."

"Cyrus?" She laughed. "We named our first-born after Ketan's father. He seemed to quite expect it! When our second son arrived, Ketan said magnanimously that this time I could do the choosing. So I did—after my father! And our third son—Gautam Gerard, who is in Junior College, known as GeeGee—was named after two very dear friends. So if our sons have oddly assorted names, there's a story behind each one of them."

"It must be so nice to belong to a family group," I said wistfully. "To have brothers and sisters."

"My dear!" Madame patted my shoulder. "I've always longed for a daughter. I shall have to wait for my sons to bring me three."

She was visibly shocked and distressed when she asked about Mumsie whom she had not met, and I told her the story. She had no words to give me, but only patted my knee several times. However Ketan Samartha might turn out to be, his wife was a darling.

Dinner was at 8 p.m., Madame told me, after our ride. Quite informal with just the family, she said. That was a relief.

There was so much time that I had a leisurely bath, and washed my hair, which I brushed dry and left in soft waves on my shoulders, thankful that the tendency to curl had lasted into adulthood. I thought it best not to pin it up into a more formal style. I chose one of the new dresses I had splurged on: Midi-length, square-necked with tiny cap sleeves, it was pale green. Good heavens, I thought, staring at my reflection in the mirror, when I had tried it on at the boutique, had it had such a low neck, which showed more of my bosom than it should? Hastily I fastened a thin gilt chain with a green stone shaped like a teardrop and put on tiny matching ear-rings. I was ready to face the ordeal.

It was only seven-twenty I saw, but why hang about in my room? As I went down the stairs, I heard something wonderful. Someone was playing a piano! I tracked down the sound to a room of immense proportions, most elegantly furnished. The dark head and back of the pianist at a magnificent instrument drew me irresistibly on. The liquid notes rose and fell, filling my being with beauty.

Very quietly I went to stand facing the pianist. He was no one I had met before. A boy rather than a man with a striking resemblance to Madame. I stood motionless, letting the music flow over me. He was rapt himself with that unseeing look musicians have when they play, as if transplanted to some distant dream world of their own.

Eventually he sensed my presence, and his eyes came to rest on me. His hands stilled over the keys, and a fleeting look of surprise crossed his face.

"Oh, please don't stop!" I begged.

He smiled. "Do you play?"

"Yes, but not like you."

"Join me," he invited, and made room on the bench. What fol-lowed was the most delightful session I had enjoyed for a very long time. Courteously, he started with the dreamily romantic 'Trai-imerei' by Schumann, then finding I was capable of more, we moved into the lilting Beethoven Minuet in G. We played as if we had been partners for years, in perfect accord. He was infinitely more talented than I was, but I did not have to exert myself to keep up. We con-cluded with my last choice, Bach's 'Jesu, Joy of Man's Desiring'. The notes died away and we sat quietly, not speaking, caught in the mood of that final, most moving selection. The sound of clapping made me swing around. I had forgotten where I was. The room suddenly seemed to be full of people.

Madame came forward "That was most beautiful!" She took me by the hand. "Come and meet the family." She indicated a boy of about seventeen nearest to us who rose to: shake the hand I offered, "Gautam, our youngest son," and then led me to a wheelchair. "My husband."

I had never come across a more striking personality than Ketan Samartha. Often featured in newspapers and magazines, I saw that his photographs failed to capture the strength and firmness that characterized the man. The light gray eyes under strongly marked eyebrows looked out with a strong direct compelling glance. Lines of pain around the mouth and running across the broad forehead did not detract in the least from one's awareness that here was a man of great stature and presence.

He leaned forward to grip my hand firmly. "A pleasure to meet Adrian Jerome's daughter."

"Tha-thank you," I stammered.

"Our son, Jai."

The figure in the open-necked black shirt leaning over the back of a chair straightened. The C.P. gave me a nod.

"How are you?" he said coolly.

"No one's bothered to introduce me. I'm Cyrus," my erstwhile piano-playing partner said.

Madame exclaimed, "You mean you don't know each other's names?"

"No," her son told her. "We made beautiful music together without words."

Nothing is necessarily as bad as one expects it to be. Despite all the accoutrements that went with their life style, I almost forgot this was the Samartha family because, more than anything, I was conscious of being in the midst of a loving close-knit group. And they did their best to put me at my ease. Madame had been kindness itself, but now Mr Samartha matched her in that. He might look formidable, but he included me in all the conversation. He: told me how they had met Daddy when they went to the Dubash Stud Farm to buy a horse. I could imagine how pleased he must have been to advise and guide.

The horse they bought on his recommendation was an excellent buy, and when they returned the following year to buy a filly, the three of them greeted each other like old friends. After that, they had run into each other at the races in Bombay and Pune.

We had moved to a smaller sitting room that was a far cry from the imposing room where we had played the piano, but most attractive and comfortable. A soft-footed manservant brought drinks. Eventually we went into what must be the family dining room, which held a table for six. Even so, the table was so polished I could see my reflection in it. In the center, a copper urn held a mixed bouquet of flowers. Pretty lace place mats, gleaming cutlery and flower-bordered dinnerware added up to a most pleasing picture. The food was out of this world. Purely Western, unlike the lunch I had shared with Madame, it was delicious to the last morsel. I had relaxed completely, and not even the presence of a certain individual across the table could ruffle me.

Conversation flowed on smoothly, interspersed by bursts of laughter. Like any family dinner, it was punctuated by light-hearted teasing and joking. Gautam was told by his mother to finish his salad before taking another roll. Casually I took one and buttered it. My opportunity came a little later when the casserole was being served for the second time. Under the table, I nudged my neighbor, and slipped the roll into his free hand. We did not look at each other. Gautam took surreptitious bites of the roll. When it was all gone, we exchanged grins. We were pals. However, we had been observed. When I glanced around the table, a pair of enigmatic dark eyes encountered mine. I looked away hastily. The C.P. did not give us away. Still, I could not bring myself to think well of him. Though he had joined in the conversation, he had spoken the least. Perhaps he is bored, I thought. Probably regrets not being in the center of a bevy of beauties, all adoring. Be that as it may, he is still my enemy. And in any case, what do I have to do with him except in the capacity that I am an Orion employee?

After dinner, Gautam begged me to play Scrabble.

We settled down happily on the thick luxury of the carpet. Cyrus joined us for the merriest session. We laughed and argued, especially over Gautam's insistence that the word "welty" did exist, though not one of several dictionaries backed his claim. The boy's parents watched indulgently. I think the C.P. watched, but I didn't look at him once. When I went up to my room that night, I sat on the windowsill for a long time, recalling every moment of this incredible day. I had been so happy, barring the one fly in the ointment—who, however, had not singled me out, so I could safely put him out of my mind—if that was possible. Hopefully, he wouldn't stay the whole time, but go back to Bombay the next day. The fact was I didn't like the way I was over-conscious of his presence all the time. True, I was furiously angry with him. At the same time, without staring, I had noted all kinds of small details—a particular tilt to his head, the gentle way he spoke to Madame, the deference to his father, and of course, those startling good looks. Well, I told myself ironically, join the throng of female admirers, Sakshi. I shook myself out of this reflective mood I had an early date with Cyrus and Gautam to go riding.

I don't know where the hours of the next day went. There was so much to do with my two companions. It being Diwali, the Festival of Lights, that night we were to have fun with firecrackers, courtesy Gautam. Before that, in the afternoon, guests dropped in, among them a lady whom the boys identified as Arundhati, their father's sister; She had in tow her college-age daughter. The lady looked me up and down as if in astonishment that the Samarthas should harbor a nonentity like me under their roof, and a Christian at that. She investigated my credentials, and then studiously ignored me. I slipped out of a side door as more people turned up. I had no place amongst these wealthy important guests who had come to offer Diwali greetings. I did not fit in. That didn't bother m. I wasn't required to. Here today and gone tomorrow was my situation.

It was to the stables that my feet led me. A beautiful afternoon, I saw, as I walked along, the sky a clear blue, the sun shining benevolently, the air so unlike Bombay's humid atmosphere. The horses pricked their ears forward when they saw me. They did not object when I stroked their faces, talked to them softly. I knelt to put my arms around the foal, which nudged me affectionately.

I sensed rather than saw someone standing at the stable door. The awareness came in the form of a prickle, a certainty. When I turned around, he was there. For a moment, our glances locked. I didn't understand why he was here rather than at the house entertaining the guests. Perhaps, though he wasn't dressed for it, he meant to go for a ride. I moved away from the horses.

"I'm sorry, Sir," I apologized. "I'm in the way."

"You're not."

It was a most awkward moment for me. I could hardly brush past him rudely. He showed no signs of going anywhere.

"Still mad at me?" It wasn't the Americanism that astonished me, but the question. "Because I didn't identify myself that evening?"

"Of course not, Sir. You were quite right not to."

"Why do you say that?" The tone was sharper.

"Because it would—have been too risky to let it—be generally known." He was waiting for me to complete that. Oh, why had I started to make that particular statement? Now I was forced to go on, making the situation worse with every word. "I mean—my employer rescued a lowly employee, was kind enough to feed her, give her a lift home. After all, she could so easily have—" I stopped in mid-sentence, appalled at myself. What on earth possessed me to say so much? These were the thoughts that festered in my mind, but I had no business saying them aloud. And to this person!

"Finish it," he said softly.

I was afraid of him now, of the repercussions that would surely follow. I said no more, looking anywhere but not at him directly. "Finish that sentence, please. She could so easily have what?"

I looked at him mutely, but the implacable expression brooked no further delay. "—risen above her station," I said miserably. When there was no reply, I dared to cast a glance, waiting for the axe to fall. He was actually smiling! I let out my breath slowly.

"I've been accused of many things—snobbery isn't one of them. I didn't tell you my name for two reasons. One, that I was rather enjoying the role of a male model. And two, if you had known my identity, you'd have stiffened up immediately."

"Instead of which, I blurted out my life history," I said bitterly. "Utterly boring and dull."

"On the contrary, I found it fascinating. I told you then, I haven't met anyone with your kind of courage. To have overcome the odds the way you did shows rare spirit." I looked at him wonderingly. "I mean that." I didn't remember having left the stables or having walked across the paddock, but there we were, leaning over the fence. "Are you enjoying your stay?"

My face lit up. "Oh, so much, Sir! It was so kind of Madame to invite me."

"The name is Jai. My parents and brothers have taken to you in a big way."

"And I to them!" He looked at me quizzically, about to speak, when we heard a hail.

It was Cyrus. "Jai, you're wanted at the house."

"Right. Excuse me." He strode away. I thought, as well as suitings, he could have modeled for jeans and shirts equally well.

"Poor Jai," Cyrus was saying. "No one gives him any peace. He's been remarkably patient about the whole thing. Being summoned back from the States. Taking on the whole burden. I think too much is, expected out of Jai."

"Will you be joining the Group?"

"I'm afraid so—later, of course. I'll be going to the U.S. after I graduate this year. Be away for a couple of years except for vacations. So Jai will have to continue shouldering most of it for some time."

"Are you looking forward to it?"

He grimaced. "Hardly. If I had my way, I'd become: a concert pianist."

"And a great one," I said warmly. "Why does your brother speak differently from you and Gautam?"

"Because," he explained patiently, "he went to Woodstock—you know, in Mussoorie and then to Columbia. After Harvard Business School, worked in the States, all in the line of gaining experience. Whereas Mama put her foot down about sending GeeGee and me away to boarding school. Sacrificing one son was enough, she told Papa. So it was St Vincent's for us. Now I'm in St Xavier's College. Bombay was as far as Mama would let me go."

"Cy, may I ask you a question? Would it be possible for me to go to church tomorrow morning?' Would your parents mind?"

"Of course they won't mind at all. As for going, I'll take you myself, and collect you later. There's a Cathedral—oh, you know it? By the way, I'm assuming you're a Catholic. Are you?" I nodded. "Early Mass?"

"Yes. But don't you sleep late on Sunday morning?"

"No, never. I hate to miss a chance to ride. Look, after church, will you come for a gallop?"

"I wouldn't miss it for anything. My last one."

My tone must have been wistful.

"By no means the last one. Mama will invite you again. No question about it. And if she doesn't, GeeGee and I will make the supreme sacrifice—go on hunger strike!"

"You're very sweet," I said unsteadily. "I can't tell you what it's meant to me to be in the heart of a family."

Cyrus muttered something under his breath. I followed his gaze. Two figures had appeared, walking away from us. The C.P, and his girl cousin. "That aunt of mine!" Cyrus exploded. I looked at him blankly. "Trying to snare Jai for Aparna for years. Keeps pushing her down his throat. That's why she sent me to fetch him now. Hideous creature!"

"The aunt or the cousin?"

"Both!" violently.

"The cousin isn't bad-looking."

"Not bad-looking! Jai should marry a princess! Not this dull plain female! Why, he could have the pick of the lot. You should see him at parties. Girls falling all over him!"

"Very bad for his ego," I observed.

Cyrus spluttered; then, catching my eye, burst into laughter.

Madame refused to listen to me when I said I could take the train on Sunday afternoon. It was all arranged, she said firmly. It was an affectionate leave-taking.

"Next time I'm going to beat you at Scrabble," GeeGee warned.

"Looking forward to playing with you again, partner," Cyrus told me.

Mr. Samartha shook hands and patted my shoulder. "Adrian would be proud of you."

I found out why the C.P. was nowhere in the place. It was his car I was going in. There was nothing I could say in protest. It would have been churlish to say one word. As might he expected, the chauffeur was banished to the back seat, and I was put in front with the C.P. The journey was uneventful. We stopped en route for a meal after which we sat in the back and chatted desultorily on the last lap of the way. He seemed to pick the most impersonal topics. I dropped off at Bandra. The interlude was over.

Inevitably there was a letdown. Then I was plunged into work, and the weekend at the Samartha home seemed to be a distant dream.

CHAPTER 7

IT TURNED OUT TO BE ONE OF ORION'S MOST CHARMING efforts. Our client was a famous manufacturer of footwear of all kinds, to suit every need and purse. We had sketched out the basic plan before Diwali, and now set to work in earnest. We conceived of having a gallery of people representing many walks of life, pictured individually wearing their own kind of shoes, sandals or *chappals.* The concept was hardly a new one, but the charm of it would lie in the personae selected. We decided to include a woman vegetable vendor, basket on head, a milkman, a glamour girl and so on.

Prem sent us out to look for the most appealing faces for some of the categories. It wasn't easy, but we were full of high spirits and enthusiasm. We found the cutest small boy whose disarming grin revealed wide gaps in his teeth, an enchanting little girl staggering about on uncertain legs. After pounding the pavements for some days, the perfect vendor was discovered, no further than a furlong away from the complex. It hardly mattered that she was a fruit vendor and not a vegetable seller since all it took was a switch in the contents of her basket. She wore a nine-yard sari, a big red dot on her forehead, and when she smiled, her broad pleasant face lit up revealing betel-stained teeth. Purva spotted a college student in a bus who, dressed up, looked a lovely glamour girl in her elegant high-heeled sandals. And so it went. Balaram was exacting about background and much effort was expended in locating the most suitable ones. Other than the baby and the glamour girl, all pictures were to be shot outdoors. The very satisfying final results succeeded in showing admirably that the manufacturer could supply everyone need.

Busy as we were, it came as a shock to me to realize the Season of Advent had begun, and Christmas was around the corner. Orion closed only for one day, on December 25th. For those whose festival Christmas was, Christmas Eve could be taken off, and made up later. It was a matter for rejoicing that Christmas this year fell on a Saturday, for then there was the bonus of having Sunday off also. Other than an office party hosted by Clemmie and myself, I had no special plans for celebration. My landlady invited me for Christmas dinner. So did Clemmie. She and I planned to attend Midnight Mass together on the 24th.

This was the time of year when my spirits reached their lowest ebb. Christmas is a time for family and friends to come together to rejoice and share in the fellowship of love: and peace. There was such a deep ache in my heart when I thought of my parents. When one had no family, what did one do? Endure the loneliness somehow.

On December 20th I was frantically busy completing an assignment when I was asked to report to Miss Kagal's office. Puzzled, I took the elevator up.

"A call for you. From Pune," the lady told me. "Just a minute." She listened a moment longer, then handed the receiver to me and left the room, having picked up a file.

I couldn't believe my ears. Stammering, I replied. Madame Samartha was inviting me to spend the Christmas weekend at Kaheksha. Oh, the bliss of being with the family once again! Of being able to ride. To play the piano. Somehow I uttered my grateful thanks, making one stipulation—this time I would come up on the Deccan Queen on the 23rd evening. After I hung up, I was so elated, I could have danced a jig, but instead I thanked Miss Kagal who had just returned, rode down in the elevator and walked sedately back to work. Everyone was busy. I had not been missed.

This time I knew what to pack. Besides my riding outfit and boots, I added a sweater and a shawl, for I knew from experience that Pune was much colder than Bombay. I treated myself to two new outfits, one a dress in a deep rich red, which did not clash with my hair, most appropriate for the Day of Joy, with sandals to match. I had my hair done, and a facial. And I shopped judiciously for small gifts that would suit my purse. For GeeGee, I found a giant poster of his favorite pop star. For Cyrus, I had the fortune to find a cassette of symphonies played by the London Philharmonic Orchestra. In a bookshop, it was not difficult to make a choice—an illustrated book on famous racehorses, which I knew Madame would enjoy, and for Mr. Samartha, hot off the press, the autobiography of a controversial Indian diplomat. Only the C.P., assuming he would be there, defeated me. I knew nothing of his interests. Ultimately, I settled for a paperweight in the shape of a tortoise. Its face was wrinkled as it peered from its carved shell, both funny and appealing.

I traveled to Pune in a spirit of gaiety. Cy and GeeGee were at the station to meet me. We greeted each other like long-lost friends, talking sixteen to the dozen. Madame hugged me, and Mr. Samartha patted my shoulder. It was a homecoming. I overheard someone say the C.P. was driving up, but had called to say he was held up and would be late.

Dinner was a lively meal. Madame said they wished to celebrate Christmas with me.

"We love any excuse to celebrate," she said.

"And to eat," GeeGee put in.

"In the garden, there's an evergreen in a pot. I thought we could decorate it. I found some decorations on Main Street. The boys will help you. And you must tell me what else we can do. Fortunately, our chef has quite entered into the spirit of the thing, it being his festival too, and has been baking all sorts of festive fare."

"How kind you are," I said warmly. "I was dreading the loneliness of having to spend the festival by myself. And here I am in the heart of your lovely family. I shall never forget the joy of being with all of you."

"My dear," she said, and touched my arm.

The three of us had a merry time after dinner. We hauled in the tree and set to work. Madame had been modest about the number of decorations she had bought. There was a whole boxful, complete with a string of colored bulbs. So, laughing and chattering, Cy attending to the taller branches, GeeGee to the lower while I gave directions, we were totally immersed in the task. Cy had put on some Christmas music, all lively favorites, and it added to our light mood. So engrossed, we did not notice a new arrival. Only the star remained to be attached at the top. Cy, defeated by its height, said he would need a chair to stand on when his eye alighted on the figure in the doorway. "Oh, Jai will do it," he said cheerfully. "He doesn't need a chair."

Startled, I swung around to meet the C.P.'s gaze. He strolled forward. "Very festive," he said. "With the music and everything, I thought for a moment, I was back in the States." He took the star from me. "Where do you want this?" In a moment, he had fixed it in position.

"I think an angel would have looked better," GeeGee observed, standing back for a critical survey.

"Hmmm. Think, if Sakshi would consent to be the fairy and occupy the place, how lovely!" Cy suggested.

"And have a total disaster?' I murmured to cover up my unease. Never was I really comfortable in the C. P.'s presence. I was too conscious of him when he was in the room. I had to be honest. It was those vibrant looks that were responsible. I did not approve of my own reaction at all.

Christmas Eve began with a thoroughly enjoyable ride in the company of the boys. It was a glorious morning, crisp and cold, but also bright and sunny. Later, after breakfast, I went with Madame into Pune Camp for some shopping. I concealed my wonder at the way my hostess bought the best without concern for the price. Having lived in the environs of Pune for many years, I was well acquainted with shopping centers. There were some places that were so expensive, Mumsie and I had never set foot there, frequenting the modest establishments we could afford. So it was in Madame's wake that I now entered such luxurious surroundings where she was recognized at once, and given every attention by the owners themselves.

I had not seen much of the C.P. except at mealtime. He seemed least interested in my activities, spending much time with his father and, Christmas break or not, at the telephone. I suppose I was hardly worth a second thought. I had a surprise waiting at dinner.

Cy enquired about Midnight Mass when the C.P. broke in.

"I'll take her." I saw the indignant look on Cy's face, and the slight shake of his father's head as he looked at his second son. "Well, okay," Cy said, then brightened. "But after dinner, we'll play, Sakshi."

And we did. Cy unearthed some music and we played part of the Hallelujah Chorus, moving into the old beloved carols and the modern ones including some calypso selections, before concluding with the soft, moving notes of 'Silent Night'. This time there was no applause, only an appreciative murmur from our audience of four.

At 11 p.m., wrapped in my shawl, I went down. I had been uneasy about my escort, but guessed that perhaps my hosts felt that if I had to go out this late, it would be safer for me to be taken by someone more adult than the youthful collegian that Cy was Certainly my companion was formidable enough to tackle any rowdies en route. The C. P. was reading by lamplight, and rose to his feet when he saw me.

"I'm terribly sorry to be such a nuisance," I said nervously. He did not answer, but led the way to where his car was parked. It was very cold, and would be colder when we returned. The C.P. was wearing a zipped up leather jacket which made him look extremely dashing.

The streets were practically deserted at this hour. As we neared the Cathedral, throngs of people, warmly wrapped, were hurrying for the Mass.

I had expected to be dropped off as Cy had done, but after parking the car and locking it, the C.P. walked by my side into the Cathedral, letting me take the lead. I had covered my head with my shawl and genuflected before finding us two good seats in the third pew, letting him sit nearest the aisle. I knelt to pray. Then I lost myself in the prayers, the sermon and the special choir numbers.

Later, the bells pealed joyously as the congregation poured out, greeting each other exuberantly, shaking hands, and embracing. We knew no one, but greeted the Bishop and attending priests at the door. It was something of an effort to get through the crowd. A strong hand enfolded mine, and led me to the car.

I threw my shawl back from my head as the car moved onto the street. Shyly I said, "Thank you. That meant a great deal to me. You were very kind, Sir."

"I hadn't been to a Catholic service before. I've attended Protestant ones frequently in the States—in Univ. chapels and some Congregational churches at Thanksgiving and Christmas. Quite a difference. The attitude of reverence is quite striking. Which is not to say it's lacking in the ones I attended." He took a right hand turn. "Incidentally, you haven't stopped 'sirring' me. I want to hear you say my name." I shot a glance at his face, and looked away at once. He was waiting.

"J-Jai," I stammered.

"That's fine," he said.

CHAPTER 8

MADAME SAMARTHA'S CHEF DID HER PROUD THAT CHRISTMAS Day. He had made all the fine foods that go with the celebration of the Festival. There was even a plum pudding with brandy sauce to end the meal. The chef had borne it in himself, and set it alight with great panache. Although he accepted our compliments without moving a facial muscle, Madame said he was well pleased.

"In which case, I hope he goes easy on those poor minions of his. Our pal is a regular tyrant in the kitchen," Jai observed.

"And temperamental too," his mother added. "But then when our guests dine royally on his masterpieces, I find it in my heart to forgive him."

We adjourned to the small sitting room. Shyly, I produced my small gifts. If the Samarthas were acting, I wasn't able to detect any false heartiness in their reactions. GeeGee went off at once to pin up his poster in his room, Cy to listen to the cassette. Their parents vowed they would start reading their new books this very day. Jai held the little paperweight, the long fingers touching it with great delicacy of movement. It would be put on his office desk as a mascot, he said. That wise look on the face of the tortoise would remind him of the adage that slow and steady wins the race. I took a quick look to see if some subtle irony was involved in that statement, but it wore its habitual bland look. I hesitated when he asked if I would join him for a ride after tea. It seemed rude to refuse. He was my boss, after all.

It was late afternoon when we pulled up the horses.

The gallop had been glorious. I had not missed the way Jai rode as if born to the saddle—which he certainly was. We halted in the same place where Madame and I had rested that first afternoon, and spent the time getting acquainted. During that short visit, anger and humiliation had been uppermost in my mind, directed against this one man who sat now, back against the broad trunk of the banyan, fine profile outlined as he gazed into the distance. My present state was one of confusion. I did not dare put it into words. But the plain fact was that from the first meeting with Jai, I had experienced this magnetic pull towards him. It frightened me so much that I told myself I was a perfect idiot, on par with those girls who developed a giant crush on some pop star or movie hero. Clemmie had gushed over him in the dining hall. Countless other women surely did the same. I scolded myself sternly. Watch it, my girl, I told myself severely. Remember who he is. If you give him the faintest inkling of your feelings, he will laugh in your face. If the Samarthas guess, they will be furious at such presumption, and stop inviting you. It will be the ruin of a wonderful relationship, and you will be the loser.

The dark head, hair ruffled by the ride and so not in its more immaculate condition for once, was turning to me. I averted my head and now stared into the distance. "You said your second name is Alexa?"

"Yes."

"It suits you. How did you acquire it?"

"I was born on July 17th, the Feast Day of St Alexius. Then my father's best friend was Alex Franklin. He is my godfather."

"Do you see him often?"

"No. He lives in Mussoorie now. We write and keep in touch."

"And your first name?"

My parents wanted a name that was out of the ordinary. They weren't satisfied with the names they had found. So they consulted the parish priest and asked him to choose a name that was meaningful. His suggestion was Sakshi—Witness."

"An unusual name for an unusual baby as I'm sure you must have been. Almost has a Japanese touch, even though it is such an Indian word." We sat silently for some time.

"Like many people, you must have ambitions, which you hope to realize. What are they?"

I knew he was making polite small talk. "I don't know if they're ambitions. I'd call them dreams—impossible ones! But a pleasure to think of them when one has a moment."

"Uh huh. Such as?"

"I'd like to paint for myself—not under instruction, or as part of a job, but for the sheer pleasure of it. Portraits especially, but also landscapes. Perhaps dabble with clay, see what I can do in the way of sculpture. Then I'd love to travel, see places. I've never been anywhere."

"Uh huh. And what else?"

I laughed. "It's as crazy as the first two. I'd love to have my very own horse."

"You could have all three."

"You mean if I won a lottery!"

"No, I didn't mean a lottery. You could have them if you married me."

He spoke so calmly that for a moment the meaning of his words did not register. Then they hit me.

"It's-it's cruel to make fun of me!"

"I've never been more serious in my life."

I searched his face. Surely this was a monstrous joke. "You can't possibly mean that!"

"Why can't I mean it? Look at me." And when I did, biting my lips to stop their sudden trembling, he went on, "I've been meaning to ask you for months. This is the first opportunity I've had."

I whispered, "But—all these months—you've never tried to get in touch with me, or come to the Orion offices when you were in the complex—or asked me for a date."

"If I had, you'd have been the center of all kinds of gossip. Perhaps even scandal. Do you see why I kept away? It was for your protection."

My heart was thudding furiously in my breast. I put a hand to my throat. There was no doubt he was serious. "But—why me?"

"Because you have the qualities I'd want in my wife. In my children. Courage, particularly. My family succumbed to them. A great sense of humor. And undeniably, you're one of the most beautiful girls I've ever seen."

"But—I don't have a rich—or influential background," I stammered.

"Do you really think I need money—a fabulous dowry?" he asked with a half smile.

I was silent, my thoughts whirling. It was still unfathomable. Jai Samartha asking me to marry him?

"What—what would your family think? They'll be terribly shocked—disappointed in your choice."

"I told them long ago. They've met you, and are supremely satisfied."

I stared at him. The great Samartha family satisfied that Sakshi Jerome, a little nobody, would be their daughter-in-law, wife to their oldest son, the C.P. himself? Was that why I had been invited to Kaheksha, to be looked over?

The sun was a red ball on the horizon. Where had the time flown? When we set out today, I had not dreamed what would happen.

Jai put out his hand and took mine away from my throat, replacing it with his own. It was the first time he touched me, and the pulse leaped under his palm.

"There's a tiny bird fluttering just here. I have been watching it," he said, and bent to put his mouth to the place. He raised his head, face an inch away from mine. "You're never to be afraid of me, Lex. Do you know I wanted to kiss you since that first evening when you crashed into me?" Very gently, he touched his lips to mine. He stood up and held out his hands to help me up. When I was on my feet, he said, quietly "I shall wait for your answer. You won't keep me waiting long, will you, Lex?" There was that diminutive again. No one had ever called me that before. I thought it was the most beautiful name in the world.

We mounted our horses and cantered off homeward. My mind was totally confused. I needed desperately to think.

When I went down for dinner that night, I felt terribly self-conscious for the first time now that I was newly aware of Jai's parents and their knowledge of his intention. Yet their manner was as normal as ever. I hadn't met Jai's eyes once though I was conscious of his on my face. When Mr. Samartha said, "Aren't you two going to play for us?" Cy and I rose with alacrity. Playing did much to soothe my troubled spirits.

Over GeeGee's protests that we were to play Scrabble, Madame carried me off to her den. I was very nervous, not sure what she wished to say. My fears proved groundless. She handed a little box to me. In it was a black velvet ribbon choker, at its center a most delicate cameo. On its raised surface, exquisitely carved, was the figure of a very young girl, bewitching in a simple classic Grecian dress. My eyes must have mirrored my delight.

"How beautiful it is," I whispered.

"It dates back to the days before I was married. A very old friend of my mother gave it to me. I thought the girl resembles you. On you it will look perfect."

"Such a precious thing. I don't deserve it."

"I look upon you as my daughter since I wasn't blessed with one."

Involuntarily, I met her gaze.

"Dear child, I think Jai spoke to you today?"

I nodded miserably. She came close and put an arm around me. The gesture was so loving, so unexpected, that the tears sprang to my eyes. She patted me. "You're not to feel alarmed. The choice is up to you. If you're worrying about our attitude, I can tell you we've never liked anyone so much as we like you. Jai has our full approval. I salute his discernment."

"You're very kind," I said unsteadily, "but I don't see—how I can accept. I see myself as quite the wrong person. I haven't any family. My ancestry is all mixed up. All I have is what I earn. A girl who marries a Samartha is surely expected to have wealth, a family that has status, social prominence."

"And be scatter-brained, frivolous, fritter away her time on silly pastimes, like playing rummy, buying clothes and jewels she doesn't need." The riposte came back swiftly. A glimmer of humor in her eyes, she continued, "Thanks to me, the ancestry of my sons is mixed up too. And the Samartha strain is going to be diluted still more. We expect our boys to choose their own partners. I have no doubt we have surprises ahead in that respect. Which is fine. Ketan and I had a love marriage. So we never planned to arrange marriages for our children. Frankly, I wouldn't know where to begin."

"He—he spoke about being attracted to me—physically. Nothing about—affection—love."

"Very remiss of Jai. Perhaps he hasn't learnt to be articulate about such things. But he'd better learn!"

"Did you—face opposition when you married?"

She laughed. "Plenty. Ketan's mother was horrified. She had a long list of 'possibles' for her only son, all carefully screened. And then he showed up with this Parsi girl! I don't think she was ever reconciled. The saving grace was that I presented her with three grand-sons. She died soon after Gee was born."

I was quiet, my head bent, thinking deeply.

"Sakshi." I looked up. "I know you're going through all kinds of doubts. For some of them, you need to talk to Ketan." My alarm must have shown in my face. "He's easy to talk to, I promise you. Go along. He's in his den. I'll be sending in the coffee tray soon."

I stood and left the room before my courage left me completely.

"Come in," Mr Samartha said when I knocked. He was in his favorite deep chair, leg on a stool, holding open the book I had given him. "Ah, Sakshi. I'm enjoying the book immensely. The fellow's an out-and-out rascal, but one has to admire his acumen. Slips out of situations like an eel. Yes, thanks to you, I have some exciting reading here."

"I'm glad," I said faintly.

Something in my manner must have caught his attention, for he looked at me keenly. He reached out and with his strong arm pulled up a chair for me next to his. At his invitation, I sat down facing him.

Characteristically, he went straight to the point.

"You're looking very disturbed, child. Do I assume Jai has approached you? And you're not sure of it at all, I take it?" In acute misery, I shook my head. "Why do you feel that way, Sakshi?"

"Oh, so many reasons." I twisted my handkerchief in my hands. "I wouldn't fit in. For one thing, I don't have the social graces Madame has."

He chuckled. "Do you think she came equipped with all the train-ing to be a gracious hostess? Far from it. It's something one acquires. An intelligent person—and you're more than that—could pick up the know-how in no time. In any case, Roza would be there to guide you."

"But what will people say? That Jai Samartha has married a little nonentity without a penny to her name."

"I dare say some fools will say that-if it's any of their business. But the majority will say that the C.P.—oh, yes, I'm well aware of what they call Jai—has captured the Komal Girl—which speaks for itself. A million young men will gnash their teeth over it!"

Involuntarily, I smiled at the picture his words evoked. Then I said soberly, "I can never give up my faith."

"Who said you'd be expected to? You may have observed that as a family, we aren't exactly religious-minded. I am partly responsible for that because I'm an agnostic. By marrying outside her community, Roza lost her title to being called a Parsi, her children debarred from being Zoroastrians. What she believes in, I really don't know. What we have endeavored to do is to give our sons values, which I hope will stay with them all their lives. So if our daughter-in-law belongs to a particular religious community, we certainly aren't going to object. In fact, that's all to the good. Unless she belongs to some weird sect, and goes around beating her breast and chanting strange chants, having first painted her face vermilion and yellow."

He had me smiling again. I looked at the strong face, the gray eyes, which must often be pain-filled, the deep lines scored in his forehead since the accident, and wondered anew that he should be sitting and talking to me so that I was fully at ease now, and could spell out my fears.

"I shan't be able to reconcile to my children not being Catholics."

"Ah, yes. I'd say that's a matter for you and Jai to work out for your own offspring. If it made them better individuals, some of your devoutness in my grandchildren would be welcome." He must have seen relief and surprise on my face. "Now before we proceed, do you think you can pour me some coffee?"

In my preoccupation with our talk, I had barely registered the arrival of the coffee tray, but now I jumped up to obey his request. We drank our coffee in perfect harmony. I thought how long it had been since I had been able to pour out my heart to someone who was in a position to give me fatherly counsel. That it should be Ketan Samartha was a less startling fact now.

I resumed, "1 keep thinking how simple a man Daddy was—just a trainer of horses. Neither rich nor powerful nor famous."

"When I think of Adrian Jerome, I remember a man of unquestioned integrity and principles. Utterly trustworthy and reliable. When he took on a task, he gave of himself unstintingly. A giant of a man in more ways than one."

My eyes stung. What a tribute to Daddy!

When I could speak, I said, "One last thing—"

"Yes?" he said encouragingly, and seeing I was finding it hard to grope for words, "Is it the thought of Jai himself that bothers you?" How had he guessed, I thought wonderingly. "My son is a rare person," he went on thoughtfully. "Too much has fallen too soon upon his young shoulders. And how well he has taken up the burden. He has more qualities of his grandfather than of mine. They both have the touch of genius. Some might call it the Midas touch. It's something inborn—an instinct which one can't acquire. It isn't that Jai is obsessed with making money. He isn't. But making a success of any venture becomes a challenge to him." He paused to drink his coffee. "But as a human being, it's less easy to fathom him. He doesn't open up easily. I suppose caution and wariness are requisites in the business world. With Jai, it probably spills over into his private life."

"Is that why—in all the reasons which he mentioned for wanting to marry me—he never said he cared for me?" I saw that I had startled him. "He said he admired some of my qualities—such as courage—that he wanted his children to have those traits. That I was beautiful. It's as if he found me a satisfactory candidate who satisfied the norms for—a—a job. So I was interviewed, and selected." I had not expected my companion to throw back his head and roar with laughter. "Somehow it's—so cold-blooded. I always thought I'd have a love marriage. This sounds to me very much like an arranged one."

Mr Samartha wiped his eyes. "Forgive me. Your simile was so apt." Then seriously, "Jai must be losing his touch. I'm ashamed of him. I'm going to ask you an embarrassing question—which you don't have to answer. You've hardly known Jai except in the most impersonal way. In a physical sense, how do you feel towards him—attracted, repelled, indifferent? Good heavens, it sounds like a questionnaire, doesn't it? Tick off the correct answer?"

I had bent my head so that my face was hidden.

Suddenly I felt very shy. He was waiting for my answer.

"Attracted," I said, very low.

He did something, which moved me very deeply—put out a hand and laid it on my head. "My dear child. We shall await your decision."

I spent a sleepless night. All kinds of thoughts kept whirling through my head. It was the most incredible situation. By dawn, I had made up my mind.

I was up very early. This time I was returning to Bombay by the Deccan Queen. I had told Madame I would have breakfast on the train. By going early, I would have most of Sunday to organize myself for the week. I had said my goodbyes the night before, expressing my deep-felt gratitude. I was to be driven to the station.

It was no surprise to find Jai waiting at the foot of the stairs. I was very calm as I greeted him, my decision having been made—. Traffic was light. It seemed that in no time at all we were at the station.

The DQ was standing on Platform One, less crowded than on weekdays, but still there were plenty of people around. Jai found me a window seat. I had declined to enter a First Class compartment. He bought me a pile of magazines. The fact that I might have bought myself one to read, while he bought an armful in the casual way of the very rich, emphasized the yawning gulf that lay between us. I wondered how many people recognized him as he stood outside my window. Dressed in slacks and sport shirt, sleeves rolled up to show sinewy arms, he looked more like a male model than ever, this time for outdoor wear, and was attracting several glances. So, I must confess, was I. Hastily, I donned my dark glasses.

The big clock on the platform ticked on relentlessly. Two minutes before the DQ was due to move, Jai looked at me, his eyes not leaving mine.

The words spilled out of my lips. "I thought—I'd tell you now. I—I can't marry you."

"Why not?"

"Because—I don't want to—play the beggar maid to your Cophetua. Because I'm the wrong girl for you. I don't fit into your social circle. And—and you—don't love me." The last words were the hardest to enunciate.

There was a last minute flurry as passengers hopped on. Goodbyes were called out, last words exchanged. Jai had reached out and taken my hand firmly in his.

"We'll have to see about that." He was walking along as the train slid into slow motion. "I shan't give up, Lex." He let go my hand, his gaze very intent. The train picked up speed, and Jai was out of sight.

I sank back limply, my head against the back rest, and closed my eyes. I felt as drained and exhausted as if I'd walked ten miles.

CHAPTER 9

I SHOULD HAVE KNOWN BETTER. ANYONE CLOSE TO JAI could have told me that once he went after something, he did not give up.

For a few days, all was calm enough. We were terribly busy at Orion, and with Prem cracking the whip, there was very little time to think during office hours. Nevertheless, I was mentally very disturbed indeed. The entire incident had left me in a dull daze. Sometimes I wondered if I had dreamed the whole thing. It wasn't the kind of situation I could discuss with Bhanumati and Prem either. I could hardly go to Prem and say, "Look, our mutual boss has proposed to me—and I've refused. What next? Do you think I'll be thrown out on my ear? And if so, what shall I do?" I was truly without anyone to turn to. I was aware that almost without exception, all my colleagues would think I was the most foolish girl in the world. Feeling as I did for Jai, I probably was. But my own conviction that all my arguments were perfectly valid, that I had done the right thing, was unassailable. Or so I thought.

Even now, I was not approached directly. Jai used the services of the Postal Department. Every few days, a small item arrived for me. The gifts came in many forms, all in impeccable taste, expensive certainly, but not outrageously so. A pretty silk bookmark. An exquisite lace-edged handkerchief. A hilariously funny card. A hair clip in the shape of a dragonfly, delicate in its iridescent beauty. A glass globe on its own stand, no more than four inches high, at its center a perfect red rose. If Jai's parents had told him what I said, then he had launched into a subtle courtship, all the more distracting because it was quite out of the ordinary.

No sender's address or note ever identified the little packages. It took all my resourcefulness to conceal them from the others. Inevitably, they were noticed. Since wild horses could not drag from me the identity of the sender, I came in for so much teasing that I was tempted to flee.

It reached the stage when I tensed up long before the post was distributed, not knowing what might arrive that day. If anything did, I slipped it instantly into my haversack. "Sakshi's secret admirer" became a standard joke.

It seemed to me that each item was an avowal of intention complete in itself. If the purpose was to make me remember, then it was succeeding admirably. I felt as if some implacable force was carrying me to an inevitable conclusion, and I was helpless to save myself. I overheard someone say that the C.P. was out of the country. After a break of some days, word went around that he was back, and at this very moment in the complex. My heart leaped in my throat. We caught fleeting glimpses of him, never alone, always accompanied by the usual coterie of executives. The girls whispered excitedly when that happened, envying the lone woman who was part of that circle.

Soon after, the post brought a somewhat larger offering. I had to squeeze the longish package into my bag with difficulty. That night, in the seclusion of my room. when I had cut open the wrappings, I could not suppress a cry of delight. It contained a little bagpiper in a kilt, about twelve inches high, complete in every detail from bonnet to sporran. He was so realistically made that one could almost hear the skirl of the bagpipes filling the misty, early morning air of his Highland home as he marched along in perfect step. I smoothed the tartan with my finger, took in every small detail. Of all the gifts, none had charmed me more than this little figure from Fiona's land.

I was waiting in line at the bus stop next evening, thankful to be seventh in the queue. When the long gleaming bonnet of the car appeared and the vehicle slid soundlessly to a stop in front of me, my eyes locked with the enigmatic dark ones looking out of the driver's window. He did not speak. I could not move. Weeks had passed since we parted at Pune Station. The impact on me of his sudden appearance was staggering. I had become almost witless, my brain refusing to function. Then I became conscious that the entire queue was watching, that in a moment cars would start piling up, setting up an ear-splitting cacophony of indignant honking. It would be a disturbance of the peace. Overcome by a sense of inevitability, I went into jerky motion like a puppet, my feet taking me willy-nilly out of the line, and off the pavement, through the car door which was being held open for me. The door slammed, and we moved effortlessly into the flow of traffic. No words had been exchanged. I sat back limply, my head against the backrest. I felt like a stuffed doll, unable to move a finger of my own volition.

Jai drove with practiced skill. I did not ask where we were going. Church gate. Marine Drive. Chowpatty, past Wilson College, and then the road began to climb I registered it all distantly. We reached the top and were now driving along tree-shaded streets where only glimpses were visible of mansions tucked deep behind tall beautifully trimmed hedges and protected by impenetrable iron fencing. The car slowed and turned into a pair of massive gates, up a drive, and came to a halt in front of an imposing stately dwelling. The sound of the door slamming must have alerted the household, for the big doors opened and a man-servant came swiftly down the marble steps to open my door. A low-voiced exchange followed. I caught the words "tea" and "dinner".

It seemed to me that I was in a veritable forest of tall trees making the enclosure green and mysterious. The top branches of several intermeshed to form a canopy. Surely they were very old. I recognized a laburnum and a Rusty Shield-bearer, Neat flower beds rioting with color, the pure tinkle of a fountain, creepers trailing up stone walls providing a burst of purple, deep pink and yellow, all lent a special aura to the place. Vaguely I recalled Madame saying this house had been built by the first Jaisingh, that Jai occupied it whenever he lived in Bombay. It was fully staffed, of course, as one could tell clearly by the way the garden looked.

"Come and see the view." They were the first words Jai had spoken to me. I followed him to a parapet. I drew in my breath sharply. What I saw was a feast for the eyes, an artist's dream. One could see the shoreline beyond which the tall high-rise buildings reared their heads, already illuminated, for the day was dying. The horizon was not quite visible from where we stood, but the setting sun cast its glow over the sea. Directly below, the breakers crashed over black rocks glistening in their wetness.

"It's beautiful," I whispered.

"As you are."

My eyes swung from the seascape to his face. I hadn't realized he was so very close, looming over me from his considerable height. I shook my head dumbly. His lips quirked in a smile. "What does that mean? That you're not beautiful?" He cupped both hands around my face. "I've been taken to task quite severely by my parents. A girl must be wooed, they tell me."

"Is that why—you sent me all those gifts?"

"Only partly. I sent them because I wanted to, because when I saw them, I knew they were for you. Did you like them?"

"Loved them," struggling not to let his closeness overwhelm me. "Especially the bagpiper."

"I got him in London last week." His hands moved to my shoulders, slid down my arms until he held both of mine. "Lex, one of the reasons you gave for turning me down was that I didn't love you." He turned one of my palms upwards and smoothed it. "I'll have to be honest about that. To me, that four-letter word spells hogwash. It's something the poets dreamed up, and eulogized *ad nauseam*. One loves one's mother, a mother loves her child. Okay, I'm willing to go as far as that. But this thing teen-agers gush over—it's all an illusion. But I do care for you. I feel concern for your welfare. I want to give you security. To give you my name if you'll accept it. "The dark head bent over my hand and I could not see his expression." And since we're being honest, I must add I've never wanted any woman as badly as I want you. And I think you're not indifferent to me, are you, Lex?" Mutely, I shook my head. "I'm probably saying all the wrong things, but I can't let you believe in something that doesn't exist. You understand what I'm trying to tell you?" I nodded again, unable to speak. I had a lump in my throat. "For the rest, I can only quote the words of the Christian marriage service—'With all my worldly goods I thee endow'—though I know very well they don't interest you. Beggar maid to my Cophetua, you said." There was a smile in his voice. "Lex?" He put a hand under my chin and lifted my face up. "When you look at me with those green eyes with those gold flecks swimming in them, I feel as if I'm drowning." I could not help the tears gathering. "My mother said I was to be more romantic, create the right setting. I can't supply the moonlight," he went on, "but I can manage the roses."

"Oh, Jai," I said, and he took me in his arms, holding me close. "I'm so frightened. Are you sure? Quite sure?"

"I'm sure," he said quietly. "You have no cause to be afraid. I'm right there beside you. As are all the Samarthas." For a long moment I hid my face in his shoulder, feeling warm and secure. Then he said, "Which reminds me. You know, we hadn't told Cy and GeeGee about my intentions. But all was revealed this time when I was home. Gee-Gee is practically not on talking terms with me. He said furiously,

'You can't *do* that! *I'm* going to marry her when I grow up!' I won't be surprised if Cy had a similar plan for his partner."

"Oh, Jai," I said, smiling through my tears, and went into his arms.

It was done. The die was cast. Over dinner that night, we made plans. I would give in my month's notice according to rules, not because it really mattered but to arouse no undue speculation. I was to tell no one. When the month was up, I was to move to Kaheksha. The details of when and where to have the wedding, we would leave till they could be discussed with his parents. If I were willing, we would have a quiet wedding, which was Jai's personal preference. That suggestion was an utter relief to me. I was unprepared mentally for the ordeal of having a grand society affair. I did raise one point. I had to tell Bhanumati and Prem. They were like my family now, and it would hurt them terribly if I didn't share the news with them. They could be relied on absolutely to keep the matter confidential. "Agreed," Jai said.

"Jai," I said hesitantly as he looked for some music to play for us, "I have to bring up something. I asked Mr Samartha about it. He said it was a matter between the two of us. I'm talk-ing—about—about our children. I—I would want them to be raised as Catholics. What do you feel about it?" He waited till the strains of Mozart's *Eine Kleine Nachtmusik* filled the room with its lovely romantic mood, and then he came to sit by me. "Did you think I would mind? Why should I? I have no affiliations to any particular religion. We were brought up that way. You'd be the mother. It's entirely up to you." I let out my breath in relief. "Now why are we wasting time like this," Jai said, "when we have better things to do?" and took me in his arms.

CHAPTER 10

THE MONTH THAT FOLLO'WED WAS A MOST EXTRAORDI-
NARY ONE for me. The first priority was to send in my resignation,
the: second to ask Prem when I could see him and Bhanumati privately. He looked at me keenly and promptly arranged to take me
with him after office hours that evening.

Bhanumati produced one of her wonderful dinners. When the
children were asleep, we settled down. They looked at me expect-
antly. When I told them, there was complete silence. Bhanumati
recovered first.

"But how romantic! Like something out of a story book!" she
exclaimed.

"The Prince and the Pauper? Or is it Patient Griselda?" I suggested
wryly.

"Oh, Sakshi, you mustn't think like that!" she scolded\ in shocked
tones. "I'd say the C.P. is the most fortunate of men to be marrying
you. None of those scatter-brained society dolls for him evidently."
Prem hadn't uttered a word. Both of us waited, I more than a little
anxiously.

When he spoke, it was slowly. "Sakshi, you've really stunned me.
Have you thought about this in all seriousness? Jai Samartha is the
last man I'd have thought of as a husband for you."

"Oh, Prem! You mustn't think I've rushed into this blindly. I've thought and thought—spent sleepless nights. I turned down his proposal once because I was so full of doubts. I know exactly what you're thinking because those were my thoughts too." I went on to outline them.

"I don't agree!" Bhanumati stated firmly. "The Samarthas are getting a pearl beyond price!"

"You're very sweet but I seriously doubt that. Mr Samartha—Madame—the brothers—have been darling to me. Do you think I'll have in-law trouble, Prem?"

"No," he said tersely. "That's the last thing that worries me. And I agree with Bhanu about their getting a jewel. No, it's the man himself-Jai-who bothers me. You mustn't get me wrong, Sakshi. I take my hat off to him for his genius in the business world. 'The Wonder Boy', some business magazine called him not so long ago. Look at the way he's taken over the running of the Group for his father. True, Ketan Samartha is constantly in touch with its workings, but it's Jai who's in control now. I appreciate the way he's done away with the obsolete, brought in innovations which have yielded 100% success." Prem took a refill of coffee. "He's never reckless about it but introduces them in the right place at the right time. Seems to have an instinct about it." He put his cup down with some force. "But the man has no warmth in his entire make-up. He's incapable of deep emotion. You know that in the Group he's called the C.P. In the business world, they've named him the I.M.—the Ice Machine. I tell you, Saksbi, where he should have a heart, there's a bloody icicle!"

"Wrong shape for a heart. Wrong color for an icicle," I tried to joke, but a shiver ran down my spine.

Prem had only my welfare at heart. What he was doing—albeit so vehemently in very un-Prem-like language—was to give me his unvarnished opinion for my own good. It was doubly disturbing because Prem was usually a man of few words.

Bhanumati said in an incensed tone, "Prem, I think you're being a horror about the whole thing! I don't believe the man can be all that you say. You're exaggerating. And frightening the poor girl out of her wits."

"No, I'm not. Every word I've said is the absolute truth." He controlled himself with difficulty. "Saksbi, all I'm doing is to put you in the picture. You'll agree I've known the C. P. longer than you have?" I nodded. "That I want what's best for you?" Another nod. "Good. My conscience doesn't permit me to stay silent on the subject. You have to be warned."

His wife protested. "Surely Jai has shown a different softer side to his nature to the girl he's going to marry? Just because he doesn't kiss you on both cheeks before every briefing doesn't prove a thing, Prem."

I thought of the man who had held me in his arms only last evening, kissed me with gentle consideration, tempering his own impulse no doubt so that the inexperienced girl he was holding should not be alarmed and perhaps take flight. Was that man really what Prem claimed him to be?

Bhanumati was saying, "And let's not forget one thing. Even if he's a bit cold now, Sakshi's influence will go a long way in changing him. And he' s so devastatingly handsome. isn't he?"

"Women!" her husband said scathingly. "As if it matters whether he's handsome or not! That's precisely what I'm trying to say. Here's a warm lovely person getting permanently linked to an icicle, and all you can talk about is the man's looks. Sakshi's influence! Nothing can change that cold fish!"

By degrees we calmed him, and managed to bring up practicalities. I mentioned Jai telling me that my resignation would be handled in such a way that no one would know. When the month was up, I was to slip away. Prem would announce my departure after I'd gone. In the remote event that news of my leaving leaked out, Prem would handle it.

But after the Chandrans had driven me back to Bandra late that night, Prem's words haunted me. And one day they would come back strongly and clearly.

My last day at Orion, but except for Prem and Naren Kaushik, no one was aware of it. I had been so happy here, I thought, made friends with all these fine young people. Rohit and Kunal were so talented, Purva not lagging too far behind. Any discerning person could see they were destined to go far in their careers. It gave me a pang to think I was no longer to be a part of this highly creative young group.

Naren had evidently been briefed about the imminent arrival of my resignation letter. Nevertheless, he sent for me. I answered his queries, or rather parried them, for Naren was extremely curious to know why I was leaving. No, I hadn't been unhappy here. Quite the opposite. A full time modeling career? Not at all. Yes, I was launching into another career, the offer for which had come some time ago. No, my instructions were to keep its nature under wraps. Had it been the Komal campaign that had brought about the offer? Well, perhaps. I really didn't know. I made a little speech about my stay at Orion, and how much I'd grown and learnt here. It was patent Naren suspected I'd accepted a film role. I kept my answers non-committal. Poor chap, a pity I could not tell him the truth. Still unsatisfied, he let me go at last.

Naren had permitted us to have extra time off, for I was giving the group a treat. It was the least I could do when I felt so guilty at keeping them in the dark. To their puzzled questions, I had only said lightly that a party from me was long overdue. We hadn't celebrated my birthday, or the spectacular success of the Komal campaign. Besides, I was in a party mood. Being young, possessing healthy appetites, always ready to have fun, they probed no further. We went to a Chinese restaurant, and had a rollicking time. I was glad. I hoped the memory of this afternoon would go a long way in making them forgive my deception. It was painful to say the usual casual farewells when we parted that evening. I did my best to keep my tone light as I responded to Kunal's witticisms and the lighthearted exchanges with the others. Then I put my head down and walked away quickly to the bus stop.

I had been surprised at Mrs Fonseca's reaction when I gave notice. Always worried that her lodgers would outstay their time, she actually showed regret. I had been a model tenant, she told me, and a calming influence on the rebellious teen-age Teresa. She did solve one of my problems. I had wondered about my furniture and household goods, my inborn thrift refusing to let me toss them all out carelessly. After all, I'd spent my hard-earned money acquiring them bit-by-bit. Mrs Fonseca offered me a lump sum for it all. From now on she would let the place furnished, and at a higher rent.

I did not touch my fixed deposit account, but I did withdraw all my savings, which I had put in a current account. One important purchase I had in mind was a wedding ring from the bride to the groom. I had no idea if this groom would deign to wear my humble offering, but to me it symbolized the bond that was to unite us. I decided that for my own satisfaction at least, I would give it.

Which thought brought me to Jai himself. I was torn between supreme joy and darkest doubts. Joy, because I loved him with my whole heart; doubt, because I did not know if I was making the greatest mistake of my life. But the die was cast and I was committed. That did not prevent me from agonized self-searching.

As Jai's hectic schedule permitted, we spent several evenings together. It was a time for getting to know each other. For all that we were to spend a lifetime together, in a sense, we were barely acquainted. Much of our time was spent talking. I listened with absorbed interest to his childhood, of school at Woodstock, of Columbia and Harvard, and the United States in general, struck as always by the wide gulf that separated us in birth, background and status. Because Jai wanted to know, I told him tidbits of family history. Fiona intrigued him very much. He wondered why Dominic had not done more to track her down. He had done all he could, I explained, which wasn't much, considering how he was hampered by geographical distances and lacked the finances to go personally to Scotland. In any case, he had still been very much in the Army. Besides, where would he have started in a strange land? As for Mynheer, we only knew his first name had been Pieter. The rest was lost in the mists of time.

In those quiet hours at Malabar Hill, I learnt that my husband-to-be was capable of tenderness and considerateness. That fact lulled my initial nervousness. If sometimes his control slipped momentarily, he took himself in hand at once. As for me, the warmth and closeness of Jai's physical presence filled me with emotions I had never experienced before. They overwhelmed me in their intensity.

CHAPTER 11

JAI

I CONFESS I BRAINWASHED MAMA. I TOLD HER THE WED-
DING would have to take place two weeks after Lex left Orion. Over
her protests that it wouldn't be fair to Lex, I told her I was so inun-
dated with work, and had an international conference coming up in
a matter of weeks, that it really was either now, or then to be postponed indefinitely.

There was an element of truth in what I said. As it was I had to
juggle my commitments around to take a week off: The fact was that
now that Lex had given in, I could not wait to tie the knot. I was not
leaving to chance any last minute change of heart.

I shall never forget the shock I experienced one day some months
ago. The afternoon had begun normally. I had been told that one of
my appointments was with the Orion duo. I thought nothing of it. It
was all in a day's work, Kaushik, often accompanied by Chandran,
attended meetings when I called them. Now we were led to a smaller
room where the seats faced a TV screen. Before the lights went off,
Kaushik made a few introductory remarks about a new soap
Coquette was launching. I cannot claim he had a hundred percent of
my attention. I had far more weighty problems on my mind than a
toilet soap. One or two executives asked questions, and then the
lights went off.

Soft, lilting music accompanied the spiel about the new soap, which apparently had been given the name Komal, extolling its virtues, Then appeared the down bent head of a girl. Lights picked out the highlights in the burnished silken cascade of hair. Some elusive memory stirred in me. A very good-looking young man was looking down at the girl. When she lifted her face to his, it was blindingly beautiful, the skin dewy as a flower, the green-gold eyes shy yet full of feeling. The fine straight little nose, sweetly curving mouth, the exquisite modeling of the face—I took them all in, drawing in my breath sharply. What really jolted me was the sight of the delicate line of throat, the bare shoulders, the way the material clung to the curves of the young breasts, clearly all she was wearing, the slim arms encircled with flowers. "No!" I felt like shouting. "You can't display my future wife like that!" All I did actually was to sit motionless and watch the man offer a rosebud, which in her shyness the girl would not take at first. Then hesitantly, she put out a slim-fingered hand and took the gift, letting her lovely head drop down once more.

The lights came on. Everyone broke into excited speech. It was extraordinary. A superb commercial, which ought to have spectacular success. Balaram's genius was unmistakable. Other agencies would be green with envy. Where had they found a girl whose looks translated the word *komal* so perfectly? Where had this unknown beauty been hidden all these days?

Kaushik looked extremely smug. I felt like punching his face in—not a desire I'd ever had before. He explained that one reason why he had shown the commercial, not a common practice, was because the model was an Orion employee. In fact, was assistant to Prem Chandran.

There were astonished exclamations. They would like to meet her, they said. See her for themselves. Oh yes, wouldn't you, I thought savagely. So that you can ogle her, think every kind of lewd thought. If I could have, I'd have flung each one out of the window to go plunging down to ground level, deriving immense pleasure from the act.

As it was, I said nothing. Kaushik was looking at me anxiously. He brought up the question again of the model being an employee. Sought permission on her behalf.

Left it a bit late, didn't you, I felt like saying with all the sarcasm I could command. The others couldn't see the least objection. Why, as a matter of fact, it was something to be very proud about. Would bring in enormous publicity, therefore a tremendous boost for Orion, and ultimately for the Group.

Having given their opinion, they waited for me to speak. When I did, I asked my questions coolly. Raised practical issues, underlining the need to make the whole thing legally watertight, the girl getting all monetary benefits due to her. I asked pointedly if she would go into professional modeling. Kaushik plunged into reassurances on that point. It was a question for which I needed an answer personally. I suppressed my desire to reprimand him for not clearing the matter first before reaching this stage, but I let that go. I could not deny it was one of the finest commercials Orion had ever created, and had been that with fine attention to detail. I had not missed even while drinking in the sight of the girl, the music, the sweetness of the voice extolling the soap, the words themselves, even the rosebud, a cream shading into delicate pink. For me to say anything critical now would be ungracious in the extreme. What stood out most was the realization that I must act fast. Once the campaign was launched, the Komal Girl would be the cynosure of all eyes. I would go to Pune to see my parents and tell them I had found the girl I wanted to marry.

Sweet as she was, Mama began preparations early. We planned a simple civil ceremony at Kaheksha without any guests at all. Lex, however, requested that she be allowed to invite Prem Chandran and his wife. The couple was very close to her, she said. This was news to me, but there was no problem about her inviting them. After all, Lex had no one else to invite. She had written to the Dubashes, then receiving no reply, had telephoned. She was told they were out of the country, visiting their son in the U. K. I had not met Mrs Chandran. Chandran, of course, was a very familiar figure to me. Orion was indeed fortunate to have him. Much of its most successful advertising was due to him. But as a person, I found he was taciturn to the point of being quite grim. If charm and a pleasant manner had been a requisite of his position, he would have been an abysmal failure.

Mama and I debated privately about inviting my aunt and family. It was an open secret that she had been trying to marry off Aparna to me for years. I had ignored the whole thing, but the poor girl was horribly embarrassed by her mother's none too subtle tactics. Aparna was a nice little person, hardly responsible for her plain looks. It was for her sake that I went along when Arundhati insisted on throwing us together at family gatherings, often lending a sympathetic ear to her problems with her parents. I didn't care for my uncle either. His laziness and neglect had put his own company into a precarious position. He drank more than was good for him, and was a womanizer. Which only served to make my aunt more determined than ever. An alliance with her brother's family would set everything right, financially at least. I was not keen to have a disappointed malicious Arundhati hovering over our nuptials like a death's-head. To add to her unpleasant qualities, she was an out-and-out snob. I doubted if she could desist from digging out all she could of Lex's background. Not that one needed to be ashamed of any of it in the slightest, but in Arundhati's value system, money counted most. She was sure to say something unforgivable to Lex, unless she was watched constantly. It was the thought of Papa's being placed in an awkward position over his sister that decided the matter.

We had no intention of sending out any formal announcements, or throwing a gala reception later. None of us realized then how much offended reproach would be directed towards us. Personally, I had an aversion to standing for hours with a smile pasted on my face,

flash bulbs going off and blinding me continually, accepting insin-
cere congratulatons. There would be loads of expensive gifts, which
I certainly didn't want. I seldom attended weddings, finding it a most
dreary waste of time. Why then inflict mine on others?

My one thought was for my bride-to-be. That first evening at
Malabar Hill when I had made love to her, I had found myself intox-
icated by her beauty and freshness, the very perfection of her. I had
found out at once and was fiercely glad that she was completely inexperienced. I saw how nervous she was, the green eyes wide with
innocent apprehension, the red lips which needed no artifice, tremulous, and for her sake I had curbed my impatience, not an easy matter. How she had managed to escape male attention was a mystery.
Probably her own lack of a family to protect her had made her wary
of getting involved with men. I recalled how when at our first meeting I had stopped to offer her a lift, she had been extremely reluctant
to accept. The Chandrans may have kept a stern eye on predatory
males too.

Lex would have to acquire a trousseau. Mama worried about it.
"I'd like to get her a whole wardrobe," she told me, "'but I don't want
her to feel offended."

"Get a pile of outfits together, Mama, and tell her it's customary to
present the stuff to the bride from the groom's side. Blame it all on
tradition. Later she can buy whatever she needs."

"Think so?" doubtfully. "Can we do the same with jewelry?"

"I guess so." On that front, I had had to restrain my impulse to
cover Lex with jewels. I knew it would disturb her very much if I did.
But I hadn't been able to resist a set I found in Hong Kong. It was in
jade and gold, exquisitely beautiful, delicately exotic. The minute my
eye fell on it, I knew I must have it for Lex. Incurably optimistic of
me when I was still a comparative stranger to her at that point, and
had spent just one evening in her company at a fast foods place. I
decided an engagement ring was a must, and had chosen an emerald
flanked by tiny diamonds, a beautiful stone in an unusual setting. To

which I added a plain gold wedding ring. Lex would surely appreciate that Christian symbol of marriage, even if the man she was marrying were not of her faith—or any faith—and this was not to be a church wedding. For the rest, I would wait. My grandmother's jewelry, some of which had gone to Mama—who never wore any of it—remained untouched, destined for the wives of her three grandsons. I hadn't known till Mama told me now. As she said, the old designs were in style again, but modern settings could be considered. From herself and Papa, she had several ideas of what she would give the child in the way of jewelry. I looked at her. "You're actually glad to be doing this, aren't you, Mama?"

"Oh, so glad, Jai! She's a very special, special girl. I recognized a kindred spirit within moments after I met her. How terrified I've been that you'd bring home one of those society beauties you're photographed with so often, clutching on to you on all sides."

"You have?" I was very amused. "But you never said one word to me!"

"How could I? For all I knew, one might already have been there in the offing."

I shook my head. "No, that was definitely out. My idea of what I wanted—someone quite out of the ordinary—was very clear. I knew for sure what I didn't want."

"The offers have poured in, Jai. Many from your father's business colleagues—and rivals, I must add. He fobbed them off saying you had decided not to marry for some time. They're going to be stunned-and mortally offended."

"Who cares!" I said impatiently.

"It's an exclusive scoop for *The Clarion* then!"

"Uh huh. All set. Salil was darned pleased. Though I didn't reveal the bride's identity. Let's see. He's a long-time friend-though his editors haven't always been very flattering to the Samartha Group."

Some time ago, on one of my infrequent visits to the Poona Club, I'd learnt from a friend that, along with a few others, mostly young couples, he was buying a plot of land in a Pune suburb, and building a house. The plots were of a substantial size, he said, with plenty of room to spread out, have a garden, swimming pool and so on. I enquired about the other couples, found they were congenial people, many of whom I knew. The plots were placed so that everyone could have privacy without being isolated. I went to see them and was pleased that they were located about half an hour's drive from Kaheksha.

I bought a plot without any clear idea what I'd do with it. In any case, it was a good investment. When the other houses began coming up, I could not see why I should not build one too. Whether I was ever going to live there was a question I did not bother to worry about. I could always sell at an enormous profit. And then in Bombay, I had the good fortune to meet a young architect who was exactly on my wavelength. Geet Adityaraj, not long back from the U.S. with a degree in architecture, was the son of the distinguished Gyan Adityaraj who had designed some outstanding examples of architecture in India and abroad, particularly in the Middle East. Geet and I communicated so well that he knew exactly what I was talking about. This wasn't going to be one of those stately mansions like Samartha House, but a modern one.

Both of us enjoyed dreaming up the house. I listed my priorities. A living room where twenty-five guests could be accommodated happily. A master bedroom. Guest rooms with attached baths, the latter to be the last word in comfort. A spacious airy kitchen where the morning sun would pour in, complete with breakfast nook. Plenty of closet space, built-in wardrobes, and storage closets tucked away neatly. A graceful staircase. Outdoors, terraces and garages. A spot selected for a possible swimming pool. A landscape architect began work simultaneously with the laying of the foundation stone.

At first, my parents were indulgent about what they considered a pleasurable pastime. If they wondered why I needed a house at all, they did not voice their feelings aloud. I had shown the plans to them, and Papa made a couple of very down-to-earth suggestions, which Geet incorporated. Mama came down frequently as the work progressed, and in time, became so enamored of the whole thing that I asked for her help in choosing floor tiles, bathroom fittings and so on. Cy dubbed the place Jai's American Dream House.

Some of my friends teased me about my future matrimonial bliss. I had never given the matter much thought. As it was, I was too pre-occupied with plans and problems relating to the Samartha Group. I thought vaguely that some day I would have to acquire a wife—the who, when and how of it I did not bother about. Until I met Lex. And then it all fell into place. The house was for her.

CHAPTER 12

SAKSHI

JAI DROVE ME UP TO PUNE, MY BITS AND PIECES STOWED IN the boot. I was given a truly heart-warming welcome by the family. Jai relinquished me into the care of his parents. From now on, having left Bombay, I would see him only at weekends.

I was swept into preparations for the wedding. Private though it was to be, Madame said a certain newspaper, the son of whose proprietor was a friend of Jai's, would cover the proceedings, taking exclusive photographs. I protested vehemently when she said that she was planning a whole wardrobe for me. It was the tradition, she said firmly. Normally, she would have done all the selecting herself, but thought it better to let me choose what I liked. Every Samartha bride received these clothes and sets of jewelry. Her mother-in-law had observed the custom as she was doing. I fell silent. It hurt my pride deeply, but what could I do except yield?

Madame must have realized what I was feeling, for she: patted my cheek. "You mustn't mind, my dear child. Custom dictates these matters. I know how fiercely independent you are. You aren't going to deprive me of this pleasurable activity, are you? I can hardly wait to get started on buying feminine garments for a change! And if I do all the choosing, and you hate it all, that'll be a real disaster! So let's have a wonderful time. The first wedding in the family, and I fully intend to enjoy every moment of it!"

And a wonderful time it was. On the first trip to Bombay, one of many, I meekly followed her wherever she led. We went to the most expensive boutiques where exclusive models were available. The one place I enjoyed most was called The Honey Bee. The owner was a lovely person, very chic, very gracious, with a delightful sense of humor. It was she who had designed some of the choicest outfits, which I fell in love with. "Call me Madhur," she said smiling, then after surveying me with an expert's eye, displayed what would look best with my coloring. As I tried on one outfit after the other, I had to agree that she was right. "You're the Komal Girl," she said in her very British accent. It was a statement, not a question. "And you're as beautiful as your picture."

She hooked up the dress I was trying on. "And a bride I heard the lady—Madame Samartha—mention Jai's name. Are you marrying Jai?"

I was very startled. "Yes," I said after a moment. "But that's in confidence. No one knows."

She nodded. "I understand. And will keep it confidential."

"Do you know Jai?"

"Well, let's say I run into him at various places. I applaud his choice." Then more briskly, "This puts a different slant on what you must see." And she brought out some stunning designs that Madame and I could not resist. We left The Honey Bee with piles of elegant-looking gold boxes decorated with a rather handsome bee. I promised Madhur I would come back so that she could design an outfit for me exclusively.

Not too confident about managing a sari, I realized there might be occasions when I had to wear one. Madame took me to dazzlingly lit emporiums where the saris too seemed dazzling to my inexperienced eye. They represented every region of India, their colors jewel-bright. The more ornate ones, heavily embroidered with gold borders and *pallavs*, were very beautiful, but not to my taste. Madame was not a sari type either, but together we chose some lovely ones. Footwear and lingerie came next. When I recalled how Mumsie and I kept an eye on sales, how Teresa Fonseca and I hunted for export rejects at bargain prices, I found it hard to believe that these delicate sandals in every hue and design, and these insubstantial drifts of silk or lingerie made of heavy satin, lavishly inset with lace, or beautifully embroidered, were all for Sakshi Jerome.

"Jai," I said hesitantly one Saturday night when we were strolling in the garden at Kaheksha, a few days before the wedding, "there's something I must ask you. I've thought a lot about it—and yes, worried about raising the matter."

"Why? Did you think I'd beat you?" he asked dryly.

"No, but you may not like it."

"Curiouser and curiouser." He stopped and took me by the shoulders. "Am I so forbidding that you can't ask me right away? Am I such an ogre to you, Lex?"

I ventured to look up, but his face was in the shadow. "It's—about my giving you a wedding ring. Would you wear it?"

"Is that all you were going to ask?"

"Not quite. I'd—hoped you'd come with me—to have it blessed. To—have the priest bless us." The words were out at last. "But—if you don't want to come—I can go alone."

When Jai did not speak, I was miserably aware that I had expressed myself badly, and probably angered him.

He surprised me. "When do you think we should go?" he asked gravely.

For a moment, I could not answer, then for the first time, I flung my arms around his neck and hugged him spontaneously. "Oh Jai, thank you, thank you!" I stammered.

"If that's all it takes to make you react like that, I think you should ask me for favors more often." I buried my face in the warm column of his throat, feeling very shy. "Lex., did you think I haven't been aware of how much it disturbs you that we are having a civil wedding?" He was holding me, cheek on my hair. "Perhaps you won't even feel it's a proper ceremony at all—that you're being made to live with me in sin." I strained to listen. "And I'm very sorry about it. It comes as no surprise to me that you want to be blessed in church. As for me, I can certainly do with some blessings. And I'll be honored to wear a ring that has been given by my bride. Does that answer all your questions?"

Having no words with which to express my feelings of gratitude, I put them all into the first kiss I had ever given him. Motionless for a moment, he then took over. When he loosened his hold sometime later, we were both quite breathless. I wondered if he was as shaken and trembling as I was. That the physical pull between us was a powerful vibrant pulsating force was undeniable.

The Cathedral held the complete peace and quiet it always did when it was empty of worshippers. I was caught up in the sacredness of the moment. To me, this was the real wedding ceremony, with Jai and I kneeling as Father Gregory laid his hands upon our heads. We exchanged no vows, but the ritual was immensely moving for me. When we had received the blessed rings, the priest put an arm around each one of us.

"I pray that you may be blessed with a very happy marriage, my children," he said as we walked the aisle. He nodded, smiling kindly when we thanked him. But a minute later, it was he who was expressing his thanks when Jai slipped an envelope into his hand. It was not a gesture I had expected, for Jai had said nothing to me. "Most generous of you," Father said. "It shall be used where it is needed most. Thank you, my son."

"My pleasure," Jai told him.

Farewells spoken, we walked silently back to the car. We were well on the way when I said, "I—thank you for coming with me. It meant more to me—than I can say. And the donation. That was truly thoughtful of you."

"You may not believe it," Jai kept his eyes on the road, "but it meant something to me too. The civil ceremony is bound to be quite soulless. This blessing provided the touch that was badly lacking."

I had leaned my head against the backrest. At this time, I missed my parents so badly, it was a deep ache within me. They should have been here now by my side, giving me their love and parental blessing. Tears stung my eyes and I closed them so that they should not spill over. When a warm hand came down to enfold mine, I opened them. Jai was looking at me. Why had I ever thought he was cold and unfeeling when I could see the profound understanding written so clearly on his face? I tried to smile, failed in the attempt, and the tears spilled out.

Perforce, Jai had to take his hand away and put it back on the steering wheel. He had not spoken.

"It's strange," he said as we approached the home stretch, "and perhaps a little fanciful of me—which is why I haven't mentioned it to Papa—or anyone for that matter—but there have been moments in my life when I've really been stuck over some vital decision, and then had this feeling almost as if my grandfather was there in person, guiding me into the right thinking. I was very close to him, you see. One might explain it away as the good sense he instilled into me—perhaps some traits I inherited from him." I had turned my head to listen, my face still tear-wet. "So it should be for you, Lex. You're thinking of your parents, aren't you? Missing them terribly, wishing they were here? In a sense, they are here, for they live in your heart. They've passed on so much that is good and fine to you—qualities that will endure all your life—perhaps be passed on to succeeding generations. I should think all their love is with their child at this moment." He drove through the massive gates of Kaheksha, up the tree-lined drive straight to the garage where he parked the car. As we took the path that led to the house, I felt my grief diminish. Jai had taken my hand in his, and I was warmed and comforted by it and by his words.

I shall regress a little at this point. There was one individual who discovered my presence at Kaheksha and was instantly outraged. No one had confided in Jai's aunt, and when she dropped in for her usual Sunday visit, she found me there. She was far from cordial and lost no time in treating me like an unwelcome addition to her brother's house. Finding me there again on her next visit was too much for her. I heard her expostulating with Madame without troubling to lower her voice. The essence of her tirade was that the Samarthas were allowing this girl to exploit their goodness. So what if she was the child of a good friend who was no more? How could Roza be sure the creature was honest? For all they knew she could be a thief! Some day they could very well discover some valuables missing! It was unlike Madame, but she quelled her sister-in-law sharply for once. After that, the lady held her tongue, but looked daggers at me. It did not help that it was Jai who whisked me out of the house within minutes after his aunt entered. Still, even in her wildest dreams she did not guess at the truth.

Such a sweet relationship had been established with each member of Jai's family that I tried not to let the unpleasantness disturb me too much. It did rankle, of course, but then, after all, I was only human. The hurt inflicted by Arundhati's words cut deep initially. Then one night after dinner when only Jai's parents were present, his father said something, which made all the difference, and brought balm to my heart.

Just as I was "Sakshi" to them, as always I addressed them as "Sir" and "Madame".

"Do you miss your friends at Orion, Sakshi?"

"Yes, I do, Sir," I said honestly, "and I miss working. But certainly not in the sense that I'm unhappy. You and Madame, Cy and GeeGee have made me feel so much at home, I could have been born a Samartha."

He looked at me quizzically. "Since you're going to be one by marriage, do you think you can try to call us 'Mama" and 'Papa'? Not if it makes you feel awkward, though." He smiled at me, eyes twinkling. Madame seemed to be waiting for my reaction. 'I have a strong desire to hear a girl's voice calling me 'Papa'. Unless you feel that would be disloyal to your own parents?"

There was a lump in my throat. I left my seat to perform the only act I could that would express my feelings. I knelt in front of Madame's chair, and leaned forward to kiss her cheek. "I'm deeply honored to call you 'Mama', but more than that, I shall love doing it." She put her arms around me, and patted my back. I could see she was too moved to speak.

On my feet again, I turned to Jai's father. "And to call you 'Papa.' Mumsie and Daddy have a special place in my heart. Both of you have another."

Mr Samartha and I smiled at each other, then he held out his hand. "Come here, child." And when I obeyed, he reached up and kissed me on the forehead. "Roza and I are happy beyond words that Adrian's daughter is to be our daughter too." I was touched to the core. Shyly, I kissed him on the cheek. He too patted me gently. The moment was so fraught with emotion that no one spoke for an interlude. There was a glow in my heart, which completely eradicated the cruel words I had overheard.

My last evening as Sakshi Jerome. After dinner, we adjourned to the small sitting room for coffee.

When the tray had been brought in, Mama dismissed the servants while Cy locked up after them. Quite oblivious of these actions, I sat quietly next to Jai, listening to Papa. I was quite tranquil now following the visit to the Cathedral, for Jai's words of comfort had stilled the turmoil in my heart. Neither Cy nor GeeGee with their irrepressible high spirits and teasing would permit any lapse into sentimental brooding. I was unprepared when Mama carrying a stack of boxes came to me. I gazed at her in surprise.

"Sakshi, I have something here for you. If Jai will let me sit by you?" She took her son's place. As she opened box after box, I sat quite speechless. It was jewelry such as I had seen only in color advertisements. She brought out set after set, the stones flashing fire in the lamplight, explaining what they were. These were gifts from the groom's family, she told me, and held a necklace against my throat, slipping a bracelet over my wrist. "A beautiful bride who is perfect in beautiful jewelry," she said with satisfaction. Then she looked at me. "You haven't said anything, dear," she said anxiously.

"I'm so overwhelmed—I don't know what to say. All this—can't be all for me surely?" I glanced at Jai. He was leaning over the back of a chair, watching.

GeeGee chortled. "Now Sakshi can model for some famous jeweler."

"Not if Big Brother has any say in the matter," Cy commented dryly.

"They're—like something out of the Arabian Nights or a pirate's treasure. I think I'm dreaming! But when would I wear them?"

"My poor innocent child! You'll need every last one! You'll see. There'll be so many social affairs."

Papa had been sitting in his big chair, amusement on face as he took in the scenario. "The object of the exercise, Sakshi, as I understand it, is to make every other woman green with envy," he told me. "Which Sakshi will do anyway," Cy added.

Mama went on "There is some other jewelry which will come to each new bride—it belonged to Ketan's mother. The settings may belong to another era, but they are very lovely."

GeeGee exclaimed in horror, "Do you mean to say my bride has to wear some of the junk?"

"Hardly junk, GeeGee! Those stones have been collected from all over the world," his mother told him.

"Then why haven't I seen you wearing any?" GeeGee demanded cunningly.

"Because, my dear fellow, I am the horsy type, and I hate to be weighted down by stuff like that. The few times I wear jewelry, it's under protest."

"Sakshi's horsy too."

"Horsy but beautiful."

"Beautifully horsy." GeeGee was so charmed with his own wit, it took him some time to stop laughing.

I put a hand on Mama's arm. "I don't have the words to say—it's all too much for me—I'm quite bedazzled—but I thank you. They're all so stunning, it will take me a long time to look at each one and really come to know their beauty. I'm terribly ignorant. I don't even know what the stones are—but I love them all."

"I'm glad," she said simply, and kissed my cheek. I kissed her back.

Eventually, the family retired tactfully, leaving Jai and me alone. Jai took my left hand and slipped a ring over the third finger. "Lex, we didn't have an engagement in the interests of secrecy, but I want you to have a ring. You didn't know it, but I slipped it in to be blessed with the others," he said quietly.

I stared down at the rich deep green stone surrounded by tiny sparkling diamonds, and fell in love with it instantly. "Jai—the stone?"

"An emerald for my green-eyed bride. I felt nothing else would do. Like it, Lex?"

"I can't—take my eyes off it! It's absolutely gorgeous!" But when his hands undid half the buttons of my blouse, and folded back the fabric on each side leaving my throat and the area below it bare, I was startled enough to look away from my ring. Jai reached for a flat box and opened it, then first took out a necklace that he fastened around my throat. My wrist was lifted next and a bracelet slid over it. Lastly, he tucked my hair behind my ears and took his time screwing in a pair of earrings. I had sat without moving till he finished. I was led by the hand to the oval mirror which hung on one wall. I stared at the girl reflected there. The gold-flecked green eyes picked up richer color from the exquisite jade and gold jewelry.

It made her look like some rare painting on a silken scroll of a court lady, and delicately exotic.

"Jai," I whispered, "it's the most beautiful jewelry I ever saw. Is it—jade?"

"Yes," the deep voice said in my ear. Hands on my shoulders turned me around. "I found the set in Hong Kong. It wasn't long after I met you. When I saw it, I knew it was for you."

"But you didn't know me then!"

"Even so, I knew I was going to marry you some day."

I gazed at him helplessly. In a husky voice, he said, "If Mama rated a kiss, what do 1 get?"

For the second time, I lifted my arms and, pulling down his head, kissed him, at first a little hesitantly, then with greater confidence, putting all my feelings into the kiss. "If that's what comes with a few bits and pieces," he said against my mouth, "then I know how to get around my fiancée—ahem, almost wife." And took over from me masterfully. If only you knew, I thought, before I let my senses drown in his embrace, that it isn't the bits and pieces as you call them, but this feeling for you which is like no other I have ever experienced.

CHAPTER 13

BHANUMATI AND PREM HAD ARRIVED THE DAY BEFORE THE wedding in Pune. Prem had said they would be staying with a cousin. I suspected that he had no intention of letting the Samarthas, particularly Jai, play host to him and his wife. Even if the cousin were not a myth, he would have: chosen to put up in a hotel. I had asked them to reach Kaheksha early so that Bhanumati could help me to dress. We were definitely short of ladies in this family, and no doubt Mama would have a hundred and one things to see to.

The ceremony had been fixed for ten o'clock in the morning, which meant getting up very early. It hardly mattered to me, I hadn't slept much anyway. Mama had suggested a professional beautician for my hair and make-up. I told her I could manage. I had learnt all I needed to know in both matters in the process of becoming the Komal Girl. When after a bath, I dried and brushed my hair vigorously, it shone in burnished waves on my shoulders, feathery tendrils curling all around my face. I used a light make-up for my face. When I looked in the mirror, it was the Komal Girl who looked back at me, eyes a little wide with apprehension. Arriving at that moment, Bhanumati distracted me from my nervous self-doubt. She herself was resplendent in a brilliant blue South Indian sari with wide gold border, heavy jewelry adorning wrists, ears and neck, flowers in her hair. Her large dark eyes sparkled with excitement. I was so glad to see her.

She hugged me quickly but warmly, taking care to keep from touching my hair and face. Then she turned to where my bridal outfit lay on the bed.

When Mama and I had shopped for something suitable, we had had a difficult time choosing. It was at The Honey Bee that Madhur had laid out this outfit for me to try on. Mama had said positively, "That one, Sakshi. Green and gold—just your colors. It could have been designed for you." It was a *salwar-kurta* in gold tissue shot with green. The price had made me gulp, but Mama had not turned a hair, and I had to admit it was unmistakably bridal. Now Bhanumati was saying in a hushed voice, "How splendid! Are you ready to put it on?" Carefully, I slipped into the *salwar* and tied it at the waist. Tightly cuffed at the ankles, it looked exactly like harem pants. Now I could sit down and put on the high-heeled gold sandals. Very carefully, Bhanumati slipped the *kurta* over my head and hooked me into it. I had to admit, the tailoring was superb, doing full justice to the lovely fabric. The gold tissue *dopatta* folded into a long narrow scarf was arranged over my left shoulder and pinned there securely from where it flowed down in a graceful fall.

Bhanumati was overcome. "Oh Sakshi, how beautiful you look! Truly a princess for the C.P.!" She frowned "But you don't have any jewelry! I knew something was missing!"

I directed her to open the closet. She did so, and seized the pile of boxes to carry them in triumph to the bed. As a true expert, it was she who recognized the gems for what they were, exclaiming aloud as she examined each piece.

"I should have guessed the Samarthas would do this in royal style! There's a king's ransom here, Sakshi!"

"I know. So straight to a safety deposit vault! You see, I'm learning!"

"Which set will you wear now?" Lovingly she turned a diamond bracelet to catch the light. It glittered with fire. "This one?"

I took one more box from a drawer. She was silent as she stared at the contents. "From the C.P." It was not a question but a statement. Her voice was hushed. "He must be crazy about you, Sakshi, if he chose this himself. How relieved Prem will be. Somehow it's more you than any of the others. And that's why the choice is perfect. You may not realize it, but it's true. You say he got it in Hong Kong?" She helped me with each piece, her admiration growing by the minute.

I said hesitantly, "I think I should add something from the other pile. Madame may feel hurt. It was all given with great affection. But T don't know what will go with what I have on."

She stood lost in thought, surveying the splendid array. Without speaking she reached for a long slender plain gold chain wrought in a rope-like design. Mama had said I could always attach a small pendant if I so wished later. Slipped over my head, it added to the jade set without detracting from it.

"There!" Bhanumati was well pleased. "Now if only some flowers—but I don't see where—"

A knock. It was Mama.

"I was held up-" she began, and then stopped when she caught sight of me. "Oh, Sakshi," she said softly.

"You are the perfect bride! We made the right choice when we selected that, didn't we? I'd love to give you a kiss, but I mustn't now." She came closer. "Jai's gift to the bride? How exquisite!" She touched my cheek with her finger. "Dearest child, I can't tell you what a happy day this is for me—for Ketan—to welcome our daughter into the family."

"You did that from the first day I met you," I said unsteadily.

Mama groped for a handkerchief. "Goodness, I mustn't get all weepy now." She turned to Bhanumati. "Mrs Chandran, how good of you and your husband to come! And thank you for helping Sakshi to get ready. I've been trying to shake myself loose for at least half an hour, but there's been a slight problem."

Bhanumati murmured a reply. I could see she was rapidly changing any ideas she might have had previously about Mama. There was
liking and appreciation, also relief for my sake, on her face. "We're
definitely short of women in this house!" Mama continued lightly,
but I knew something had disturbed her. There must have been a
question in my eyes for she said reluctantly, "Arundhati and menage
have arrived." The five words spoke volumes. Mama forced a smile.
"Cy and GeeGee have appointed themselves your security guards.
The Registrar is expected any moment. And the groom is waiting!"

Bhanumati hurried to lock away the boxes. Mama took me by the
hand. She led us out of the room.

At the top of the stairs, I held back. I thought suddenly that I
should be dressed in white, wearing a veil, going up the aisle on
Daddy's arm, the scent of flowers all around us, and on the altar
white candles, their flames beckoning, the organ playing the stirring
music that welcomes the bride's arrival, while the priests waited to
perform the sacred ceremony. In the first pew, Mumsie would be
smiling, wiping a little tear, but so happy for her child. A wave of
such desolation swept over me that I groped with outstretched hand
for Bhanumati. She caught it in a comforting grip.

"Sakshi," Mama was saying anxiously. "What is it, dear? Are you
feeling faint?"

I looked all the way down. At the foot of the staircase, three figures
waited, faces turned up. Flanked by his brothers, Jai, almost unrecognizable in a cream *kurta-pyjama* outfit embroidered at collar and
cuffs in gold thread, gold *mojris* on his feet, every inch the C.P.

Cy said something to his brother. Jai stared for less than a
moment. Then he was mounting the stairs swiftly, eyes never leaving
my face. Bhanumati drew in her breath sharply. When Jai held out
his hand to me, my companions released their hold. In his strong
warm grip, the desolate feeling dropped away. Down below, Papa
was there, and a whole crowd of people. Flash bulbs popped.

There was a complete hush as we reached ground level. The wheelchair moved forward. Papa clasped our entwined hands in both of his. He had spoken no words, but this was his blessing to us. The small sob instantly choked back was Mama's. Then we were moving *en masse* into the big hall.

It had the unreality of a dream. Part of my mind registered the magnificent display of flowers in the center of an enormous table, chairs for the guests, lights going off in my eyes in a continuous barrage, chatter, laughter, movement, excitement. Jai and I going through the civil ceremony. The rings produced by Cy with a flourish from his pocket. And then suddenly I was Sakshi Alexa Samartha receiving warm embraces, kisses, handshakes, *namaskars* from the domestic staff. Mama reached up to cup her son's face in her hands and kiss him tenderly. Jai bent to receive his father's embrace. Only one face looked bitterly unhappy, but Arundhati kept her distance. The group around us probably served as a clear deterrent. Bhanumati was having the time of her life with Cy and GeeGee. Even Prem was seen to be talking to Papa in a corner.

We had moved to the other end of the hall where a grand banquet had been laid. It was quite informal with everyone helping himself, consuming the delicious food the chef had produced. He himself was very much in evidence, directing the show.

I had a quiet moment with Prem. I asked how the Orion crowd had reacted when they discovered I had gone.

"Hurt. They couldn't understand why you hadn't told them you were leaving. I had to tell them you were launching on a new career—which is stretching the truth, but not untrue. Sakshi—has it been all right?"

I knew he spoke out of deep concern for me. "Yes," I said simply. "I hope I look as happy as I am."

He gave me a searching look. "Then I'm satisfied. You will remember Bhanu and I are always there?"

I nodded, very moved. Dear Prem, always so strong and support-ive. Mama came up to put an arm around my waist and ask Prem if he'd eaten enough. The photographers were waiting to take pictures of everybody. We went with her.

When I go through the album now, pure nostalgia overwhelms me. Papa out of his wheelchair, sitting next to Mama, unquestion-ably the head of the clan. Mama smiling sweetly. Cy and GeeGee so smart and youthfully correct in suits and ties. Grim-faced Arundhati striking the single sour note, Aparna shy, her father bleary-eyed as usual. Bhanumati resplendent in her shining silk sari, Prem not seri-ous for once. And in the center of them all, my very own C.P., so proudly, heartbreakingly handsome, his chosen bride by his side, hand clasped in his. A record of a marriage, which started out with every promise for the future. And the promise was fulfilled-for some time.

CHAPTER 14

JAI

IT WAS, WITHOUT DOUBT, THE HARDEST THING I'D EVER DONE. Resuming the burden once again a bare week after we were married became a major effort on my part. I had not expected it to turn out that way, assuming I would slip back into the groove with my usual ease after a brief break. What I hadn't anticipated was that I would be loath to leave Lex. She had come back to Bombay with me to stay in Samartha House, but I was fully tied up, returning home late every evening. All day while attending to a myriad matters, I could not stop thinking of her, longing to throw everything aside and go to her. Which I couldn't possibly do. It was upsetting to think of her alone in the house on Malabar Hill with little to occupy her. Vishwas had served the Samarthas for a very long time, and the place under his rule ran on oiled wheels. For someone like Lex who had had a full schedule, the hours of the day must drag on endlessly.

The Clarion had come out with its exclusive color photographic display and report. The account had surely been written by a woman, and a romantic one at that, for she waxed lyrical over the beauty of the bride, the dashing handsomeness of the groom, and added quite a bit about the Samartha history. Coyly she suggested how the eye of the groom had picked out his most beautiful employee. KOMAL GIRL CAPTURES CROWN PRINCE'S HEART, the headline read, and a brief paragraph explained how the Komal Girl had burst into the public view in all loveliness to launch Coquette's newest product. An entire page inside was devoted to photographs in which Lex looked like a fairy tale bride. The media had hardly been pleased with the scoop of a rival paper. J had left it to my P.A. to handle the complaining calls from other dailies and periodicals.

It was less easy to shake off reproachful calls from friends and business contacts, all demanding a grand reception and an opportunity to meet the bride, and to give us their blessings—which really meant coming to snoop and conjecture. I'd have to consult my parents about that, I told them, and so put them off. In the meantime, I went home each evening, glowing anticipation in my heart.

It had been a time of discovery for me. I had thought I knew Lex well enough. As it turned out, I had not realized that my wife was a creature of spirit and fire and dew. Certainly I had known she was extremely frightened, very shy, about the physical aspects of the man-woman relationship. Mama had pulled a surprise after the wedding was finally over, and we were leaving for the secluded retreat I had borrowed from a friend of mine. She had found a moment to be alone with me, and laid a hand on my arm. "Jai, you will be—gentle with her, won't you?" It had surprised me till I remembered Mama had taken over the role of mother to Lex. "I will be," I had assured her, for I could see only her own concern for the girl she had accepted as a daughter prompted her to overcome her natural reticence, and speak to me on such a delicate matter. In any case, I hadn't needed Mama to remind me. I had drawn upon all my experience to be, in my mother's words, gentle, holding myself firmly in check. I had every intention of making our relationship richly meaningful to us both. That I had succeeded in awakening Lex was proved by her shy hesitant response to my lovemaking, until one night after an interlude which had shaken us to the core, we were struggling to resume normal breathing, the green eyes looked at me in dazed wonder before she buried her face against my throat, and whispered shakily, "Jai, oh Jai," in disbelieving way.

Even before we were married, I had always liked the way Lex listened when I reminisced, sitting at my feet, delicate chin propped on her palms, elbows on her raised knees, large long-lashed eyes fixed on me unwinkingly. I had never opened up to anyone else, or talked so much as I did now. It was Lex who begged, "Jai, tell me-" and, as she had asked, I would speak of my childhood, or about my life: in America. With such flattering attention, I needed little coaxing. It gave me a very special pleasure to evoke her delightful little chuckle. Inevitably, the moment came when my voice trailed off, and unable to hold back a second longer from the smooth fragrant young skin, the sweetly scented silk of her hair, and the lovely curving form, I would scoop her up into my arms. Then everything else receded into nothingness, and there were only Lex and Jai.

The house I was building was coming up rapidly. It was now that I told Lex to start thinking of how she wanted to furnish it. At first, she was horrified at the idea. "I wouldn't know where to begin," she said helplessly, but gradually as the edifice rose before her eyes, excitement gripped her. Now began an absorbed hunt on her part to track down what she wanted. It became clear that the artist in her reigned supreme as she selected furnishings of every kind. I was glad as I watched her immense pleasure in the task that I hadn't requisitioned the services of a professional decorator. After all, it was Lex's house, and I wanted her to do it up as she liked. I had given her *carte blanche* in every way, but Lex shopped with great thrift, checking and comparing prices instead of ordering lavishly as she could have easily done. On the weekends when we went home, it was Mama who accompanied her. Sometimes I went along. My presence was quite superficial. The two of them had a ball, engaging in earnest discussion over swatches of fabric for curtains, or considering the merits of this throw rug against that. It touched me that they shared so fine a

rapport. Clearly, Mama had missed having a daughter, and was losing no time in making up.

Speaking of rapport, Papa had fallen under Lex's spell completely,
going under without a murmur of protest. Few people had seen him
unbend the way he did with his son's wife. He chatted with her for
hours on dozens of topics. It relieved the monotony of his days, for
though he had plenty to do, he was still a prisoner in his chair. Since
his accident, entertaining had come to a virtual standstill at Kaheksha. There was an occasional impromptu guest, but Mama refused to
tire Papa out in any way with even the smallest party. Indeed, it
would have been a major effort on his part to play host. His leg gave
him considerable pain, some days being very bad ones. Talking to
Lex took his mind off for a while.

A problem Mama had agonized over related to Papa's diet. Always
a hyperactive man who was ever on the go, he had loved riding as
well as playing a vigorous game of tennis as time permitted. Now his
enforced lack of movement resulted in an increase of weight on a
frame that had never had an ounce of superfluity. The increase surely
couldn't be good for him. The chef was certainly heavy on ingredients like butter. The problem was how one could go about tactfully
into convincing him to cook meals that were not loaded with calo-
ries. He was just the type to take umbrage, and do the disappearing
act. Good cooks were hard to find. Lex took him on. She told him his
pastries were heavenly. Would he teach her how to make them?
Greatly flattered, he gave her lessons whenever we came up from
Bombay. Casually she brought up the matter of salads her mother
used to make that sometimes comprised an entire meal. When he
evinced an interest, she promised to try one out with him. It was
loaded with the freshest vegetables, had a low calorie dressing, and
was colorful and as healthful as anything one could devise.

His chest swelled visibly when she dubbed it "Salade a la Joachim".
The salad was the forerunner of many low calorie dishes. Lavish
praise was heaped on Joachim, for a new strategy had been born

with the family clamoring for this speciality of his or that. He never caught on that he was making very different foods, as for example, desserts, which were now built around fresh fruit instead of loaded with cream and nuts. Mama heaved a sigh of great relief.

As a special wedding present, my parents had given Lex a filly. The whole family went out to see how she reacted. Lex fell in love with her at once for she was the prettiest creature, lively and intelligent. Lex named the filly Astra On the spot because she said she was a heavenly creature.

My parents watched the pair fondly and indulgently. Then my wife flung her arms around them both and kissed them. Papa was visibly pleased. He patted her gently. In fact, the incident set a pattern, for whenever we were saying our farewells, Lex kissed my parents. Whether she missed her own people so much, or whether mine felt they now had a daughter of their own, I do not know. I guess it was both. As for Cy and GeeGee, it was a warm informal relationship they shared with my wife, enjoyable for all to watch.

It must not be supposed that Lex was all sweetness and light. The gleaming dark red of her hair indicated she had a temper and lost it when she felt strongly about anything. She hated cruelty and injustice, especially to the weak. That included animals as well as humans, particularly children. The only time I saw her flare up in the stables was when one of the horses had not been rubbed down after a ride. She did it herself while a shamed stable hand protested. Vishwas was less than pleased to find a couple of stray cats and a mongrel being fed at the back door of Samartha House every day. As for me, there were times when she put forward spirited arguments. I enjoyed the battle of wits, finding her views refreshing.

At first in fact, I didn't catch on when she sometimes responded with an "Uh huh". It was always said demurely. Then once, catching the hint of mischief in the green eyes before she lowered them, I realized she was imitating me. I hadn't been conscious that the Americanism was so much a part of my speech. And there were other phrases and expressions she picked up from me quite unconsciously. I was tickled, for on her lips they sounded cute.

I was proud to escort my beautiful wife to the innumerable business dinners, which were part of my life. If the guests were foreigners, and had brought their wives along, I found soon that I could leave Lex to entertain the ladies, take them sightseeing or shopping. To me, it was a real contribution, one which I appreciated very much. I didn't appreciate equally the male attention she inevitably received. Compliments covered her in confusion till she learnt to take them in her stride. At the clubs in Bombay and Pune where I was a member, Lex made friends with several young couples. Sneha Chitradhar and she hit off. particularly well because Sneha was a J. J. graduate too.

She was a lively sort whose indulgent husband had set up a handicrafts shop, which she ran in partnership with two other ladies. Akash Chitradhar didn't need the financial returns the shop brought, but it provided his wife with an outlet for her considerable handcrafting talents.

Lex and I had talked about having a family. I guess it was expected of me as the eldest son to have children. For now, however, I was content to postpone having them. I didn't want to share Lex for some time to come. I knew Mama and Papa would love to have a grandchild or two to spoil. They would have to wait. In the meantime, life took on a special new meaning for me, all because of this extraordinarily lovely girl whom I held against my heart each night, watching the tender innocent beauty of her face as she slept deeply in my arms.

CHAPTER 15

SAKSHI

OUR HOUSE WAS READY FOR OCCUPATION. IT WAS TRULY THE most beautiful house I had ever seen, but more than that, it was Jai's and mine. When Jai's parents were building theirs, Mama had wanted an unusual name, nothing run-of-the-mill, and had finally chosen Kaheksha, which meant a cluster of stars, something in the order of the Milky Way. Hence the mural at the entrance. On a clear night, once could see the heavens in all their glory so the name was an appropriate one. It seemed to me that for our house I could not find a better choice than Iona, inspired naturally by that special feeling I had always for my Scottish grandmother. Iona was the name of an island of the Inner Hebrides off Western Scotland where St Columba had landed in 563 A.D. and it had been an early center of Celtic Christianity. I wasn't sure at all if Jai would approve of my choice, but he did, quite wholeheartedly.

Did he think it was rather foolish to use the name of a place many thousands of miles away? Why on earth should it be, he responded. In the States, immigrants who remembered the motherland with nostalgia and homesickness had named their towns and cities after those in the Old Country. And then there were the Biblical ones. He particularly liked the names of Native Indian origin, as for example, Minnehaha—Laughing Water. Never one to lose an opportunity to

ask him questions, I demanded examples from the first two categories he had cited. Jai obliged, patiently reeling off English
names—New York, New Jersey, Cambridge, Guilford, Birmingham,
Lancaster—French ones like New Orleans—and the Biblical Siloam
Springs, Bethel and Bethlehem.

Since the property had been landscaped early, tall neatly trimmed
hedges already formed a protective shield from curious eyes. The
exterior of Iona had been given a creamy off white paint with green
trim. Bougainvillaea creepers in all colors, for which Pune was
famous, were reaching up to climb the walls in pink and white, crim-
son, magenta, deep yellow and purple. The young saplings of flower-
ing trees had taken firm root. Asoka trees, still growing, would stand
sentinel all the way from the gates to the house.

Jai had advertised in the local daily, and to our good fortune, we
acquired a fine middle-aged couple, the Gonsalves, to work for us.
Their children had grown up and left home so they were happy to
find a niche with us, especially since a cottage on the premises went
with the job, Thelma was a superb cook, one of those rare persons
who actually enjoyed the challenge of cooking for a party.

Gonsalves took on the role of a kind of man-of-all-work-butler,
handyman, occasional chauffeur. Thelma had helpers in the kitchen
and to clean the house, while a *mali* took over in the garden.

Of great delight was the gift to me from Cy and GeeGee of two
male German Shepherd puppies, beautiful, tan and black, and full of
mischief. They won my heart instantly. I named them Romulus and
Remus, Rom and Reem for short. Dogs were a must in this area, for
the residents lived at some distance from each other. Already a stone-
wall was coming up to surround property, and a night watchman
employed. Jai installed an intercom between the house and the cottage so that the Gonsalves could be called upon if necessary.

Nothing gave me greater satisfaction than to enter the rooms I
had personally decorated. I knew Jai's preference ran to the modern,
and indeed, the house demanded it. I had never cared for steel or

chrome, preferring the warmer textures of woods in their natural grain. To me, color coordination was all-important, and I had been particular about choosing schemes for each room that were a delight for the eyes. I went wild with cushions that made a striking note, heaped on sofas, adorning chairs and stacked in piles on the gleaming floors, the covers representing in brilliant color every region of India. I had scoured out-of-the-way places for wall hangings to make a stunning eye-catching focus. For the master bedroom, I had thrown all discretion to the winds, choosing green and gold as the colors, repeated in the rich bedspread I had been fortunate to find. I was gratified to hear the compliments on my abilities as an interior decorator. Perhaps the final accolade came from the young architect who had designed Iona. When an individual as sophisticated as Geet Adityaraj said that I had made the interior perfectly attune to the spirit of the house, then I knew I had done a successful job of it.

Jai had become a commuter, plying between Bombay and Pune like thousands of others. Most of the time he went by train, because it was far less complicated, but on occasion made it by car. It meant several hours of traveling, but he wouldn't have it any other way. In turn, I averaged two days in Bombay, usually Thursday and Friday, so that we came together for the weekend to Pune.

This pattern evolved over a period of several months because when Jai was away on inspection trips, or out of the country. There was no point at all in my staying on in Bombay by myself. In Pune, I could paint and ride, spend time with my in-laws, but I missed my husband with a deep ache in my heart. I never let him know how I felt. He was on duty, and sentimental feelings on my part must not prove a hindrance. So I packed for him, saw him off with a smile, and counted the hours till his return.

It was Sneha who found me an interesting occupation to fill the gap. Talking to a regular patron of her shop, she had discovered that the lady yearned to have her child's portrait painted. Sneha thought of me at once because I had done a little watercolor of her baby son. It was a challenge for me, and I applied myself with all the skill I could command. The result delighted the lady, and as time went on, other similar requests came in. However, I did not confine myself to portraits, but tried my hand at landscapes, particularly the view from Malabar Hill of the sea and the skyline and rural scenes depicting villages and people that I saw when I moved outside Pune.

Once Jai took me with him when he went to Hong Kong and Tokyo. It was the first time I had ever flown, and he seemed to enjoy initiating his novice wife into the joys of foreign travel. I drank in everything with wide eyes. One memorable journey came about a year after we were married. Jai had to go to the U.K. for consultations, and I went with him. Considering that I had never been there before, I don't know why London seemed so home-like to me. The greatest pleasure was yet to come. From England we took a three-day holiday in the U.S., spending most of it at the farm of one of Jai's dearest friends. They owned a huge sprawling spread in Connecticut. I loved meeting Mary Anne and Greg Sealey and their three adorable tow-headed children. I loved being in America, and thought wistfully how "super" it would be to stay on longer in the country, which was second home to my husband. I knew Jai would have loved nothing better.

But as it was, we were fortunate to have even that much time. We were to leave via Boston, and were able to spend a few hours in that historic city exploring. Jai took me to Harvard, and I imagined him carefree and unencumbered as a student on this campus, little imagining how soon he would be called upon to return home and take on such arduous responsibilities. And then we were homeward-bound.

Since Jai was going to be away for some days, I asked him about a desire which I had long wished to fulfil. Of course I could do it, he told me smiling. I need not have asked, he added. And so my wonderful crowd from Orion, bursting with high spirits, so pleased and excited at being invited, some of them never having been in Pune, came up for a fun-filled weekend. They had such a good time, devoured Thelma's cooking with such gusto, leaving that lady gratified and beaming with pleasure, they completely forgave me for past sins. I took them to see Papa and Mama. Awed at first, they lost their stiffness under Papa's skilled handling and Mama's gracious welcome. I could see Papa enjoying their keen mental processes and youthful enthusiasm. Like small children released from the prison of a classroom when we left, they left their assumed decorum behind and recovered their boisterous spirits as I drove with them around Pune. In return, they brought me up-to-date with all Orion news, which I listened to avidly.

"Thank goodness the C. P. isn't here," Kunal said. "I'd be petrified."

"Sakshi isn't petrified, that's for sure," Rohit pronounced. "She looks every inch the radiant bride."

"Still," Clemmie said wistfully, "it might have been fun seeing the C. P. at close quarters in a different milieu—at his own hearthside, so to say."

"Mmmm, that's a chance we missed," Purva agreed. "You know, Sakshi, once we got over the shock of learning about your marriage, we all had to agree the two of you are made for each other. The C. P. had to marry a girl who was different. Beautiful anyway, but not like anyone else, and certainly not a painted society doll. And for our Komal Girl, only a prince would deserve her," Rohit said seriously.

"So we were glad for you! Though we miss you so much!" Purva put in.

Another time, I had the Chandrans up. With so much open space and fresh air, the children had the most wonderful time. They romped with Rom and Reem, sat on horseback, clutching on to me for dear life. Even Prem enjoyed the peace and quiet, while Bhanumati and I had so much to talk about. But no matter how much I loved these visits from my friends, I was ever in a state of waiting for my husband to come home.

CHAPTER 16

ANY WORDS OF MY OWN WOULD BE TOTALLY INADEQUATE TO introduce what surely must be the most incredible, and yes, heart-rending experience of my life. I can only let Byron speak for me when he says: "'Tis strange-but true; for truth is always strange. Stranger than fiction."

In actual fact, I was oblivious of what was happening, and it was Jai who was the first to hear of it. As it was, he told me about it after it was all set. When the call came from the Scottish Presbyterian Hospital, it was referred to one of the Group officials. There is always a lunatic fringe people in Jai's position have to contend with—cranks, disgruntled types, beggars—and the official usually handled them with brisk efficiency. However, this time it was a request he could not dispose of so easily. The business was of a personal nature. Eventually Jai's P.A. apologetically brought the matter to him. Intrigued, Jai had him contact the Hospital. The conversation that ensued made him cancel all appointments for the day. He awaited his visitor with interest.

A Scotsman, Jay thought, when the stranger spoke. He was tall and red-haired, about Jai's age. He introduced himself as one of a team of surgeons visiting the Hospital to demonstrate new surgical techniques. He was here for a fortnight, of which one week had passed. Interesting, Jai thought, but the man still hadn't stated his business.

"You will wonder why I tried to contact you, Mr Samartha. I am here on a mission. Before I came to India, I corresponded with friends here—who kindly did some investigating for me. My search has been for a Col. Dominic Jerome, and for his son, Adrian. The trail through certain retired Army officers led finally to Poona."

Jai had sat up now, listening with his full attention. "I learnt with regret that both these gentlemen are no more. A great disappointment, I must add. However, I was greatly cheered to learn that there was a Jerome—Adrian's daughter—who, I believe, is married to you, Mr Samartha."

"Why are you looking for the Jeromes?"

"It is on behalf on my great aunt." Jai waited, almost sure of the revelation that was coming. "My father's aunt, Fiona Cameron, who was married to Dominic Jerome." Involuntarily, Jai's eyes went to the bright head of the man.

"Fiona," Jai murmured almost to himself. "Utterly incredible!"

"Yes, isn't it? Incidentally, my name is Dougal Cameron. When my aunt heard about this trip of mine—about eight months ago, and that Bombay was my destination, she begged me to try and locate the Jeromes for her."

"Then—your aunt is still alive."

"Yes, indeed. But sadly in a fragile state of health. Last winter, she had double pneumonia, which left her greatly weakened. At her age, not a happy condition." Dougal Cameron looked at Jai keenly. "You're aware of the story, Mr Samartha?"

"My friends call me Jai." A smile broke over the visitor's face. Simultaneously, they both put out their hands for a warm handshake. "Yes, I know the story. So you are my wife's cousin! I find that hard to take in. She's always believed that she had no family left. You say that you're here for just one week? Then there's no time to lose. I shall ask my wife to come down at once—she's in

Pune—Poona—and she should be here in a matter of hours. I can't imagine how she's going to react."

When Jai called, I took his request in my stride. It was not an unusual one. Some foreign business contact must have arrived, and I would have to entertain his wife.

With the minimum of fuss, I was ready within an hour, and en route to Bombay. At Samartha House, I had a quick bath, dressed up, and was ready for any assignment Jai had for me. My toilette was complete when Jai's call came. So I had arrived. Good. No, he didn't have anyone's wife for me to take under my wing. He was bringing home just one visitor. We would take him out for dinner later. Tea? Possibly. All unsuspecting, I went forward to greet the two men.

I took in the stranger's appearance. Younger than many of Jai's business contacts. I noticed, the man was looking at me with keen interest. Jai put an arm around me. "Lex, I've brought home a great surprise. I'd like to introduce a kinsman from Scotland—Dougal Cameron."

If it hadn't been for Jai's supporting arm, I couldn't have stayed upright. I could not believe my ears. In a daze, I placed my hand in the outstretched one, felt it being shaken with great warmth. I took in the soft burr, heard the voice say what an immense pleasure it was to meet me—the end of a search. Somehow we were in the ornate sitting room, and I could sink into a chair. I kept tight hold of Jai's hand as explanations were given. Fiona! Fiona was still alive! She had wanted to find Dominic and Adrian! This Scots surgeon with the blue eyes and red hair was my cousin!

"...I'd almost given up hope. I didn't know what I'd tell Aunt Fiona."

I found my voice at last. "I'm sorry. It's too much for me to take in. I've always had such a special feeling for my grandmother. Spun endless fantasies about her since my childhood. Please, tell me—" I begged, and sat back to listen.

"I'm not quite clear about the first part of this story," Dougal began, "because it was spoken of in hushed whispers by the older members of the family sometimes. To my sisters, and me it was something from the distant past, from the annals of family history. We call her Aunt Fiona though she is our grandfather's sister. She retired some years ago. Was a district nurse, known far and wide for her tireless devotion to her patients. To come back to what I was saying, we were vaguely aware that she had been married to someone in India, and that the marriage hadn't worked out. It all came into sharp focus early this year when she found out I was coming to India. I was sent for, and that was when I learnt the facts. I didn't have the heart to discourage her, but I had few hopes of tracking down the Jeromes. I knew it meant so much to her. My fears were well founded. Letters flew back and forth, every possibility carefully explored but leading to a dead end. And then in early August, was told that one last lead was being investigated. Two former Army officers who had retired in Poona gave the relevant information. I decided to wait till I was in Bombay to try and get in touch with the one Jerome whose whereabouts had been reported. Only to find that I was being regarded with suspicion—probably suspected of being a terrorist, or something of that order. It took all of one week to reach the person I wanted. It was well worth the effort. Here I am face to face at last with Aunt Fiona's granddaughter."

Jai had chuckled at the sly reference to terrorists.

"Dougal, you say the lady isn't very strong?"

"Yes. When she had pneumonia, it was discovered that she had a heart condition. That's why it was imperative for me to begin my search in all earnestness."

"You're here for a week. On which day do you fly out? I see. British Airways? Let's see if there's a seat available for Lex. If not, then on the first flight possible after that."

Dougal stared. I could see he wasn't used to such quick high-powered decisions. In any case, the words made me dizzy. He laughed suddenly. "I suppose this is how captains of industry work. I won't even say that it's terribly difficult. If you succeed, then all our immediate problems are solved."

We took Dougal to an exclusive restaurant for dinner where the mere sight of Jai had the waiters bowing obsequiously. Dougal proved to be the exact opposite of the dour Scotsman image. He had a delightful sense of humor. The three of us had established such a rapport with each other that we might have been old friends. But throughout that enjoyable evening, my head was in a whirl.

It was a long flight, but it hardly mattered because during its course, my cousin and I spent the hours getting acquainted. Then too his fellow surgeons were so gallant about looking after me; dare I say it, so different from Indian men—with the exception of the Samartha brothers and a very few others. The team was to have a week off after their stint in India, so Dougal was free to escort me all the way to Inverness. We were met by his sisters, Elspeth and Catriona, and driven straight to their home. Jet lag would probably take its toll later, but I was too elated to feel it. I was actually in Scotland! These were my kinfolk! Soon I would meet my grandmother!

Elspeth whisked me off to my comfortable room at once, bringing me a cup of tea, and giving me time to bathe and dress. A long soak in a hot tub was wonderfully refreshing so that by the time we assembled for dinner, I was ready for adventure. Elspeth was the oldest, Cat the youngest. Elspeth was a commercial artist, very capable and sensible, obviously in charge of the household since their parents had been killed in a ferryboat disaster near Skye. From what Dougal had said Elspeth had a devoted admirer, a widower with three children, but for some reason, she had not yet allowed him to take her to the altar. As for Cat, so lively and pretty, several young men danced attendance on her. For all that, she was an excellent P.A. to a wool manufacturer. Both were red-haired like their brother, but Elspeth's eyes were not blue like the other two, being an attractive hazel.

When I joined the trio, I sensed the excitement in the air. Indeed, I felt it too. I was glad of Dougal's now dear and familiar presence, for he led us through the first awkward moments. Suddenly, the ice was broken and we were talking and laughing non-stop.

"We didn't know what to expect," Cat said frankly.

"I tried to pump Dougal on the phone, but all the wretch said was that you and your husband were lovely people."

"I've asked Dougal about a thousand questions. I fared better than you did. Please, won't you tell me about my grandmother?"

Elspeth said, "Dougal must have told you she's in a convalescent home. When I went to tell her about the call from Bombay, she didn't speak at all, just gripped my hand, face very white, eyes burning. We'll take you to her tomorrow morning."

"And her state of health?" I asked anxiously.

The sisters glanced at Dougal who said, "Sakshi knows about the heart condition."

"Will—it tire her out to see me?"

"Not if we take it in small doses. We'll be told how long you can stay at one stretch. If anything, meeting you will make her feel infinitely better."

"The first thing that will strike her is that you have the same eyes," Cat observed. "There's an overall resemblance one can't miss. Amazing really."

Dougal chuckled. "So amazing that when Jai took me home, I saw this girl in Indian attire, but unmistakably a Cameron! I thought I was dreaming."

That night, lying in the big bed under the comforting warmth of a goose down quilt, I tried to assimilate everything that was happening to me. In a matter of hours, I would be face to face with the one person I had not in my wildest dreams expected to meet. Suddenly, I wished Jai were here to give me the solid security and strength of his presence. He should be sharing this moment with me.

The night before I left, he had held me close, talked softly in my ear as I clung to him, overwhelmed by it all. Not once did I make known my need and longing to have him come with me. A Samartha wife simply did not take her husband away from his duty. With the International Trade Fair looming large, and the Group exhibiting its own products, there was no way he could take off at this stage.

Mama and Papa had been excited for my sake. She had helped me to choose clothes to pack, and to select gifts to take. I had to smile at GeeGee's request. He had asked me to find out what Edinborough Rock was. The thought of him lifted my spirits, and I fell asleep.

I must have presented a calm enough exterior, but my fast beating heart threatened to burst, as I followed my cousins into the garden behind a Sister in starched uniform and cap. It was a sunny morning, and other convalescents were seated in the warmth outdoors, one on crutches, and another in a wheelchair. Our progress was watched with interest. In a secluded spot, wrapped in a plaid rug, was a figure stretched out on a lounger. I was dimly aware of the Sister's brisk voice, then of Dougal's mingling with those of his sisters. They spoke very briefly, then Elspeth reached out and drew me forward.

The first shock was an impression that I was looking into my own eyes, the second being the snow-white hair that softly framed the thin face. It was the expression in the eyes fixed on me almost in supplication as if doubting my reaction that broke my heart. I needed no urging. The look drove me to my knees beside her. I spoke a single word spontaneously—"Grandmother?"—and saw the mouth tremble and the eyes fill with tears. A fragile hand reached out and I took it in my stronger one. At some point, the others must have slipped away tactfully, but I have no memory of their doing so.

"I thought—you might not wish to see me," painfully. "How could I not! You've always had this special place in my heart. To meet you in person—I haven't the words to tell you what that means to me."

"My dear." She put out her other hand and touched my face and hair. "You're so lovely. You must have a beautiful mother."

"I always thought I've taken after you in looks."

She shook her head. "The eyes, yes. And the hair. But I never had your beauty. Passably pretty perhaps, No, that delicacy of face, and the grace you have must come from another source—perhaps from the Indian side. They call you—?"

"Sakshi."

She repeated it softly.

"And my second name was chosen because I was born on the feast day of St. Alexius." I told her about my godfather.

She was silent for a moment, and then roused herself.

"Will you believe it, my father's name was Alexander—Alex they called him."

I smiled at her. "That's a wonderful coincidence." She made me get off the ground and pull up a chair close to her. "Can you tell me now—about Dominic—and Adrian?"

As I spoke, her eyes seldom left my face. Only the movement of the hands betrayed her, sometimes clenching into fists—when I told of my grandfather's tragic demise. She lay back then and closed her eyes. When she opened them, I looked at her anxiously, not knowing whether to continue, but she nodded wordlessly. I could see she was close to tears, but she bit her lip and controlled herself. My face must have glowed when I described Daddy. When I came to the incident with Tammie, a sound left her lips. My voice became unsteady when I came to Daddy's passing, and I fell silent. She drew my head down, and we held each other in shared grief. I experienced such a feeling of comfort, as I had never felt before. It took us some time to recover. Then very briefly, I concluded my story with the narrative about Mumsie.

"My dear child!" The words burst from her lips. "I'm sorry! So very sorry!" It seemed more than an expression of condolence. It was as if she was trying to convey something more.

"But now I've found you, and I'm not alone any more," I said simply. And now the tears spilled out, sliding down the pale cheeks. "Oh, please. I didn't mean to distress you." I was upset.

"I'm all right," she said when she could speak.

I glanced at my watch. "I don't think I have much time left."

"Oh, they mustn't take you away so soon!" She wiped her tears away. "Why, we've barely begun. I want to know every little thing about you. Your childhood. Your life. Do you have photographs?"

"Stacks of them. I brought them for you. And a camera to take pictures of you." I wanted to lighten her mood before I left. Perforce I had told her enough sad things. "You know, I love the way you speak. I wish I could learn to speak in that delicious way."

She smiled indulgently. "Now why would you want to do that when you speak so beautifully yourself?" Her eye had gone to a point behind me. I turned to see the Sister. She cast a keen eye over her patient, but apparently saw nothing alarming. Wistfully, my grandmother wished I could stay longer, or at least come back in the afternoon. "Tomorrow," Sister said firmly. "You've had plenty of excitement for one day. Besides, they're waiting for the lass."

I bent to kiss the soft cheek, felt the thin arms around me. "I'll be back," I promised, as loath to go as she was to let me depart.

Jai called that night. He listened with deep interest to all I had to tell him. So happy to hear his voice, the words spilled from my lips eagerly. His next call would be from New Delhi, he said, for he was leaving shortly for the Capital and the Trade Fair.

Perhaps it is not appropriate for me to speak of matters that do not relate to my grandmother. Certainly everything else pales in comparison with the momentous reality of our finding each other. But nevertheless this account would be incomplete if I did not at least touch upon some of the other wonderful things which happened-wonderful because they were all a part of my heritage.

The days took on a pattern with the mornings reserved entirely for visits to the Convalescent Home. One of the Cameron sisters dropped me off, but at my insistence, I returned by bus. Elspeth did all her artwork at home so she was always there to greet me. Dougal had gone back to Edinburgh, but promised to return as soon as it could be arranged. To my delight, other members of the family came to welcome me. Occasionally, the exact relationship eluded me, but it hardly mattered when unfailingly they were all so kind. They promised a grand reunion as soon as Dougal came back. Almost every day, one or the other would take me to their homes and entertain me royally.

I learnt quickly about Scots hospitality. If it was high tea, then the table groaned with such delicacies as oatcakes and scones, finnan haddie and much more, accompanied by very hot strong tea. For lunch or dinner, I was initiated into those hearty filling examples of Scots cuisine, Scotch broth or cock-a-leekie. Everyone was amused when I said that if I continued to stuff myself this way and waddled back to India, my husband would disown me.

When I look back, I remember clearly that the first feature of the Highlands that struck me was the air, heady as wine. Everywhere I was taken I filled my senses with the magnificent beauty of lochs and glens, mountains and great salmon rivers, which I had encountered so far only in story and poem. Since this was autumn, heather drenched the hillsides with purple. I learnt that the brilliant splashes of color were of the scarlet berries of the rowan. And with my own eyes I saw Scotland's own emblem, the thistle.

How can I describe the quickening of my pulses when I was taken to the battlefield of Culloden where in 1746, Prince Charles Edward, known in legend and song as Bonnie Prince Charlie, made his last stand? Imagine my delight at being taken to Loch Ness. Och, but the beastie failed to oblige by making an appearance. Inverness itself is set on the banks of the Ness. I discovered that the castle where Macbeth murdered Duncan had once stood in Inverness, but that Malcolm who avenged that death had it razed to the ground in the 11th century. I was told that I had just missed the Braemar Gathering where judges and performers alike wore kilts. Here I could have seen traditional competitions such as tossing of the caber, ball and hammer throwing, piping and dancing. Another place I did not get to was that sacred isle, Iona, where both Duncan and Macbeth are buried. My cousins comforted me with the thought that I could explore to my heart's content during future visits. I looked forward to that time, but for now the all-important factor of this visit was my grandmother. I had been the receiver of such bounty, from my very presence in Scotland and finding my father's mother to acquiring an entire branch of family, that I could only feel the deepest gratitude to the Almighty.

I have to confess that I always thought of my grandmother as Fiona. Even now, though I addressed her with the respectful title due to her, she was still Fiona to me. When on my second morning, I took the piles of photographs to show her, we spent all our time over them. I sat quietly when she stared for a long time at the pictures of her husband, and of her son in every stage of his life. I turned my head away when I saw the slim pale fingers touch and smooth the glossy prints. Sometimes she bit her lip, and I knew she was controlling her tears. I left them with her so that she could see them again whenever she wanted to. On subsequent days, I dredged my memory for every interesting detail about my grandfather and father to tell her, going on to my own life. She was the easiest person to talk to because she drank in everything I had to tell her with flattering absorption. Quite frequently, a look of sadness or pain brought shadows to the green eyes. At such times I tried to find something amusing to relate, and bring the smile back to her face.

And then one day, greatly daring, I asked my own questions, not knowing if I would elicit the answers. But I had to clear up some haunting mysteries from the past. "What made you go away, Grandmother?" I asked about four days after our first meeting. When she did not speak, I said gently, "You don't have to tell me—but I should so like to know."

She opened her eyes, which she had shut. "You have every right to ask. It's just that—the memories are painful. I—haven't let myself think of that time often. I've—I've carried—this burden of guilt for so long, you see. I can't atone for the grievous wrong I inflicted on Dominic or my son. It's been a kind of punishment even if not expiation. But the story must be told. You must know."

"You can tell me whenever you feel ready."

She shook her head. "No. I've waited too long as it is. I don't know how long—" She lay back in her armchair, for it had turned cooler and we were sitting in her room. Through the window, a puffy white cloud was visible. Then she began to speak as if she had summoned all her strength.

"Sakshi, I tried to adjust. To tell myself that this was part of the life I had chosen, that for the sake of my loved ones, I must learn to accept it all in the right spirit. You see, for Dominic and me—well, it had been love at first sight. He was so good looking in the way some Indian men are, with very fine features. The dark eyes and hair, the exquisite manners, the uniform, all added up to such charm that it contributed to the annihilation of all my native caution and good sense. I had never been a romantic at heart, and I was bewildered by my own emotions. My father wrote letters, but my mother's pleading ones hurt me most. I shut my ears to all arguments. At the Hospital, almost no one spoke to me civilly But I was young, so much in love, ready to withstand anything for the sake of the man I loved. We were married and I became the wife of Major Jerome.

"Our marriage was idyllic. Life had never seemed so rosy. Then it began to disturb me that I was doing so little that was worthwhile. Never domestic by nature, I managed to entertain and run the house in the style expected of me. Between Dominic's orderly and the servants, it wasn't very difficult. But I had been used to the arduous duties of a Sister Tutor, while here my greatest responsibility was to plan the next dinner party.

"I don't want to give the impression that I felt I was superior to anyone, or that I looked down on the other officers' wives. Far from it. To use a more modern expression, this new way of life wasn't my thing at all. Dominic was away frequently. When he was there, I managed to push my feelings into the background. Other small things surfaced which added to my unhappiness. For instance, on Sundays, we attended separate services. Naturally, there was no such thing as a Scots kirk. I went to the Anglican Church while Dominic attended Mass. Unfair of me, of course, when I had married a Catholic. It came to me gradually that this was Dominic's world, and he loved it. I was the misfit. My thoughts made me ashamed and I did not say anything. Much later, I thought I should have discussed them with my husband. At least he would have known how I felt. When I learnt about the baby, I felt trapped, a prisoner under a life sentence. Yet when Adrian was born, I loved him. He was so big and bonnie, almost ten pounds at birth. The way he thrived was enough to bring joy to any mother's heart. His advent did not compensate for the rest. I sat in the first pew of the Catholic Church and watched the priest baptize my son, feeling the wrath of all my stern forebears weighing me down. Still, it took me two years to come to a decision. I prayed over it, Sakshi. Asked for divine succor. Came to the point where my mind was made up. For the first time in my life, I resorted to stealth. I wrote to the Matron of a Scottish Hospital in North India. She was from Inverness, and knew my family well. I took her into my confidence and asked for help. It was prompt in coming. She made arrangements for me with friends in Bombay, booked a flight for Fiona Cameron and infant.

"My greatest pain stemmed from the fact that not only was I abandoning my beloved husband, but taking his son from him. Was that not the height of cruelty? Yet how could I leave my baby behind, perhaps never to see him again? It was an agonizing time for me, Sakshi. In the end, you know what I did.

"I did not permit myself the release of tears. Not when I wrote my letter to Dominic. Not when I held Adrian in my arms for the last time. Not when I left Indian soil for the last time, and set foot on Scottish ground. The reception that awaited me was hardly what I expected. My mother wept and embraced me, but my father told me sternly that I had failed in my Christian duty to my husband and child. He did not need to tell me that. It is a knowledge I carry with me to this day. I had no respect for myself left. I missed Dominic so deeply. My arms ached to hold my child and rock him. I told myself not to intrude in to their lives, to leave them strictly alone. In time, they would forget me."

Fiona's voice had dwindled almost to a whisper. I poured her a glass of water and held it to her lips. She drank before lying back quietly. Footsteps heralded the arrival of a coffee tray. We did not speak till our cups were empty. I was glad there had been a break in the conversation, for the narrative had taken a toll of Fiona's strength. Still I could not leave it at that. I had something to say and this was the moment for it. I began to speak.

"I was only four years old when I lost my grandfather." The green eyes opened. "But one memory is very clear. It is of sitting on his lap many times and looking through the album of your photographs. He pored over them by himself for hours. The name 'Fiona' became a part of me because of that, and because he told me I was like you. That's how you came to occupy a very special niche in my heart." The eyes were misty. "This grandmother was mine in a very important way."

The words were whispered. "Then Dominic didn't hate me?"

"Never even for a moment. You were the most wonderful thing that had happened in his life. He carried your photograph in his wallet at all times. He would take it out and look at it at least once a day. It was his talisman."

"Oh." The word came out in a sigh.

"So you must never feel he thought ill of you. He cared for you till his last breath."

She was silent. Then she uttered a single word. "Adrian?"

"My father was incapable of holding a grudge. It was simply not part of his nature. In any case, he was too young to have any actual memory of you. He and my grandfather—well, it was most beautiful to see the rapport they shared. That is how I look at it now after so many years. Yet Daddy spoke of you with pride. I was about twelve when I asked him why he didn't try to find you. He said, 'But where would I start, little one? Don't think I haven't wanted to. Perhaps some day—' So you see, the wish was there, but he hadn't the faintest idea how to go about it." I reached out and took the thin hand in mine and held it to my cheek. "Grandmother, did you never want to get in touch?"

The answer came painfully. "At first, I wanted to so much. To write and give Dominic a fuller explanation. Then I'd think that would be prolonging the agony. Over the years, I'd say to myself, 'Dominic must have been promoted to a higher rank,' or 'Adrian has started school.' I'd imagine him growing into boyhood, then into manhood. Wonder if he was married and had children. No, I saw no purpose in opening old wounds."

"After so long, what made you ask Dougal to try and find the Jeromes?"

It took her a while to reply. "Last winter I was very ill. During my convalescence, it came to me—that I was only too mortal. If I—wanted to make my peace—I must not waste time. Dougal's impending visit to India seemed like divine intervention. I did not underestimate the problem. The trail was probably very cold by now. I was asking Dougal to take on a most difficult task—but I could not rest until we'd tried." Her hand tightened its clasp on mine. "Dearest Sakshi. My child. You've brought me more joy—and peace—than I can tell you. I shan't ask for more." I was very close to tears, but I controlled them with effort. "My one sorrow is that I have nothing to leave you."

I hoped she didn't detect the tremor in my voice. "You've given me riches beyond compare. I've told you what Jai said when he asked me to marry him about the qualities I possessed, which set me apart. They're there in my nature for all time. Not just the physical resemblance; but also something far more precious. Jai said he would like our children to inherit them. As for material goods, I have too much of them."

She stroked my head. "You make me feel—I haven't lived in vain."

"How could you ever think you've lived in vain! Why, I've heard from so many people of your selfless devotion to your patients. It was one of the first things Dougal told me. How you could have worked in some big city hospital, but chose to be a district nurse, going out in the most awful weather conditions to remote homes in the hills."

A sweet smile lit up her face. "But I loved my patients, you see. Delivering babies most of all."

I lifted my head to listen. "I hear the crackle of starch. Sister is on her way to eject me." I leaned over to kiss her, and we held each other for a long moment.

On the way home, however, I was downcast. Was it my imagination, or was Fiona become more fragile each day? I knew she lived for my visits, for the Sister had told me so, but surely though I took care not to overstay my time, every session drained her of the little strength she had. Elspeth welcomed me with a warm smile. Her keen gaze must have noted my woebegone face. Lunch in half an hour, she said. Casually she mentioned that a package had arrived for me, which she had put in my room. Puzzled, I went in. The curtains in the bedroom were drawn. Strange, for when I made the bed earlier, I had opened them to let in the light. When my eyes became accustomed to the unexpected darkness, I understood. Jai was fast asleep under the goose down quilt.

I had never been so happy to see anyone in my life.

When much later, Jai explained that he had preplanned this, and Dougal had known about it, I hardly listened. Indeed, Jai said, his flight booking had been made at the same time as mine, timed in such a way that he would be there for the first part of the Trade Fair which was the more important one. Elspeth and Cat took to Jai in a big way. Relaxed, looking many years younger, having left all his arduous responsibilities behind, he was his suave but altogether charming self. For the most part, I was the listener, enjoying the lively exchange as much as the other three participants. It was only after everyone had retired for the night and we were alone that, my voice tremulous, I unburdened my heart to him about Fiona.

Jai cupped my face in his hands. He said softly, "We have to be prepared for all eventualities, Lex."

Fear clutched me with icy fingers "Why—why do you say that? Did Dougal—say anything?"

He drew me close, resting his cheek on my hair. "Only that her heart is in bad shape. Her illness didn't help."

I closed my eyes and clung to him. "Jai, I can't lose her now!"

"How has she seemed to you?"

"Oh, Jai, visibly weaker than when I first saw her. She tires more easily. Do you think meeting me is the cause—that I've exhausted her?"

"Not for a moment. I think you've brought her more happiness than she dreamed of."

"She said—I'd brought joy—and peace."

"So there you are. I think no accolade can be finer. Lex," gravely, and when I lifted up my head, he looked directly into my eyes. "You've never lacked courage."

I was silent, standing very still. Then I nodded. I felt him draw me back against him, and I lifted my face to his.

The sunshine that had welcomed me to Inverness had taken a holiday. This morning when Elspeth drove Jai and me to the Convalescent Home, it was misty and somehow depressing.

Fiona's eyes widened when she saw my companion, but within minutes I saw she and Jai had taken to each other without reservation, almost as if they recognized each other. She smiled when he said he would have known she was Lex's grandmother anywhere. The full approval and pleasure on her face warmed my heart. Happy too was the feeling that she seemed stronger.

She said softly, "I'm so blessed, not just to know my child but also her husband. I hadn't expected to."

"Ah," said my husband gallantly, "I couldn't have kept away for anything. I had to meet the lady who's been so important in my wife's existence. And now that I've met you, I can understand why. Will you believe *it*, she told me about you at our very first meeting?"

"Tell me about yourself."

She listened to him quietly, eyes on his face. He spoke briefly. I knew he had taken note of her fragility.

"A different world," she said at last, "but what a fascinating one. And you have the best of both worlds. I understand why you have such a distinctively American accent. Sakshi has told me about your fine family." Then almost to herself, "It's good to know my child, my Sakshi, has found a safe harbor with you." She roused herself. "You call her 'Lex', I noticed. Alexander was my father's name. Very stern and uncompromising. I was never close to him. But I love the name 'Sakshi'. It has a lovely sound. She tells me it means 'Witness'. I pray that whatever she witnesses in her life from now on will have much goodness. We cannot bypass the bad, but she had so much to bear in her short span." She smiled at Jai. "With you by her side, I shan't worry."

"Does it disturb you that Lex is a Catholic?"

"No. Perhaps many years ago, it might have done so. But I've come to realize that religious schisms are man-made, that we are all children of the same Creator. If Sakshi has become the fine sweet person she is because of her religious upbringing, then I am glad of it."

"Yes. I've always thought the courage with which she has taken adversity has come from you."

"Not from me, Jai! Why, I was an arrant coward. I ran away instead of staying and facing my problems."

"I don't think so. Being only human, we all make errors. Besides, had you stayed on, your husband, and perhaps later your son, would have known you were miserable, and that would not have been a happy situation for them. It took courage for you to take the decision. And I think the rest of your life has shown you to possess all the courage of your race."

Fiona was silent, and then she took my hand, "My child, you have a husband with wisdom beyond his years. He's put a new slant on matters, which I had not thought of."

Before we left a little later, Jai shot several pictures of us. Sister was roped in to do the clicking so that Jai could join us. She was mightily pleased when he insisted on taking a shot of her. I realized for the first time, that she could actually smile. When Jai bent to say his farewells, Fiona took his face in her hands and kissed his brow. Gently he kissed her cheek. When my turn came, the thin arms held me longer than usual. When she let me go, her eyes were full of tears. "Bless you both," she said softly. At the door, we turned back to wave. She was still looking at us. A pale hand lifted in farewell.

That night, happy that Fiona was stronger, that she had met Jai and they had liked each other so much, and that Jai was here, I curled myself into his warmth, and slept soundly. In my state of dreamless oblivion, I failed to hear the knock, or Jai answering it. I missed the low-voiced exchange. Then dimly, as if from a great distance, I registered Jai's voice calling me. I opened my eyes and found him leaning over me. "Jai?" dazedly.

"It's Fiona, Lex."

I struggled to sit up, my heart drumming in my chest. "It was very peaceful—in her sleep."

And thus did the promised family reunion take place with kinfolk coming from far and wide to pay their last homage to Fiona Cameron. I sat in the church with my cousins on one side, and Jai on the other, and listened to the eulogies spoken by humble people—farmers, crofters and shepherds—whom she had served with boundless devotion. As one of them said, there must have been at least twenty-five present there at that very moment who were her "bairns", whom she had ushered into the world, often in the most difficult conditions. I was fiercely proud then.

Perhaps it was Dougal who spoke the final words of a chapter in my life. It was at the airport in Edinburgh when hesitantly I asked if he thought my visit had strained my grandmother so that it was the cause of her passing.

"No," he said emphatically. "Not for a moment. All or us knew how grave her condition was. Don't you see, when she heard about you, she held on to the slender thread of life that was all that was left? She was a nurse. She knew how it was. Jai knew, for I had told him there was no time to lose. She was waiting for you, Sakshi. You touched her last days with gold."

I bit my lip to control my tears. "As she touched my life. Do you think—she knew that day? She blessed us both."

"Who knows the answer to that, dear girl? From the way she looked, she was at peace. That's what you gave to her. A gift beyond price." Dougal hugged me. "And you must go in peace, Sakshi, because that is what she would have wanted for you. You have two homes now—one in India, and the other here in Scotland. Will you remember that the doors are wide open for you at all times?"

I could only nod.

CHAPTER 17

ABOUT EIGHTEEN MONTHS AFTER WE WERE MARRIED, THE EVEN tenor of our days came in for a change. Negotiations were in progress to finalize the details of Japanese collaboration in the production of a new line of software. This I learnt only from a reference here and there in exchanges between my husband and father-in-law. Jai never discussed affairs of the Samartha Group with me, or shared his problems. Perhaps he thought I would have no understanding of them. It hurt a little that he should keep me out so completely. True, I would be of no help except to be a good listener. And I was not illiterate. I possessed what I hoped was a reasonable intelligence, which would enable me to grasp the essentials. Be that as it may, Jai was frantically busy, having to stay on in Bombay much of the time, or take off for Tokyo at short notice. He was in constant touch with Papa by telephone. Jai put his foot down about my coming to Bombay in these hectic days. He would feel happier, he said, if he knew I was in Pune, close to his parents, with plenty to keep me busy and happy. He himself was hardly at Samartha House, and then only to drop into bed and sleep.

There were rare occasions when he came up to Pune for a few hours, but always exhausted. I put off all small parties, which we often threw, to give him complete peace and quiet, letting him sleep as much as he could. Often he slumped in a chair and said, "Lex, play for me," and I played softly, only to turn around and find he had fallen asleep. I will not deny I did not approve at all of the killing pace at which he was driving himself. I did not mind that he was too fatigued and preoccupied to say a few bare words to me, and was closeted in with Papa for discussions. But it worried me that his health might suffer. But what could I do, except hold my tongue, see he had every comfort, and pray for the days when Cy and GeeGee were ready to share the burden? I had heard of business tycoons who developed ailments from ulcers to heart conditions. Jai was still a young man now, but how long could a person take it?

When I found Mama in tears one day, I was shocked and distressed. She was learning over her desk, face buried in her hands, and sobbing her heart out. All I could do was to hold her and wait for her to calm down. Papa had had a very bad night. His leg had given him no respite, and by morning, he was exhausted, drained of all strength. How long was this to go on, she queried piteously. He simply refused to listen to a word about an operation.

This was one subject that had never come up between Papa and me. As far as he was concerned, it was taboo. I waited till he was better, having slept the clock around, and then went to visit him. Propped up in bed against a nest of pillows, he still looked tired, the lines deeply scored on his face. Compassion threatened to overcome me. He seemed happy to see me, and motioned me to a chair. I hated to hit a man when he was down, but the situation cried out for shock tactics. I was about to use the most powerful argument of all.

"Today was the first time I've ever seen Mama weep," I started off. He looked taken aback. "She's always so brave, but today she broke down," I went on, pressing home my advantage, and feeling horribly mean. "Her whole concern is for you, Papa. She loves you so much, and it's almost more than she can bear to see you suffering. It seems so needless to endure such agony—for you physically—and for her mentally." He lay back on his pillows, and did not answer. Summoning all my courage, I plunged on. "Why do you refuse surgery, Papa? You've already had several operations. Why not this one?"

He had closed his eyes. When he spoke, his voice was so low, I had to bend my head close to hear his words. "I—have been thinking of it, Sakshi. Lying here today—thinking of Roza and what I've put her through for the last two years and more—I've come to the conclusion that if for no other reason, I must do it for her sake." I had reached out involuntarily to touch his hand as it lay on the sheet, and he closed it over mine. "Everyone—probably thinks I'm a stubborn fool. Perhaps, I am one. It isn't easy when—you've been strong and upright, always in rugged health, to think that some day you might be minus a leg—a cripple. You will think it foolish—but I can't help thinking—if they decide the leg cannot be saved, I shall be—just half a man." He fell silent. I held back my tears with difficulty, and waited till I was sure I could speak coherently, holding his hand in both of mine.

"But if you have the operation, you'll be totally free from pain, won't you, Papa? And be able to resume a fully normal life?"

"Confined to a wheelchair for the rest of my days."

"You are that now, Papa, but you won't be then. There are wonderfully designed artificial limbs now—you'd be fully mobile, wouldn't you? And after all, the leg may be saved."

He turned his head and gave me a tired smile.

"I'll go now and give you a chance to rest. And, Papa," hesitantly, "I know you don't believe in such things, but I'll be praying for you. As I always have—but especially now, Papa." I kissed his cheek and went away.

To Mama, I said nothing about this conversation. If Papa had made up his mind, then he should be the one to tell her. But on Cy's next trip home, I talked it over with him. As a matter of fact, Cy had become a true pal, the brother I never had. When he gave advice, it was surprisingly mature. It was in Cy I confided when I felt unsure of myself in some situation, who bolstered my self-confidence in a very concrete way. I appreciated the way he demolished my complexes with a few pungent remarks. Then too I enjoyed his droll wit. Above all, I had the assurance that I could turn to Cy in trouble. My one sorrow was that he was leaving for the United States shortly to do a Master's in Business Administration. I would miss him greatly. Now about Papa, he regarded me with astonishment. I had actually succeeded where everyone else had failed in making Papa discuss the matter, and agree! It must be something to do with my green eyes—a spell I had conjured up! Cy was not inclined to accept my explanation that Papa had made up his mind even before I met him. There was a surgeon in the United States, Craig Marshall, eminent for his success in such surgery. If Papa had really made up his mind, the ball would have to be set rolling at once to set up the whole thing. What a blessed relief Papa's acceptance was! I was nothing less than a miracle worker! Useless for me to deny it vehemently.

With that settled, there was something else I had to attend to urgently.

In the business section of a newspaper, I read that the Samartha Group had completed all details of the collaboration with the Japanese multinational corporation, and that production would begin shortly. A strange way for the wife of the man who was setting up the whole thing to find out, but that was the way of it. It was good news, I thought. Now Jai would be able to relax a little, and some of the tension he had been laboring under would leave him. Best of all, I would see more of my husband. To my sorrow, problems cropped up at one of the units Jai called from Bombay so say he was leaving at once with some of his executives to settle the matter. It was no use waiting for him to be freer. I must attend to my problem myself.

I hadn't been very well for a few weeks. At first, I'd shrugged off the loss of appetite as a result of missing Jai. I was only half alive when he wasn't around. Lately, on the rare occasions when I saw him briefly, he had been so preoccupied that it would have been cruel on my part to ask him to accompany me to a doctor. I made my appointment, drove myself, went through tests, and came to know what was wrong with me. I had never needed Jai so much as I did now. It was his right to know I was going to have a baby. I suppose I could have tracked him down and phoned him, but somehow I felt such momentous news had to be told to him in person. So I was quietly jubilant, waiting for Jai to return. We would break the news to the family together, I thought in secret joy.

Jai should have been here by now, I thought to myself on the evening he was expected at last, and suppressed a small nagging worry. Perhaps the plane is late, I told myself. I carried a glass of fruit juice to the terrace and sat on the parapet with it in my hand. An hour later, dusk had given way to night, and I had to quell a rising sense of panic. Gonsalves appeared in the doorway. I could see he was worried.

"I don't think you should wait, Gonsalves. Tell Thelma I'll serve dinner when Sir comes. He seems to have been held up."

Over his protests, I sent them both off, promising to summon them if necessary. As I knew very well, Thelma had been cooking all day in preparation for tonight's dinner. For that matter, so had I made ready the house, filled it with fresh flowers, and set the table for the meal. I had bought myself a lovely dress some time ago at The Honey Bee, but had saved it for a special occasion. It was white chiffon over a satin under slip, dotted with gold sequins with very full sleeves and a full-length skirt, which twirled in soft folds around my legs. I had left my hair loose on my shoulders in a burnished cloud, as Jai liked it. I had looked at the slim reflection in the mirror and grinned to myself. Soon nothing in my wardrobe would fit me—and I was delighted at the thought.

It was close to ten o'clock when I heard the car. When headlights appeared, I ran down the steps, joy in my heart. Jai emerged from the car. He brushed his lips over my cheek before turning to remove a single bag, not unlocking the boot for the rest.

"We'll worry about it in the morning," he said.

"I can call Gonsalves."

"No need."

When the living room lights fell full on his face, I saw he was very tired.

"I'll go straight up and have a shower. I'm filthy. Down in ten minutes."

I watched the long legs take stairs three at a time, and slowly made my way to the kitchen. I switched on the oven, and took out the salad ingredients Thelma had placed in readiness in the refrigerator. I hope there's no trouble brewing, I thought, that the problem has been settled. Jai didn't want me to go up with him as I usually do so that we could have talked, caught up with news. Probably needs sleep desperately.

The oven was just heated enough. I slid in the chicken in wine to heat. I would warm the rolls minutes before we were ready to eat. A pity, I told myself, that Jai is too weary for a celebration dinner. I should have anticipated how tired he was sure to be.

I had just finished tossing the salad when I heard his footsteps coming down. I left the salad bowl on the kitchen counter, and hurried to the living room. I was surprised to see he was dressed in slacks and shirt. Normally, Jai liked to wear a favorite old dressing robe to relax in.

He took the glass I handed him, and sank into a deep chair, stretched out his legs, and took a long draught.

"Was the plane late, Jai?"

"Not really. I was held up by something else." He leaned his head back and closed his eyes.

"Astra had her foal."

"That's good," but did not open his eyes.

"And I have a wonderful secret to share with you."

His eyes opened. Obviously he hadn't registered what I had said. He stood up abruptly. "Lex, I have something to tell you."

Suddenly I was afraid. It was a premonition of something terrible.

"Jai," I whispered, "it isn't—your health, is it?"

He glanced at me. "No, no. Nothing to do with that." He went to the window and stared out into the blackness. "I don't know where to begin. More than anything, I hate to hurt you."

"You can tell me anything, Jai," I said steadily.

He turned around and looked straight at me. "I want a divorce, Lex."

If he had stabbed me with a dagger, I would not have felt the impact more. I felt I was slowly bleeding inside. I had braced myself, but not sufficiently, for my legs gave clean away, and I sank into a chair. So it's come, I thought, and did not realize I had spoken aloud. There was complete silence for some time.

"Am I—allowed to ask why?" I asked at last.

"Because there's someone else."

I sat motionless. With an effort, "Do I know her?"

He lifted a hand and let it fall. "Of course. You've met often. Ila Anjan."

In my mind flashed the image of a tall pencil-slim woman, very smart, hair cut very short like a cap, the epitome of efficiency. P.A. to Srikant.

"I see."

"I've waited for weeks—not knowing how to break it to you. I realize how great a shock it must be for you. It's a wretched mess. I take full blame for it."

I drew on every ounce of courage I could summon to lift my head, and meet his eyes directly. "You needn't fear I shall make a row over it, Jai. Somehow I suppose I guessed it might happen some day." I tried to smile. "I—shall get over it." I stood up slowly to find my legs were still functioning. "If you don't mind, I think I'll go upstairs."

"Lex—"

"It's all right, Jai."

I shall never know how I made it to the stairs, but I managed. I was halfway up when he called from the foot of the stairs. "You said you had something to tell me?"

I looked at him blankly. "Oh, that. Nothing important. Quite irrelevant now." And I continued upstairs.

I closed the bedroom door behind me. Some impulse made me push the bolt, though not because I thought Jai would follow me. I leaned against it, breathing deeply, trying to assimilate the implications of what Jai had told me. It was as if I'd been living in a golden bubble, beautiful but ephemeral. It had needed only the lightest touch to burst it. Prem's warnings kept ringing in my ears. I must keep calm, I told myself. Think what I would do now. For a moment though, my spirit quailed within me. Where would I go? Unconsciously, my hand spread out over my abdomen. I wasn't alone any more. It wasn't just myself I had to think of.

Tripping more than once, I stumbled across the room to the big bed, sank slowly to my knees, burying my face in the silken cover. The thoughts and needs were there in my mind and heart to overflowing, but they would not formulate themselves into any coherent words. Then at long last, like a dam bursting, they poured out.

"My God and Father, please give me strength and courage to do what I must. If Thou are by my side, I shall not be afraid."

I undressed slowly, made my preparations for bed, and lay down quietly. When I closed my eyes, I could feel the darkness beating against my lids. My thoughts marched on relentlessly. One fact, which stood out starkly was that I had failed Jai. He had chosen me to be his wife for specific reasons, and I had fallen short of all his expectations. I struggled to analyze it, but no answers came. This woman, Ila Anjan. He had been attracted to her because they were two of a kind. The same interests, the same world. Besides, she had those provocative looks. No man could miss them. Why then had Jai not married her years ago? Ila was about his age. She was very much a part of his circle as P.A. to Srikant. Now, when I thought back, I recalled she had been a guest at many parties Jai and I attended in Bombay, along with other top personnel for the Group. Had Jai been speaking the truth when he said he had wanted to kiss me that first evening when I crashed into him by the lift? When I turned down his offer of marriage, he had spoken of the chemistry between us. And it had been there. One look across a crowded room was always enough to scorch me, set my heart to beating faster. Here in this very bed, how often had I been lost in the dark sorcery of Jai's love-making, held his head against my breast as he slept *in* exhaustion after a particularly grueling week, lain held securely in his arms while we both slept?

Mama. Papa. Cy. GeeGee. They had taken me in and made me part of their family. If I had been born a Samartha, they could not have cared for me more.

I heard a car door slam, the sounds of an engine starting, then receding into the distance. Jai, Perhaps he found it unbearable to stay under the same roof with me a moment longer. The very thought must repel him.

I knew what I must do.

I was up at dawn, showering, slipping into shirt and pants. Soundlessly, I went downstairs to the kitchen and plugged in the kettle for tea. A faint scorched smell lingered in the air. I turned my eyes away from the pot of soup that still reposed on the range, the salad bowl on the counter, and the napkin-covered basket. Strangely, though I hadn't eaten since lunch the previous day, I wasn't hungry at all. But I drank a cup of tea thirstily, and another, then I went to the big window to watch the slowly lightening sky.

There was no sound of footfall, but the ESP, which was such a strong force, warned me. I felt the pickle. Jai was somewhere behind me.

"Tea is ready," I said without turning around.

Sounds indicated that a cup was taken from the cupboard, liquid poured. A spoon tinkled.

"Lex?"

"Yes?"

"We have to talk, Lex."

"Not now please, Jai."

After a moment, "Very well. Tonight then, after I get back."

I did not answer. I went to the stairs and began to climb them steadily. It was going to be a busy day.

CHAPTER 18

INTERLUDE

GEEGEE CAME BOUNDING UP THE STEPS TO THE TERRACE AT THE rear of Kaheksha, where his parents were having afternoon tea, and flung his books on a chair. He laid a fairly large box on the table in front of his mother.

"For you, Mama. By courier."

Roza was astonished. "What on earth can it be?"

"It isn't your birthday. And our anniversary is in June." her husband observed. "Well, open it."

"Probably a nice un-birthday present," GeeGee said cheerfully. He helped himself to a sandwich after noting from the corner of his eye that his mother was too preoccupied to notice he hadn't washed his hands.

Having cut the tapes, Roza tore away the heavy wrappings and lifted out the envelope from the top where it lay with her name on it. More puzzled by the minute, she slit open the envelope and unfolded the single sheet of paper. Her eye scanned the lines rapidly. Mouth stuffed with cake, GeeGee was horrified to see tears streaming down his mother's face. He nudged his father urgently. Ketan came out from behind his newspaper

"Roza, what is it?" he asked, urgency in his voice.

"Mama!" Gautam had run to where she sat, one hand at her throat. He picked up the sheet of paper and handed it to his father. Slowly Ketan read it aloud:

∽

Dearest Mama,

I suppose I really have no right to call you that now, but that is how I think of you. Last night Jai asked me for a divorce. You must not be angry with him. The failure is mine entirely. You said these sets were for your daughter, and gave them to me with love. Since I can no longer claim to have that title, I am returning them to you.

I carry away with me the most golden memories of the way you took me in and made me a part of your family. I can't tell you what it has meant to me. You. Papa. Cy. GeeGee.

If my mother were still on earth, she would pray for me now. Since she is not, I ask you to. I need a mother's prayers.

You must not worry about me. I shall be all right. I have learnt how to fend for myself.

You will be receiving another package from me. I send it with all my love. Half the contents are for Papa. I leave him to guess which one.

My love to each one, and to you, my dearest Mama.

SAKSHI

No one spoke for at least five minutes. GeeGee felt like throwing himself on the floor and bawling. Ketan reached out to lift out the contents of the parcel. He flicked open each box. Catching the rays of the afternoon sun, the jewelry winked in brilliant hues.

"Bloody fool!" Ketan spoke at last. "What can have possessed him?"

"Do you think—she's gone? The note sounded—so final somehow." Roza said bleakly.

"We'll find out now. I'm calling Jai."

In a moment, the terrace was deserted.

Within minutes, Ketan was in contact with Jai. Mother and son listened with all their attention.

"Jai? Your mother had a note from Sakshi. It says you've asked for a divorce. It's too incredible to believe. Some misunderstanding? A tiff between you two? What! What are you saying! Why, why, why? Who? No! Not that woman! You've gone raving mad! What have I got against her? IJa Anjan, my dear son, is an immoral woman. A nymphomaniac. It's common knowledge. What? No, of course it's not malicious gossip. Ask anyone. Why, the woman rarely sleeps in the same bed twice! Aha, you refuse to hear such talk. At any rate, I want the woman off my payroll. I don't give a damn! That's your decision. Find the way. And now your mother wants to speak to Sakshi. What do you mean she isn't there? Good God! Has she mentioned where she's gone? No note? Jai, Jai, what have you done? That sweet child! What will she do now? To whom can she turn? She's returned all the jewelry your mother gave her. This is worse than anyone thought. Hmmm. If you have the slightest clue, inform us immediately. And get busy about the woman."

Ketan hung up the receiver to see two pairs of eyes fixed on him. He limped to a chair and sat down heavily. It was some moments later that GeeGee wondered aloud, "Where could Sakshi have gone, Papa?"

"I wish we could know that, son."

"Do you think," Roza said slowly, "that she might have gone to the Dubashes? They know her and would surely help."

"It's worth a try."

But a dejected Roza reported having talked to Sohrab Dubash himself. Sakshi had not talked to them or even approached them. In fact, they had not been in touch for a long time.

"Dreadful thoughts come into my head, Ketan. You don't think Sakshi will—"

"No, I don't think so at all," he told her gently. "She has too much courage for that. And it's against all her religious beliefs." He patted her shoulder. "We shall find her. She may write again."

"Do you think she might think of seeking help from the Camerons—go to Scotland?"

"Even if she did, there hasn't been time enough since Jai sprang this on her last night. Though we can't preclude that as a possible solution."

They sat in silence, lost in thought.

CHAPTER 19

JAI

I COULDN'T PUT MY MIND TO ANYTHING THAT DAY. I HAVE
NO memory of the people I spoke to on the phone, the letters I dictated, or what I said to those who had appointments with me. Ila
came up on urgent business for Srikant, trumped up, of course. As
always, she came through Monica, all very straightforward, armed
with a folder. I had gotten up, and she threw herself in my arms,
locking hers around my neck. Her eyes gleamed with triumph.

"Jai, this must be the happiest day in my life!" She pressed her
mouth to mine in an avid kiss. "Aren't you going to tell me what she
said?" The vision of another face rose in front of my eyes, the green
eyes darkened with shock and pain.

I detached Ila's arms. "I don't want to talk about it."

"My poor Jai." She stroked my cheek. "Did she rave? Weep? Have
hysterics? Why so secretive? I want to know. Everything."

When the buzzer sounded, I had never been so grateful to Monica. "Yes?"

"The representative from Nand Works is here, sir."

"Right. Send him in." I was back in my chair behind my desk.
"Sorry about that, Ila. I'll call you later."

Acute disappointment was written on her face. But the door was
opening, and Monica was ushering in a dapper middle-aged man.

Schooled to be discreet, she showed no signs of having noticed Ila's expression as she brushed past her and went out. Perhaps she thought I'd administered a reprimand.

Unflappable as Monica was, she didn't turn a hair when around noon I asked her to cancel all appointments for the rest of the day, and summon a cab for two o'clock to take me to Pune. This was one time I would not wait. I just had to get home to Lex. I owed her a complete explanation.

In the cab on the way to Pune, last night's events kept unreeling behind my closed eyes. I hadn't missed the way Lex looked in some filmy white material, arms and shoulders gleaming through it like warm ivory. Her hair was worn loose the way I liked it best. Most unmistakable was the way her eyes shone in eager welcome, her face mirroring delight that I was back. It hadn't made my task any easier. I avoided meeting her gaze; made the excuse I needed a bath badly. Under the shower, letting the water beat down on my upturned face, I knew I had to do it first thing after I went down. A clean thrust was better than dithering over the whole thing.

It was her expression when I told her, and the question about my health that cut me to the quick. She did none of the things one might have expected. The first words she uttered were more to herself, but I heard them clearly. "So it's come," as if she had always expected something of the sort. They pierced me to the core, condemnation as explicit as a sentence.

I watched the slender beautiful form ascend the stairs. Nothing could dim my appreciation of her beauty.

Reaction was setting in.

Something was burning smell shook me from my reverie. I experienced none of the relief, even elation, I should have felt. Only this awful empty feeling deep In the kitchen, I yanked open the oven door. Whatever it was had burned and blackened beyond recognition. All I could do was to turn the heat off. My eye fell on a bowl and covered basket on the counter, a pot on the burner. All my favorite foods, no doubt. I turned off the kitchen lights, and went to do the same in the dining room. It was the table that caught my eye. I stared at the tall white candles waiting to be lit, the centerpiece of deep red roses. A celebration to welcome me back. With a flick of my wrist, I plunged the room into darkness so that the sight would be hidden from my eyes.

Irresolutely, I stood at the foot of the stairs. What must Lex be doing? Was she weeping at last? I wanted to go to her, to kneel down beside her, to beg her to forgive me for inflicting such hurt on her. To assure her she was not to blame in any way. Only the thought that she might not want to look upon my face stayed me.

When the telephone shrilled, I jumped. On the third ring, I had the receiver in my hand. And was shocked.

Taking care to keep my voice low, I said furiously, "I told you never to call me here!"

"I couldn't resist! Did you tell her?"

"Yes."

"And?" Did I detect the faintest gloating?

"It's okay. I shan't say more now. I'm hanging up."

Suddenly I felt stifled as if the walls were closing in on me. I went out of the house. Rom and Reem came bounding up, tails wagging furiously. The car was where I'd left it. The night watchman saluted as I went through the gates. Intensely fatigued though I was, I went for a long drive, letting the cold night air play over my hot face.

I drove to the foot of a hillock and parked. Climbing to the top, I sat down and stretched out my legs. The city of Pune lay spread out in front of me, lights twinkling. I sat for a long time, past midnight.

When I returned, it was extremely quiet. No light was visible under our bedroom door. I stared at it for a long moment, fighting the impulse to open it, and go in. I went into one of the guest rooms, undressed in the dark, and lay down.

The cab made good time. It was just past five when we arrived. I paid the man off at the gates.

Gonsalves was taken aback when he opened the door to my ring. "Sir!" he exclaimed.

"It's okay. I came by cab." I glanced around, and then lifted my head to detect any sounds from upstairs. "Where's Madam?" When he did not answer at once, I turned to look at him in surprise. He wore an odd expression on his face.

"Madam—isn't here, Sir."

"You mean she's gone out?"

"Gone—away, Sir."

I stared at him. "What do you mean?"

Lex had left the house around three, Gonsalves told me. She had been very busy all morning. He had packed and nailed down a crate of canvases, then delivered it to the Chitradhar home. Madam had gone out in the car, and come back at noon. She had sent off something by courier. Thelma had been worried when Madam told her not to make lunch, for she had had no breakfast either. She had ordered dinner for one. Unhappy about it, Thelma had come back at two-thirty to coax Madam into having a bite. Gonsalves had come back with her. They had been just in time to see Madam coming downstairs carrying a bag and the little typewriter. She had seemed surprised to see them.

"Madam, are you going on a trip?" Thelma had exclaimed.

Madam had put down her things and come to put her arms around Thelma. "Yes, I am."

"But—Sir?"

"Not this time. Will you give him his dinner? And, Thelma, look after him. Give him good things to eat. He's under so much strain."

"When will you be back, Madam?"

Madam had not answered for a long time, and then she said, "I shan't be back. This isn't my home any longer." Thelma had started to cry, and Madam had tears in her eyes. She had kissed her, and hugged Gonsalves, then asked for a rickshaw.

I hit my fist on my palm. I could not take it in. Lex gone? But where? She had no family to go to, no parents to whom she could turn.

"Did she leave a letter for me?"

"A package, Sir."

It was more a heavy brown envelope, sealed with tape. I tore it open. Several key rings fell out, each neatly labeled. Bank books. Check books. A slip of paper with a number written on it. I recognized it. It was the combination of her safe upstairs. No note. Had she left a letter there?

I tore upstairs, bursting into the bedroom. I took down the oil painting that concealed the safe, used the combination, and swung open the heavy door. Piles of boxes greeted my eye. I lifted one out. It contained the jade I had given Lex as a wedding present. All the jewelry I had given her was intact. And now I hunted feverishly through the little desk for a note, a clue. Nothing. Pens and pencils in their crystal holder. A desk calendar. A tiny jeweled clock. All there. Only the little portable and Adrian Jerome's bronze horse were gone. I yanked open the top bureau drawer. A carved box inlaid with mother-of-pearl held all the small gifts I used to send her—a brooch, a handkerchief, the rose in the glass globe. I slid back the doors of the wardrobe. Rows of clothes hung in perfect order on their hangers. On the racks were pairs of shoes and sandals, including the pretty ones Lex had been wearing last night. Flacons of perfume, rows of toiletries stared at me impassively from the bureau top.

The late afternoon sun slanted on the green and gold bed cover. I flung it back and threw the pillows aside, groped over the mattress. Again nothing.

The message was clear. Lex had taken me at my word. She had taken nothing that had been bought with my money, and gone out of my life.

I was halfway down the stairs when the telephone rang. It was my father. At that moment when my mood was so black, the call was ill timed. If such a thing was possible, I felt infinitely worse when I hung up. How malicious people were! Ila was a mod woman with liberal ideas but she wasn't promiscuous as Papa claimed she was. She'd told me herself about the two affairs she'd had, broken off because neither man had really been able to comprehend her interests or thinking, the type of woman she was. In the very nature of her job, she was almost exclusively in the midst of men. Why even we had been very circumspect. I had never been unfaithful to Lex.

Still, I had spent long years in a more permissive society, and I would have been very naive to expect Ila to be inexperienced in sexual matters. But it was utterly wrong to call her immoral, and worse, a nymphomaniac.

Gonsalves brought in tea. I gulped down three cups of the hot liquid thirstily. What I needed was a drink, but I refused to let alcohol become a prop. And I had to make a visit.

Night had fallen when I parked outside the Chitradhar home. When Akash quickly opened the door, his eyes nearly popped out. But he let me in, and disappeared. Sneha burst in through the door.

"You have a nerve coming here, Jai!" So she knew.

"I've come to ask if you know where Sakshi is."

She looked at me as if I were demented. "Why?"

"Because I want to see my wife," I said steadily, holding in my temper.

Sneha laughed scornfully. "Wife? What a term to use when you couldn't wait to get rid of her! I don't know where Sakshi is—and if I knew, I wouldn't tell you!" She burst into tears and ran inside.

Akash had been a silent spectator. Awkwardly, he said, "Great friends, you know. Sneha's very upset."

"Akash, Sakshi was here earlier, wasn't she?"

"Yes. When I was away at the office. Sneha was weeping when I got home."

We had started walking towards the car. I stopped and laid a hand on his arm. "Akash, I swear to you, I shan't harm her in any way. I just want to talk to her. Work things out for the best. Make arrangements. You can understand that, can't you?" He nodded. "Won't you tell me where she's gone?"

"I don't know where, Jai. She didn't tell Sneha either. Said she would get in touch. Terrible it was. Left her canvases with us, you know." He touched my shoulder. "Sorry about it. The whole thing. Lovely girl. Ideal couple."

I said nothing. Lifted a hand in farewell, and drove away.

CHAPTER 20

IT ISN'T IN MY MAKE-UP NOT TO FACE AN ISSUE SQUARELY
and at once, but I avoided going to my parents' home. I knew neither
of them would mince matters. Lex was their beloved daughter, and
related though I was to them by blood, it would make no difference.
I knew a new medication was keeping Papa comparatively free from
pain until his operation in the U.S. scheduled for next month.

As always, Ila and I were very business-like in public. If I met her
at all during office hours, she came invariably accompanying Srikant
for conference sessions with several other people. One could not
fault her performance. She had every piece of information at her fingertips, anticipating every need of Srikant almost before he asked for
the data. Our meetings were in a little tucked-away restaurant in a
suburb of the metropolis, or on a secluded beach we had found. It
was in the latter place that I told her *it* would be better all around if
she worked elsewhere for the time being. As expected, she was livid
at first, but I won her around. If she wasn't working for the Samartha
Group, I reasoned, there would be none of the constraints that
bound us now. I had come armed after some investigations. A business colleague had mourned he was losing his valued P.A. who was
getting married. I had pricked up my ears, and told him I might be
able to find him another. It was a feather in Ila's cap, as a matter of
fact, a promotion to work directly for the Chairman of an important

company with the salary and perks to go with it, instead of continuing to work for a lowlier General Manager. It was poor Srikant who really lost out on the deal, losing the best assistant he had ever had. In truth, the Group was losing one of its best people. I could not let that deter me. Papa would act swiftly if I did not. Rumor would be rife, and who knows what conjectures made.

Belatedly, I was beginning to realize that I must brace myself for a barrage of gossip items. For the duration, only our friends knew Lex was away. They had accepted it, but for how long? The Chitradhars would say nothing, I knew, but gossip starts insidiously, and no one knows where and how. The scandal sheets would have a field day with Jai Samartha when the full truth became known, as it would sooner or later.

I had not made it back to Iona for about two weeks after Lex left. The Police Commissioner whom I had met had instituted discreet enquiries, but not a clue had turned up. I was in a most restless frame of mind, wracked by uncertainties, fears, and guilt. I could not bear to return to our empty home. There was nothing there for me now.

I had to face the music some time. I was constantly in communication with Papa, of course, even several times a day on occasion, but our conversation revolved around purely business matters. With Mama, there had been no communication at all. No question about it. I missed my family. Mama's birthday falling on a Sunday, I went up to Pune that Saturday.

Thelma had a superb dinner waiting for me. For her sake, I ate as much as I could—which wasn't much. These days I didn't have the same interest in food. The house shone, the garden was in full bloom.

I had avoided going into the master bedroom scrupulously, using a guest room instead but when I needed some casual clothing to slip into, I was forced to enter. Going straight to my wardrobe, I lifted out several items, hangers and all, not looking left or right. But there was something in the room, and I couldn't get over the overwhelming impact of it. In spite of myself, my eyes went to the bed made up immaculately.

Instead of the green and gold bedspread, I saw the perfect curving form of a girl with unblemished skin, hair spread out on the pillows in a fiery glory of disarray, green eyes with that soft heavy-lidded look after my love-making, tender red mouth curving in a sleepy smile. The girl stretched out her arms to me. The image receding, and my vision clearing, the only thing there was the distinctive pattern of the flower-leaf weave.

I turned away abruptly. Someone was moving about the room. A man. The reflection was clearly there in the mirror. I went close. The man's appearance was truly impeccable, the shirt snowy white in spite of being worn all day, the tie quietly elegant, the coat sat with perfect fit on the wide shoulders. Gold cuff links and tiepin glinted.

"Won't you be late for your photography session?" a fresh young voice was asking.

For all the way the man in the mirror looked, I disliked him intensely. The unsmiling face, devoid of expression or warmth, belonged to a man of little feeling. Was it my imagination, or was there a hint of cruelty in the curl of the mouth? I turned away abruptly.

Picking up my clothes, 1 went out, closing the door very quietly as if not to disturb in the slightest the memories that lay within.

My parents were in Papa's den. A coffee tray, still untouched, sat on a little table by my mother. They appeared flabbergasted to see me. I bent to kiss my mother, but did not receive the loving pat she usually gave me, or her sweet welcoming smile. She looked at me with grave eyes. When I straightened, I met a sardonic gray glance.

"Return of the prodigal," Papa said, mouth twisting in a smile, which held no amusement.

Mama was still looking at me. I recognized that look. It was the one she wore for months after Papa's accident. It smote me. I let my gaze wander away as if it was the first time I was in this room, which I knew from my childhood. Anywhere but at Mama. And then I saw it. It had been given pride of place. Mama on Jupiter. The artist had captured her graceful posture exactly. She was minus her cap, which she held loosely in one hand, and the wind was blowing through her hair. It was her expression that caught the eye most. The humor was there in the mouth, the merry look in the eyes, as if she was sharing something most amusing with the observer. What came through was the loving attention to detail. Every stroke of the brush proclaimed it as Lex's work. My breath strangled in my throat.

"One of the two Sakshi sent as gifts. This one to Papa. The other one—Kaheksha at sunrise-is mine." Mama spoke for the first time.

"Then she's been in touch with you! And you didn't let me know!" The words jerked out.

"No, Jai. They came by courier."

I stared at her. "But the sender! The courier could have told you!"

"Did you think we didn't enquire? They were sent by Akash Chitradhar."

I sat down abruptly. Papa reached for his stick, hauled himself out of his wheelchair to go and sit by Mama. "I fail to understand why you're so bothered about Sakshi's whereabouts, Jai. Having driven her away, why don't you just keep out of her life? As it is, you've ruined it."

Angry words rushed to my lips, but I held them back.

"To think," Mama said sadly, "that we—Ketan and I—were party to inviting the child up. Nurturing the whole thing. I blame myself so much."

"You should never have involved her in a sham relationship, Jai. She was perfectly happy as she was.

The Komal ad opened doors for her—even film offers came her way. Didn't accept any of them, of course. But a beautiful girl like that—why, any man of taste and refinement would have considered himself unbelievably fortunate to win her. I believe Prem Chandran and his wife protected her from all undesirable males. Who were queuing up, I learnt. Chandran goofed though when he should have been most on his guard. Yes, in time, Sakshi would have found herself a fine husband"

"Who would have cherished her as she deserved," Mama added.

"What makes you imply I didn't cherish her?" I said hotly. "I care for Lex. I did my utmost to make her happy. Even she must admit that."

Papa shrugged. "What price all that cherishing when you went and shattered her life?"

"I fully intend to provide her with all she'll ever need A financial settlement, which will give her an income for life. The house is hers anyway. And whatever else she might ask for."

"It hurt me so much when she returned all the jewelry we had given her—because, she said, they had been given to our daughter—and now she no longer had the right to be called that."

"When did she say all this?"

"In a note."

So Lex had written Mama a note, but left not a line for me. Only the mute message via the package of keys and checkbooks, I thought, the knife twisting a little more.

"I don't suppose you'd let me see it."

"Why not? Here." Papa tossed a bunch of keys at me. "Left hand. Third drawer."

They were silent as I rapidly scanned the words on the paper. I read it once, and then again more slowly, keeping it in my hand. Other than a brief mention at the beginning, I did not figure in it. But I was there through every line, right in the dock.

"Asking me to pray for her," Mama wiped her eyes with her handkerchief. "We should have trusted her instinct. It told her this wouldn't work."

"I sat with her just there," Papa pointed to his leather chair, "when she came to consult me. And I, like some seer, went methodically through each reservation she had, and made her see her fears were groundless," he said heavily. The phone rang. I picked it up and nodded to Papa. It was a call from London. He got himself into his chair, and wheeled himself forward.

Mama poured out two cups of coffee. "Jai," she said softly, "what did Sakshi take with her?"

For a moment, I did not speak. "A small bag," I said softly. "Her portable. Nothing else. Left everything."

"I was afraid of that. Has she enough money?"

I said wretchedly, "I don't know. Why do you think I've been trying so desperately to find her?" The words burst out of me. "Mama, I've been imagining her with nowhere to go—no money. "She put a hand on my arm, the first time she had touched me. "She took nothing. Left her keys, the jewelry, check books—all her clothes—whatever had links with me. Why did she go away like that, Mama? I wanted to explain, to ask her forgiveness."

"She doesn't blame you, Jai. Only herself. The note says so."

I looked down at my hand. The sheet of paper was still with me. I wondered if I would be allowed to keep it. Had it been written in gold on vellum, it could not have been more precious to me—the last link with Lex.

The London call was obviously drawing to a close.

Well, so was the confrontation. The chastisement, which I had postponed, had been expected. I was glad it was behind me. I was wrong. It wasn't over.

Papa hung up. "Rascal, that Branscombe." He snorted. "Thinks he's pulling the wool over my eyes." Without warning, he asked, "What have you done about that woman?" I told him briefly. "Good thing. You handled that well. Didn't get her measure yet, did you? She lassoed you in expertly. Filed for divorce yet?"

I was still seething.

"No," I said shortly.

"How come?"

"You may recall I've been somewhat busy," I said ironically.

"Rusi Sethna, I suppose?"

I didn't answer. I wasn't prepared for what happened next, Gee-Gee burst in "Mama, I—" and then saw me.

"Hello, GeeGee," I said quietly. I hadn't seen my kid brother for more than a month.

I froze into immobility when, face contorted, he shouted at me, "Monster! Devil! Murderer!"

Shocked, Mama was on her feet. "GeeGee!"

"I hate you! I hate you!" He looked at me wildly.

"GeeGee!" Mama said again. He turned and ran out.

I was more shaken than I realized.

"I'm sorry about that, Jai. He misses Sakshi terribly. As we all do." Mama sighed.

I couldn't take any more. I stood up. I looked down at the note in my hand for the last time, laid it carefully on Papa's desk. I felt his eyes upon me. A few minutes later, I had taken my leave, and was out in the cold night air.

The reference to Rusi Sethna had reminded me that I had to see him. I didn't understand why I had needed the reminder. The appointment was not made through Monica. I did not want her to know why I wanted to see an eminent divorce lawyer, nor the switchboard girls to overhear a word. Two days later, I was in Rusi's offices.

The Sethnas and Samarthas were friends, moving in the same social circles. We were members of the same clubs. Parvez Sethna was a close friend of Lex, as Rusi was of mine. Rusi listened to me. The silence was eloquent.

"And Sakshi is agreeable?"

"Yes, she is."

"I'd like to talk to her."

I hesitated. "That won't be easy."

"Why not?" When I told him, he stared at me.

"Don't look at me like that! I haven't murdered her!" I said irritably. "We'll find her, then you can talk to her. Till then, can't you proceed—the preliminaries, at least?"

He leaned forward. "Jai, you haven't told me why you're doing this? It can't be a *cherchez la femme* thing, can it? It is? Not really? You'd better tell me who it is."

I didn't reply at once. After Papa's reaction, I had become extremely wary about mentioning Ila's name.

Rusi was looking at me steadily, his clever lawyer's face impassive. When I spoke the name, his jaw literally fell open. Then he recovered fast.

"I see. Well, I'll be touch, Jai. Work on it. You realize Sakshi *is* the other half of this case, and her presence is vital. We can go so far and no further."

I rose to my feet. "I understand. Look, I'll be out for several days. Bangalore first-~we're opening a new department store there, and then I'll be in New Delhi. Back on the 17th, I hope."

He made a notation. "Fine," he said briefly.

"I'll call as soon as I get back."

"Right."

It was when I was in the car driving back to the office that this disturbing memory came back to me. I had slowed somewhat waiting for the traffic in front of me to move on, when I heard this soft voice speaking with an unmistakable Scots accent. It said, "It's good to know my child—my Sakshi—has found a safe harbor with you. She had so much to bear in her short span. With you by her side, I shan't worry," It took some frenzied tooting behind me to arouse me to the fact that I was holding up the line of cars behind me. Even so, several seconds went by before I could drive on. The recollection had pierced me to the core.

CHAPTER 21

THE OPENING OF THE NEW DEPARTMENT STORE IN BAN-
GALORE went off without a hitch. New Delhi was a different matter
altogether. After three horrid days of coming up against bureaucratic
red tape, I was extremely exasperated. I kept in constant touch with
Papa by telephone, and with all the unit heads. When I called Ila, the
exchange was necessarily brief. I could give her no assurance about
returning on the 17th.

Then unexpectedly on the morning of the 15th, I was summoned
to the Ministry. When I walked out thirty minutes later, I was quietly
elated. I wasted no time in informing anyone since I was able to get
an early flight back to Bombay that afternoon. I could contact Papa
and Ila that night.

At the airport in Bombay, I almost decided to call Ila and tell her
of my return, but chances were that she was out for the evening. And
I was weary, longing for a bath, a meal, and relaxing with some
music. I thought Ila and I could spend the next evening together.
Traffic was as frenetic as ever. The cab crawled along. When the cabbie swung into a side lane to avoid the congestion, I realized we were
not far from Ila's apartment. Impulsively, I told the man where to go,
I bade him wait in front of the building block where Ila had her
apartment. Outside her door, I pressed the button, waited a couple
of minutes, and tried the bell again. So, as I'd guessed, Ila was out.

About to turn away, I heard movement from within, then bolts being drawn.

Ila peered around the door. "*Kaun?* Who is it?"

Then her eye fell on me. "Jai! But you weren't coming till the 17th!"

"No, I was given the green signal this morning. Took an early flight back."

Crazy really, but I had the impression she actually looked frightened. After a pause, she held the door open. Did I imagine reluctance on her part? Certainly she had no plans to go out. She was wrapped in a robe, obviously donned in a hurry, hair disheveled, face minus make-up. I thought she looked positively ill.

"Aren't you well, Ila?

"A migraine," she said with difficulty.

"You poor thing! Have you taken something for it?" She nodded "I shan't stay. I guess you were asleep. Sorry I disturbed you." I smiled at her. "I'll call you tomorrow. Depending on how you feel, we'll see what to do in the evening. Okay?"

She was patently in such discomfort, I reached out to touch her shoulder in sympathy, but my arm froze in mid-air when a man's voice said sleepily, "Get rid of him, whoever it is, Ila. Shobha will be livid if I'm late for the third evening in a row."

My arm fell by my side. I turned around to take in the towel wrapped around the man's waist, the legs and torso bare.

"It's okay, Shyamsunder. I was just leaving anyway." Ila was close to fainting. "So that's your migraine," I said pleasantly. "I'll leave you to it."

After a squeaky "Sir!" Shyamsunder had vanished precipitately behind the bedroom door.

I did not wait. Out of the apartment, not waiting for the elevator, I raced down the stairs. I thought I heard my name being called.

The cabbie was waiting patiently. "Malabar Hill," I told him.

An hour later, I had showered and eaten the omelet Vishwas had made for me. Then I stretched out on the settee—and closed my eyes, letting Rachmaninoff's Second Piano Concerto flow over me. But if I thought it would prove a soothing distraction, my purpose was defeated.

The ugliness of the evening's encounter played behind my lids in every unsavory detail. Humiliation first, then fury had been my immediate reactions. Strangely enough, the one feeling I had not experienced was jealousy. That I should have been such an absolute fool, such a complete idiot, never noticing what was right under my nose! Papa had spelled it out for me most clearly. Instead of heeding his words, I had in my anger and disbelief stopped visiting my parents. I had determined to stand by myself, as I looked at it, abandoned by my own.

Over the years, how many men had Ila been involved with? Possibly she did not know herself. Was she a nymphomaniac, or just a very liberated modern woman who made her own rules, and lived by them? It really didn't concern me. How clever she had been with me though, totally convincing that the physical side of our relationship was sacred, and therefore to be postponed till we were married. In the meantime, she had been in and out of bed with probably every top executive in the Samartha Group, and the concern she was working for now. And judging from her partner this evening, not limiting herself to that level. And this was the woman who would have married the grandson of the legendary Jaisingh Samartha, besmirching the very name.

Vishwas was saying something. I opened my eyes, put out my hand to lower the volume, and seeing who was behind him, switched off the music. The sight brought me upright, swinging my legs to the floor, and to my feet. "What do you want?" I asked coldly.

"Jai!" She came forward, hands stretched out, lips quivering. Dispassionately, I thought she looked every bit her age. Her makeup was a mask, which did little to hide the fact that she was thirty-four, two years my senior.

"Jai, let me explain—"

"You owe me no explanation."

"How can you say that!" she exclaimed. "Jai, it wasn't what it seemed. Shyam was just—"

"—discussing the latest stock market situation," I completed, "As I say, it's none of my business. I've had a very grueling day, Ila. Will you go now?"

"But I have—"

"Spare me," I said icily.

It wasn't that easy, of course. This kind of exchange continued for some time. I became icier by the minute, she more voluble, excited. It wasn't difficult to see she was fighting for what she had lost in one single stroke this evening. My inopportune visit had sent all her castles in the air plummeting to earth, all her scheming and ambitions tumbling into a void from which there was no return.

I had stopped taking any part in the conversation. Ultimately, she ran out of breath. She stared at me, chest rising and falling. I noticed irrelevantly how flat it was. Her face, normally attractive, had taken on an animal mask, which made her look positively ugly. I couldn't bear the sight and turned my eyes away. She recognized the revulsion. That more than any words I might have spoken convinced her that she had lost. From explanations and pleading, she became vituperative. What poured out now were remarks about me personally. I let her rave on, keeping my face blank, though the barbs stung. No one likes to be dissected, have a cruel character analysis thrown at one's head. When she came to a panting stop, I only said politely, "Are you through now?"

She began to cry, ugly tearing sobs that shook her thin frame. I went to stand by the window, looking out, hands tightly clenched in my pocket. The sounds tapered off eventually.

She said slowly, "I'm so glad that green-eyed witch deserted you. That's what you deserve. I hope you never find her."

I did not move. "Better go now, Ila. I'm sure you wouldn't like Vishwas to throw you out bodily."

"I'm going! And I hope you suffer the torments of hell!"

I heard the sounds of her departure, the front door opening and closing. Vishwas came anxiously, coffee tray in hand, to ask if I needed anything more. No doubt he'd heard the woman's raised voice. I told him not to let her in again ever. And for tonight I was at home to no one.

He stammered an apology. I told him to forget the whole thing and bade him goodnight.

Then I sat down and let relief take me.

I was snowed under with work the next morning. Problems had piled up in my absence, unit heads had to be met, Papa to be given a report on the Ministry's approval. The one person I forgot completely was Rusi Sethna—until he called around mid-afternoon after the lunch break.

"Jai, you were supposed to see me."

"Yes, I know." I explained what had held me up.

"I have to see you urgently."

Suddenly alert, I asked why.

"An epistle arrived in your absence." For a moment I could not speak. "Jai?"

"I'm on my way," I told him.

Rusi lost no time in handing me the letter. I read it still standing up, my eye leaping from line to line. The writer said she guessed that Rusi was handling the case, and therefore the enclosed documents were being sent to him. From her side, he could count on the fullest possible consent to the divorce. She would send a declaration to that effect later, and hoped that a brief delay would not hamper progress of the proceedings. She wanted neither alimony, nor a financial settlement, and was making no claims of any kind on property, monies or material goods. The enclosed document spelled out in detail that she, Sakshi Jerome, d/o the late Adrian Jerome, wife of Jaisingh Samartha, son of Ketan Samartha, was hereby relinquishing all rights. Included in the list was the house in Pune, jewelry, all assets and shares in the Samartha Group, etc, etc.

I read it with feverish haste. When I came to the bottom, I re-read the whole thing again.

"Ought to please you," Rusi was saying dryly. "Makes things easier all around!"

"There is no sender's address!"

I had turned the paper over frantically. I looked up. "The envelope! Surely there's something on the envelope!"

Silently he passed me a long brown envelope. It bore his address neatly typed. I struck my fist on my hand in frustration. The smudged postmark, barely legible, was Bombay.

"Bombay! God, has she been here all the time? Where could she be found in this teeming city if she chose to keep out of sight?"

"Jai, I fail to see why you're so desperate to find her. She's being extraordinarily generous—magnanimous. In fact, I can set the ball rolling on the strength of this letter. And she promises one more document shortly."

I whipped around in fury. "For God's sake, Rusi! I *don't want* you to set the ball rolling! Can't you understand that?"

He stared at me. "I must be particularly dense today. You'd better explain why ten days ago, you came to consult me, asked me to handle a divorce for you, and now you do a *volte face*." He must have seen something in my face. "You'd better sit down. You could do with a stiff drink. But we'll have to settle for coffee." He spoke briefly into the intercom. I sat motionless. He did not speak, but went through some papers on his desk. When the coffee came, Rusi moved me to the comfort of the sofa grouped with some equally comfortable chairs, flanking a coffee table. I gulped the liquid thirstily and felt better. "I'm taking a lot of your time, Rusi." I roused myself.

"No problem, I have no appointments this afternoon. The rest will keep."

"I'm sorry I barked at you."

He waved a hand. "A friend's privilege."

I tried to smile. "Some privilege! You're legally entitled to bark back at me when you feel so moved."

"I'll do that,"

"Rusi," I said slowly, "I no longer know what's with me. In fact, I've been so muddle-headed over this whole thing, I don't think I'm fit to be helping run the Samartha Group." He did not interrupt. "They say confession is good for the soul. As a lawyer, you've heard countless sob stories. Here's another."

"I'm not a lawyer now, Jai. Just a friend."

I put my head in my hands. "I don't know where to begin."

"Try the beginning. I always thought you and Sakshi had one of the most successful marriages in our circle."

"You thought right. We did."

"When did things start going wrong?"

"That's the point. They didn't. Go wrong, I mean. One of those inexplicable situations. A select team of Group execs was on extensive tour, checking on various problem situations that had been reported to us. Srikant was there, and with him as indispensable right hand, Ila." I linked my fingers together. "She's been around for years, as you know. Thought of highly. Razor-sharp mind. Invaluable asset at meetings and conferences. I confess I'd never thought of her as a woman. Just as a highly efficient machine, to be admired and appreciated. This in spite of the fact that she was very much there at business dinners, even social whirls, accompanying Srikant on behalf of the Group. You may well recall seeing her at countless shindigs. But on this trip, things became different. In Ahmedabad, Srikant caught a bug of some kind—his stomach—and had to keep to his hotel room. Ila took over effortlessly. That evening, the others went off in different directions—one to see friends, another to visit family members, etc. I had dinner with Ila, and later, we went out just to while away the time. I discovered she was good fun as a companion. We stopped at a place where they had a floorshow and dancing. It felt pleasant to unwind. We danced, strolled along window-shopping. There was a subtle shift in our relationship. I was now seeing her as a woman." My voice died away. This confessor wasn't finding it easy, no matter how good it was for his soul.

"Well, I didn't sleep with her, if that's what you're thinking." Rusi had raised a skeptical eyebrow. "You're thinking I could have without much resistance from the lady? You're wrong. Ila made it clear from the start that she wasn't ready to give up her principles on that score." If possible, Rusi's eyebrow went even higher. He snorted. "I respected her feelings. Ila was certainly attractive in her own way, but we had clicked on a very different level. Spoke the same jargon. Talked shop most of the time. She was as knowledgeable as any man where business affairs were concerned. Frequently, she put her finger straight on the root of a problem that had been vexing us." I picked up an ashtray from the table and balanced it on my hand. "I don't know at what point marrying Ila came into the picture. It seemed to be a slow but natural progression. But I had one big mountain to scale—and I dreaded the prospect of telling my wife."

I was up, pacing from Rusi's desk back to my seat. Gripping the back of a chair, I continued, "I couldn't fault Lex on even a single count. I don't have to tell you what a warm, lovely being she is. Beautiful to look at, with an irrepressible sense of humor. After I came back from the States—my father's accident, you'll recall, everything fell on my shoulders. I coped. But I soon forgot how to laugh. It was Lex who brought laughter into my life again. My family adored her. Since this thing came up, I've been *persona non grata* at home—with my brothers at least. My father and I have had this special bond, my brothers having appeared much later. I guess it's a common enough phenomenon with the eldest son. That closeness has been spoiled now—and it hurts. My mother—ever gracious—is more forgiving, but deeply sorrowful. To them, Lex was the daughter they never had. You won't know it, Rusi, but Lex is alone, except for kinfolk in Scotland. Lost her parents tragically, and had to learn how to fend for herself. That was the main deterrent. I couldn't bear to hurt her when she's been hurt so much already. She's been a wonderful wife to me. It was Ila who lost patience with my excuses. She threatened to confront Lex herself and tell the truth." I went back to my seat, and looked down at my hands. "I did it."

After a moment, Rusi asked, "How did she react?"

"How else but stunned—dazed? Asked the reason, asked if she knew the person I wanted to marry. Told me not to worry. She wouldn't make any trouble. Left the room."

"Was that when she went away? In the night?"

"No. I encountered her next morning briefly. She didn't want to talk then. I said we could talk that night. I came back early just for that. She was gone."

Suddenly I felt exhausted, as if I'd been through the whole experience again. I sank back in my seat.

"And Ila? What happened there?"

I said tiredly, "I went to see her unexpectedly. Passing by on my way to Malabar Hill from the airport. Just off the plane from New Delhi. Thought I'd just say hello, let her know I was back."

"And discovered what anyone could have told you years ago," Rusi said grimly. "The moment of truth." I said nothing. "Are you very disappointed? Dejected?"

"About Ila? Enormously relieved. If I'm dejected, the reasons are quite different. It isn't easy for a man who prides himself on his judgment of character and situation to accept that he's been completely bamboozled, you know."

"Nothing's wrong with that faculty of yours. You've just been taken in by a very clever scheming woman."

I shook my head. "I can't blame her. I'm a grown man, not an untried boy. Goodness knows, I've had enough experience with women."

"Will it make you feel better if I tell you now—belatedly—that in our particular social circle, the women have been twittering for months about Ila's intentions towards you? Parvez always mentioned it—and all of them were incensed about it."

I stared at him. "They're crazy! There's been no such thing! We've had a very correct employer-employee relationship."

"You mean, you've had," Rusi said dryly. "What the lady in question had in mind was quite different."

I was quite bemused. Could this be true? And if there had been such clear signs, what were they? How come I hadn't noticed them? I put the queries to Rusi. "Jai, dear pal, this is one area in which we are completely retarded. Being mere men, we don't have that kind of insight. You know the saying—set a thief to catch a thief. Well, here it's set a woman to assess another." He shrugged. "How do we know how they detect these things—a look, a word, a gesture. Leave them to ferret out anything if it exists." He grinned. "Or imagine it, if it doesn't. You know, Jai, if I'd had an inkling of what was happening, if you'd sought my advice before you approached Sakshi, I'd have told you to sleep with Ila—get it out of your system, You couldn't have found a more willing bedmate."

"I'm shocked at you, Rusi! What would Parvez say if she heard you!"

He spread his hands. "What's so surprising? I can' t keep track of the number of our so-called friends who play musical beds regularly."

"Anyway, you're mistaken," I said wryly. "That was one thing she made clear from the outset."

"That she'd withhold her favors, as they put it, till you were married? Sheer genius on her part." He looked at me. "What next, Jai?"

"I have to find Lex, Rusi, She's my wife," I said simply. "Can you advise me on that? The police enquiries have come up with precisely nothing."

He was thoughtful. "Amazing," he mused, "that someone with that distinctive beauty—the coloring—and so well-known—should not have been spotted by now. The Komal Girl whom millions would recognize. She's stayed well hidden. I can put you in touch with a private investigator. A husband who wanted evidence of his wife's infidelity brought him to my attention. Want me to attend to it?"

"If you will, Rusi," I said gratefully.

"Right. I'll get on it right away. Can you let me have the details, plus photographs? Good."

PART II

Leave the fire ashes, what survives is gold.

—Browning, *Rabbi Ben Ezra*

CHAPTER 22

SAKSHI

THE STATE TRANSPORT BUS DEPOT AT PUNE'S SWAR GATE
swarmed with people. I paid off the rickshaw, and carried my suitcase and typewriter. I was wearing my most unobtrusive clothes. A
scarf covered my hair, and I wore dark glasses. There was no direct
bus for Mahableshwar at this hour, but a Wai-bound bus was leaving
within five minutes. From Wai, I could find another bus to Panchgani where I was bound. It was imperative that I be on my way
before my disappearance was noted, and perhaps a search begun.

The bus was quite full, but the conductor waved me to a seat at
the back where two women, mother and daughter, sat. I sank down
and waited tensely till the bus driver got in. Doors slammed, a rum-
bling and throbbing told me we were about to move. For several
miles, I was much too overcome with relief to think of anything else
but the fact that I had managed to slip away.

I was very weary, having been at it since dawn. Before the day
began in earnest, I had written my letter to Mama and sealed the
envelope. I was conscious of Gonsalves getting the rest of Jai's bags
out of the car, and bringing them upstairs. Some time later, I
answered his knock and took in a tray of tea. When I heard Jai leave,
I did not go to the window to see the car drive out of the gates. I
could now start sorting through the contents of my locked desk

drawer and the safe. Eventually, I had collected almost everything. When Thelma came up to ask about breakfast, I told her I would have some toast later. I was very busy, I said, and did not want to be disturbed. I saw she was about to burst into speech about last night's ruined dinner.

I forestalled her. Reluctantly she went down again.

When I went down later, I made straight for the studio, taking a willing but puzzled Gonsalves with me. It took time to sort out the canvases, but at last it was done. The two portraits that had been commissioned were packaged separately. Into some crates went my other canvases, and painting materials. And finally I had Gonsalves pack the two paintings that had to go to Kaheksha.

It was late when we finished. I dashed upstairs to shower and dress. Gonsalves had followed my instructions and loaded the crates into the back of the van. I told him where to deliver them. I had called Sneha earlier to say I was sending some stuff, and would be grateful if she could store it in their garage for me. Also that I myself would be dropping in later. My next stop was the bank.

It was a time-consuming affair to get everything out of the safe deposit vault. I could see the Manager was dubious about it and not pleased either, but what could the poor fellow do? From the bank where I had my very own money, proceeds of the Komal campaign, I withdrew the entire sum. If I was very frugal, it should see me through for quite some time.

The meeting with Sneha was fraught with emotion. I told her the barest details, controlling my own tears when hers began to roll down her cheeks. But at last, after she'd promised to let it go no further than Akash, I was able to get away.

One more thing remained to be done, to get my own personal things together. I found Daddy's leather suitcase just where I'd tucked it away deep in the recesses of the wardrobe. I refused to let the sight of it make me break down. I had given away most of my pre-marriage clothes, but I hadn't been able to part with everything, my inborn strain of thrift no doubt prompting me. Now I had reason to bless the trait from my grandmother, for there was enough there to fill the suitcase. I worked quickly now, for it was already mid-afternoon. About to close the bag, my eye fell on the large framed photograph of Jai and myself. In color, it had been taken by Cy as we stood by the paddock. Jai had his hand on my shoulder. He had that unsmiling expression, and looked ravishingly handsome, while I, my head flung back, was laughing. "The Two Models" we had dubbed it. My hand went out to lift it from the bedside table and lay it on the top of the pile of clothes with Daddy's bronze horse. And then I was ready to go.

The ST bus had climbed up Katraj Ghat, and was now in the tunnel. By the time it emerged, I became aware of a sick feeling in my stomach. The diesel fumes were no doubt responsible. That, plus the fact that I hadn't eaten since lunch the previous day. It was a sharp reminder of my condition. Along this same route I had gone up with the Samarthas or with Jai at least a dozen times, and not turned a hair. I took out my handkerchief and pressed it to my mouth.

"*Gadi lagthe ka, bai?* Does the bus make you sick, lady?" I hadn't really registered the other passengers on the seat, wrapped as I was in my own misery. The woman who was asking if the bus made me feel sick was a village woman wearing a faded nine-yard cotton sari. Her face was all sympathy, I nodded. She turned her head and spoke to the quiet teenage girl sitting in the window seat. Obediently, the daughter got up to exchange seats with me. The air blowing in my face helped enormously. After a while, I felt infinitely better. When I looked at the woman, she smiled and nodded. I smiled back. How could a simple illiterate woman be so kind? At the next halt, I bought cookies and gave one packet and some candy to the delighted girl. I ate the whole other packet myself. I must have fallen asleep because my next recollection was that it was late evening and the air was much cooler.

From Wai I was able to take a bus on the last lap of the journey. I was so tired, I was ready to drop. It was dusk when I trudged from the Panchgani bus stop to Binty's home, my feet dragging, the suitcase feeling heavier by the minute. Then at last, there was the small white washed cottage with its fenced-in garden and little wicket gate.

Binty was watering the garden. She looked up startled, saw me, and dropped the hosepipe. Then she was hugging me, taking me inside the warm, cozy little interior. I did something unexpected. I fainted.

Hours later, I lay still in my narrow bed. It was very quiet except for the distant barking of a dog. I had been washed and fed, and allowed to stretch out on the ancient old-fashioned settee. For the first time since last night I was completely at peace. Binty had asked only one question—if I was pregnant, and nodded in comprehension when I said I was. She had pottered around, doing her small chores, and then settled down with her knitting. Painfully I had told my story. She had looked up at the word "divorce".

"Stay here," she said briefly. "It is no problem at all." Visitors rarely got to this section of Panchgani any way. In the unlikely event that anyone of the family was passing through to Mahableshwar, they would hardly expect me to be here. I was to avoid the busier areas, and keep strictly away from the main road through which cars and buses had to pass. She had made no comment on my husband or his family.

Now in the bed, I thought I must concentrate on my health. Binty would see to it that I ate properly, but I must take long walks early in the morning and after dusk. Still making plans, I fell asleep.

I shall not linger over what happened in the next few months. Suffice it to say that Binty took over my life at this point. It was she who took me for regular check-ups to the doctor, made me eat properly, drink plenty of milk, which I detested, and made me take my walks. I swallowed vitamin pills, took iron and calcium. Once when I tried to stammer my gratitude, she said to me, "My dear child, I can't tell you what joy it is to have you here. Don't get me wrong. I'm happily settled here. I have my pension, the house is mine, my friends are good to me. But having you under this roof is to have my daughter come home to have her baby in the traditional Indian manner. I never had my own husband and children. Your presence has compensated fully for that. It isn't just Rebekah's grandchild we are awaiting. I feel it's mine too. So no more talk about the trouble you're giving me, or of gratitude."

I hugged her, but could not speak. I had found a haven.

I suppose I was happy. Certainly the beauty of the place could not be faulted. One matter I had taken care of was writing to Rusi Sethna. I had decided to send him the final document after the baby was born. Foolish of me, I knew, for I was well aware a divorce takes time. But I was taking no chances. My child had a right to its paternity. I must stay legally married to its father at least until its birth. I had no intention of making any demands on the Samarthas. This child was mine and mine alone. But it would be legitimate. If its father had rejected and spurned me, that was not the child's fault.

If in the hours of the night, I often lay awake, unable to halt the memories that flooded my mind, only I knew. Unbidden they passed before my closed lids, a whole cavalcade of them dominated by a single figure, smoothly arrogant, wearing the faultlessly tailored clothes on the splendid framework with careless elegance. My ears heard the deep timbre of the voice.

My son was born in the little cottage. Binty delivered him with the help of a friend who was a nurse, and who had alerted for the event. It was an uncomplicated labor.

The small room resounded with lusty roars. Both women were smiling as they attended to us.

"Doesn't look like you or the Jeromes," Binty commented, as she dusted the small body with baby powder after the first bath. When a few moments later, she placed the fragrant bundle by me, I gazed at my son and recognized clearly the stamp of Ketan Samartha on the tiny face. Newborn though he might be, the face was not wrinkled like that of so many babies. It would be a strong face, I thought, the nose already well defined. I touched him with my finger, tracing each feature in wonder at the perfection of him.

"Has your skin color. And the hair—not much of it—is like yours," Binty observed. "And we'll know about the eyes only when he opens them."

I regained my strength rapidly. With the exercises I did, my figure went back to its former shape. Now that the baby was born, I had to make a new beginning, start to plan for the future. Whatever I decided would be dictated by the fact of the child's existence. Had there been no baby, the options were many. I could have found another position like the one I'd had in Orion. Modeling would certainly have figured on the list. Working on a magazine as illustrator was another possibility. All three 1 set aside as impractical. I wasn't exactly panicky because I'd used little of the money from my nest egg.

Over her vehement protest, I had insisted on paying Binty for my maintenance. Thanks to her, there hadn't even been a hospital bill. But even so, I couldn't just sit idle, and draw on what I had. Then something came my way in a most unexpected way.

Binty had neighbors. The houses weren't close at all, not really next door. Helpful as she was, the neighbors often consulted her, or called upon her when someone in their families was unwell. She always responded with copious kindness, even nursing the patient if necessary. Occasionally, they dropped in to see her. They were aware that a niece of hers had come home for delivery since her parents were no more, and thought nothing of it.

One morning, a lady neighbor dropped in to consult Binty about a persistent cough her son had. She brought with her a small daughter. I had just finished feeding the baby in the bedroom, when I noticed the little visitor staring at me. I coaxed her in, showed her my son, and made friends in no time. When her mother called, she went reluctantly, glancing back longingly at the baby. It was much later that I spotted the book she had forgotten on the bed. I picked it up to take to Binty, but something made me stop and examine it. It was a story about animals, and profusely illustrated. The drawings were good enough but not as delightful as they should have been. A thought struck me. I found and then made a note of the publisher's name. It was a Pune-based firm, specializing in children's books. I sat down and wrote at once, enclosing sketches I had done. The reply came sooner than I expected, almost by return mail. The publisher was more than interested. Terms were mentioned. If I was willing to accept them, when could I start work? The net result of the correspondence was that a steady stream of assignments came to me. So pleased was the publisher that other established publishers commissioned me. I soon graduated to illustrating book covers. Certainly, the total income was less than what I'd earned at Orion, but then, thinking of the marvelous convenience the arrangement offered me, I could not complain. As I said before, my needs were simple.

The days went by quickly. Between looking after the baby and my painting, plus helping Binty with household chores and cooking, I didn't know where the time went. There was little time to brood. But there were small reminders of the past, which cropped up unexpectedly.

There was the night when after dinner Binty and I were sitting peacefully, she knitting, and I holding the sleeping one-month old infant. Out of the blue, without warning, she asked without looking up, "Child, who's Jai?" My head jerked up as if I'd been shot.

The name had not been uttered aloud for months.

It had a tremendous effect on me. Suddenly I felt like weeping, something I had not allowed myself for a very long time.

"Why do you ask, Binty?" I said after a long time.

"You were calling for him," gesturing to the baby in my lap. "That was the name you cried out when the last contraction came and he was born."

I could not speak. I hadn't been conscious of doing it. Acting as a catalyst, the name brought a storm of weeping, the tears streaming down my face, falling on the little blanket, my body shaken with sobs. I felt Binty bending and taking the baby from my lap, then coming back to pat my back gently before taking me in her arms. What she said had no meaning, but the murmur was soothing, and gradually the weeping diminished.

I was made to drink Binty's sovereign remedy—a cup of hot sweet tea. Much later I told her quietly, "Jai is—was—my husband." She had never asked to know the name though she had been aware of the last name.

"I see," she said, but made no comment.

I did not know what had precipitated the bout of weeping. One of the first things I had done when I was up and about had been to send the promised document to Rusi Sethna. I knew nothing of legal matters, and was hardly in a position to find a lawyer, but I had stated that of my own free will, without any coercion whatsoever, I was giving my full consent to the divorce. I repeated the statement made in the earlier document declaring I wanted no financial, or any other aid in any form whatsoever, that I was making no claims. As with the first communication, Binty had asked a friend of hers to post the envelope when he went to Bombay. There was something very final about that act. It was symbolic of the end of a chapter. Now there were just two of us. Sakshi and son.

I named the baby Adrian Anton. If that was an odd name for Jaisingh Samartha's great-grandson, I thought with grim humor, it was no stranger than the fact that the said great-grandson had been born in a tiny unpretentious cottage instead of in some fabulously expensive private nursing home, his birth attended by a team of doctors, each with a string of foreign degrees to his name, and born amidst much fanfare and rejoicing as the first boy of his generation. My normal sense of humor reared itself again for, out of whimsy, I bestowed on the baby the nickname Scotty. Whimsy alone did not account for the choice. A tribute to you, Fiona, I thought, saluting my beloved grandmother. No one had honored her in any way, poor lady. After all, I was the inheritor of her green eyes and russet hair, and who knows how many other qualities had been handed down to me from my Scottish forebears. Always close to her in spirit, after meeting her in person and coming to know her, she was enshrined forever in a very special corner of my heart. When Scotty was ready for school, I would register him as Adrian Anton Jerome.

Each day, Scotty brought Binty and me new delight.

Under her supervision, he thrived on the diet he was given. He put on weight at a steady rate, arms and legs becoming strong and firm, cheeks rosy and round. Binty predicted he would grow to be a tall man, for he was large for his age. In any case, what could one expect with my father being so large in size, and both of Scotty's parents much taller than average? The small scalp merely sporting some wisps at birth was now covered with reddish hair. But the facial structure, the distinctive shape of mouth and nose, and most noticeably, the gray eyes, made his resemblance to his grandfather, Ketan Samartha, unmistakable. Sometimes with a pang, I thought how much Mama and Papa would have loved him. Perhaps some day, they would meet him. By then, no doubt, they would have other grandchildren, perhaps Scotty's step-brothers and sisters. But for the present, I could not contemplate such a move. I had to remain incognita.

CHAPTER 23

SAKSHI

SCOTTY WAS FOUR MONTHS OLD WHEN SOMETHING HAP-
PENED to bring drastic changes in our lives. I was watering the little
garden one evening when a car drew up. The driver hailed me.

"Excuse me," he said courteously in English, "but I seem to have
lost my way. Can you direct me? I want to get back to the highway."

"Of course." I gave him the instructions and he thanked me. To
my surprise and then alarm, he did not drive off as expected, but
went on looking at my face. He was about my age, a Parsi, and good-
looking with a pencil-thin line of moustache. I was terribly uneasy.
How could I know if he was related to Mama? In the event that he
was a casual passer-by, such open masculine interest was definitely
unwelcome. I turned so that I was not exactly facing him, the
hosepipe giving me sufficient cause to do so.

I jumped in my skin when he said, "Sakshi?"

It was the name that did it. I whipped around swiftly.

"I thought I recognized your eyes. Aftab Dubash." For a moment I
simply stared, then I broke into my warmest smile. He was out of the
car, shaking hands, as pleased and excited as I was. It was the kind of
meeting between childhood companions who have not seen each
other in years. Words tumbled out of us as we caught up with news,
and finally just stood and beamed at each other.

Binty returned, and insisted on Aftab's coming in and having a cup of tea. I had to grant it to him He didn't turn a hair at the unpretentious interior. We were still talking non-stop. I could see, however, that Aftab was more than a little puzzled at my habitat. I had to tell him the truth. That I had been married. That I had a baby. Binty had taken me in, I said, and I was doing work for a publisher. He made no comment. When Scotty woke up, Aftab held him gingerly, and we all laughed. He rose to go. His parents were in Mahableshwar, and his mother would worry if he were too late. But he promised to come back soon. Hesitantly I asked if he would see to it that information about my whereabouts did not go beyond his parents. A quick look at my face, and he gave me his word.

The unexpected meeting left a glow in my heart. It brought back some of the happiest days of my life. I realized too I had missed meeting someone young, used as I was to the crowd at Orion and my circle of friends. I looked forward to Aftab's next visit.

It came sooner than I had expected. He was back the very next day. To my great joy, he had Uncle Sohrab with him. Lean as ever, his hair now gray, he was still the same. He kissed me lovingly, and kept his arm around me. I suppressed my tears with difficulty.

"Little Sakshi! My dear, I can't tell you how pleased Gulnar and I were. We bombarded Aftab with questions. I couldn't wait to come down to Panchgani. Now, can you come up with us? Spend the day? Oh, I know you have a baby. Gulnar is longing to meet him."

I said slowly, "I'm sorry, but I don't think I can. There's nothing I'd love more. But you see, if I came to Mahableshwar, I might be recognized, and I must avoid that at all costs."

He looked at me thoughtfully. "I see. The car, as you see, has tinted window glass. Would it convince you if I say I shall see to it that you're completely unobserved?"

"Go with them, child," Binty urged. "You haven't had a change since you came."

I capitulated. It was too exciting a prospect. I felt like a small child bound for a picnic. Binty helped me to gather up Scotty's needs, and pack them into a basket. I gave her a loving hug. She patted me on the back.

As the car moved smoothly up the twelve miles of winding red road to Mahableshwar, famed hill resort, as was Panchgani. I held my sleeping son with mixed feelings. Thus had I come so often in the past. Entering M'war, the car halted for clearance at the check post. In front of us lay Venna Lake. A few boats were already on the water. Bearing a bamboo from which hung a basket at each end, a man came to the window. He was lifting a lid to display the enticing red strawberries nestling in green leaves. He could see nothing through the glass, of course. Small children selling their wares tried their luck—wild roses, bright orange carrots, purple *jambul* fruit, and the purple-black of mulberries. I had a lump in my throat. It was all so familiar, so dear to my heart.

Aunt Gulnar came down the steps of the Dubash home. She took Scotty from me, and when I emerged, kissed me with deep affection. "My dear," she said simply, "a happy day for me. How beautiful you've become! And this young man," looking down, "is completely adorable."

I can't describe the feeling of security, which lapped me. I felt as safe and loved as if I was in my own parents' home. There was so much to talk about, so many gaps in time to be filled. Scotty had been whisked away by a maid after I attended to his lunch. I was told he had gone to sleep. So it was in a relaxed state of mind that I could consume with relish the delicious meal we were served. For the first time in months, I discovered I had missed elegant living.

After lunch, we sat on the porch, which commanded a celestial view of the mountains. A streak of silver in the far valley was actually a river. I breathed deeply of the pure mountain air. It held a touch of moistness unknown on the plains below.

I had set down my coffee cup. I turned to my hosts. "'I can't tell you—how wonderful all this is. You're so kind. I feel I'm back with Mumsie and Dad."

"In that case, won't you tell us what is wrong, child?"

"We'd like to do all we can, Sakshi. You know whatever you say will be absolutely confidential," Aftab nodded to show approval of his parents' words. I made up my mind. Haltingly, then with greater confidence, I told them.

They were very quiet after I finished.

"Roza and Ketan Samartha. How well we know them, Run into them at races and horse shows often. They've bought horses from us," Uncle Sohrab mused. "Now their children—they must have been around, but I can't quite recall—"

"Firoza Samartha is a lovely woman. I can understand why you love her," Aunt said thoughtfully.

Aftab leaned forward. "Sakshi, you realize, don't you, that you can't hide away forever. You're too young to stay so isolated. It isn't good for you. Yes, I know the lady—Binty-has been a savior, but you'll have to make up your mind to start a new life again."

"Where can I go, Aftab? I have Scotty to think of. Had I been alone, things would have been different. I can't let J-anyone know about Scotty. He's all I have in the whole of India. My only blood relative here. That's why Binty's home has been ideal."

"Come to us," Uncle Sohrab said.

I looked at him incredulously. "To the Stud Farm?"

"Yes."

"How can I! That's right outside Pune! I'd be spotted within a day!"

Patiently the three of them outlined their plan. Behind their house at the Farm was a small, furnished bungalow. It was used for occasional tenants who needed quarters for a short spell, often a foreign scholar attached to the University. It was empty at the moment.

"I'm not offering you charity, child, but a job." Uncle Sohrab saw the unbelieving look on my face. "And not one I'm cooking up either! You'll be expected to train selected horses for shows and contests. Timings to be adjusted to the little one's needs. You may continue with your painting, if you wish. There's enough to do on a stud farm, as you know very well."

Aunt Gulnar took my hand in hers. "And I need you. It will be so lovely to have another woman around. And the baby, I adore him already."

I was afraid to believe it. It sounded too good to be true.

Aftab added, "That point you mentioned—about being right in Pune. It's something like Poe's 'The Purloined Letter'. It won't occur to those folks that you're right under their noses. They're surely imagining you're a thousand miles away."

"It's like this, Sakshi," Uncle Sohrab told me. "You need a helping hand, right? But I need you too. No one has your rapport with horses, your touch. In that, I'm just exceedingly fortunate to have found you again."

"The lady who's been so kind—she can come and visit you as often as she wants, if that's bothering you. And you're not to worry about babysitting. Goodness knows there are enough servants floating about doing nothing."

What was there left to say? I lifted a trembling hand to my face. "It sounds so wonderful! I can't believe it!" I said unsteadily.

"Better believe it!" Aftab said firmly. "We're leaving the day after tomorrow!"

CHAPTER 24

INTERLUDE

GEEGEE CAME SHOUTING FOR HIS MOTHER, EXCITEMENT palpable in every line of his body. He burst into the small den, which was Roza's special domain. "Mama, I saw her! I saw her!" He could be referring to only one person.

Roza's pen dropped from suddenly nerveless fingers. Shakily she rose to her feet. Hand at her throat, she whispered, "Sakshi?"

"Yes, Sakshi!" he said triumphantly. "Better sit down," he told her, noticing her state, and chastising himself for not being less exuberant. Then, unable to contain himself, he poured out his story. He and Bhiku, the chauffeur, had been driving back from the outskirts of the city, and had stopped for a red light near a shopping center. A crowd of pedestrians had darted across the road, and that was when he saw her. "I couldn't trust my own eyes, Mama, until Bhiku said, 'Did you see Young Madam?' So I knew it was real. When she lifted her face to glance at the traffic lights, I saw her eyes, and there was no doubt left at all."

"How—how did she look?"

"Absolutely beautiful!" enthusiastically.

"I mean—did she look—prosperous?"

"Have a heart!" GeeGee protested. "We only caught a fleeting glimpse. She was wearing pants and some kind of jacket." In a different voice, "One thing though, Mama. She was pushing a baby. You know—one of those things with wheels. A pushchair, I think it's called." His mother did not show the shock his words caused. "Could be a neighbor's child?" he suggested hopefully.

"I don't know, GeeGee." Roza hid her dismay. Her relief and joy that Sakshi was well and apparently settled was badly jolted. Only later with Ketan did she voice her doubts.

"Not surprising," he said thoughtfully. "Have you forgotten how beautiful the girl is? It would be the natural thing for anyone—all kinds of men, young and not so young—to fall in love with her. We can't forget she left bruised and battered. If some man offered her a helping hand—gave her solace at a time when she needed it most—it would be natural for her to turn to him. Besides, I think she's under the impression that the divorce is an accomplished fact. That Jai is married to another woman now. That being so, she was free herself." He sat back. "Still it's a mess, isn't it? An unholy mess."

"At least we can be thankful *that* woman is out of the picture. Jai never told us why he broke off with her. It's not the kind of thing one can ask about."

"Jai is nobody's fool. He may have found out for himself what she is. As you say, it's the one bright spot in an otherwise dismal scene."

"Ketan—the crossing where she was seen—could it be that she lives somewhere in the vicinity—or goes there frequently?"

"We'll find out. But, Roza, don't put too much faith in finding her again, will you?"

She shook her head mutely.

If the surveillance did not yield results, Fortune smiled on Roza at long last when she was least expecting it. GeeGee and she drove to an annual equestrian sports meet one Sunday a month later. It was one of those events they both enjoyed thoroughly, and never missed. There was a time when Roza herself competed. Now she took special pleasure in watching talented amateurs taking part, knowing exactly how it must be for them. In a spirit of anticipation, mother and son settled in their seats, blood fired by the crowds, the color and excited expectations. Glancing down at the program in her hand, a name leaped out at Roza. Jumping Normal—Sakshi Jerome. Further down the same had been entered for the most difficult event of all. She sat stunned for a moment, before showing the card to GeeGee who stared at it round-eyed.

Neither mother nor son remembered much about the first events later, though they clapped mechanically. And then it was time. Legs flashing, Summer Lightning cleared the heights, totally in tune with his slender rider, with the utmost ease. Unconsciously, Roza clasped her hands together in wonder. The crowd fell silent as the pair approached the highest bar, and then roared with approval, waved caps and handkerchiefs after the pair had soared over it gracefully and effortlessly.

"Oh, good girl!" Roza said aloud. GeeGee squeezed her hand.

It was with bated breath that they watched the next event in which girl and horse took part, again with matchless precision. When they cantered off the field, the horse was taken over by a groom. A tall young man lifted Sakshi off her feet, and kissed her soundly. The girl emerged from the embrace, breathless and laughing, her cap having fallen off, hair tumbling down. An older man wearing a cap also kissed her warmly. The trio went up to the fence of the enclosure to watch the remaining competitors. It came as no surprise when Sakshi Jerome was announced as the winner in both events. The crowd shouted in approval. Clearly, Sakshi was a favorite with them.

After the show was over, GeeGee did not wait to consult his mother. He darted off, running after the slim figure. Roza saw Sakshi turn around, stare incredulously.She waited anxiously. Then with a smile of the utmost sweetness, the girl reached up to hug GeeGee. They spoke together, and then Sakshi scanned the crowd. When she caught sight of Roza, she began to run. They fell into each other's arms, neither able to utter a word When they finally moved apart, both had tears in their eyes.

"Ah, Mama, I can't tell you how good it is to see you! Oh, where can we go and talk? I know! The cafe."

It was a heart-warming session. Eagerly, Sakshi asked her questions. GeeGee was almost out of college! And Cy would be back from the States in six months! The surgery on Papa's leg had been successful so that now he spent four days in Bombay, keeping office hours! What wonderful news! And Mama was spearheading a fund-raising drive for a new Hospital Children's Wing!

How lovely she looks, Roza thought. She always was, but now she has a special glow about her. The new love interest in her life, no doubt. And why shouldn't there be, as Ketan says? That young man—unmistakably a Parsi. The way she looks now it should surprise no one if a line of men was beating a path to her door.

"Will it shock you if I tell you I have a baby boy?" After a pause, Roza said inadequately, "How nice!" "Yes, isn't it?" She smiled at Roza's confusion.

"Is he sweet?" casting about in her mind to find words.

"Very sweet. And a bundle of mischief!"

"Does he look like you?"

"No, though he has my coloring. Quite different."

To GeeGee, "I almost didn't recognize you! That height—to say nothing of the moustache!"

He grinned and smoothed his upper lip complacently. "Has the girls swooning!"

"Oh, I don't doubt that!"

"You mustn't mind if I ask you, dear, but are you—all right? Financially, I mean? You won't hesitate to tell me if you're not?"

The green eyes were misty. "You're a darling. No, I'm quite solvent. Thank you for caring."

"You have a job?" from GeeGee.

"Several jobs. And I love all of them. I've even gone back to some artwork."

"Not for Orion?" Roza asked startled.

"No. Not that kind of work. Something quite different. I get more assignments than I can handle."

Roza put down her cup. "My dear, we mustn't keep you from the little one. I can't tell you how precious a time it has been this afternoon. To see you again. To know you're well and happy."

GeeGee handed back the riding crop banded in silver and the horseshoe-shaped ashtray, which were Sakshi's prizes and which he had been admiring. "For me too."

The women kissed each other with deep affection. Sakshi reached up to kiss GeeGee's cheek. Shyly, he returned the caress.

"It's meant so much to me to meet you. Give my dearest love to Papa."

"We shall."

"Mama? I'd be grateful if you didn't mention meeting me—to everyone."

Roza patted her shoulder. "I understand. And I don't need to tell you we're there if you need us."

"You're so kind. And I shan't forget."

On the way home, wrapped in their own thoughts, mother and son were silent. Oh, what went so wrong, Roza thought in silent grief. They had everything going for them, she and Jai. They seemed to have adjusted so well. But why didn't Sakshi stay on and fight? Why did she slip away so completely, give up? And now the other woman was no longer in the picture and it was Sakshi who was involved elsewhere. Had borne another man's child. If anything, that was the hardest thing to accept. But the child was a reality, and one could not wish it away. Jai, my dear, dear son, my firstborn who has a very special place in my heart and his father's. Such a beautiful child, so intelligent and receptive. It broke my heart to let him go away to Woodstock. But his grandfather insisted, said it was best for the boy's future, and what could I do? I think Jai realizes what he lost—something irreplaceable. Or else why would he keep searching for Sakshi?

Roza roused herself, for GeeGee was asking, "Did you notice, Mama, that Sakshi didn't mention her address, or offer to let us see her baby?" His mother nodded. "Do you think—she's living with someone? I mean, a man? The child's father?"

"I don't know, dear. But it seems very possible."

"And it doesn't bother you?"

"I can hardly sit in judgment, GeeGee, when it was my son who treated her with the utmost shabbiness, creating the situation in the first place. I haven't the right to condemn her. Yet, it does grieve me that I've lost my beloved daughter. But if she's found happiness again—as she appears to have—then I find it in my heart to rejoice for her sake. I can't begin to imagine what she's been through. Somehow she found the courage to start again, to fight her way through out of the bleakness. And for that I applaud her."

"Oh, Mama, I do too."

It was not in character for Ketan Samartha to leave it at that. Discreet enquiries about Summer Lightning and his rider brought the answer. It dawned on Roza that the older man she had seen wearing a cap that day was Sohrab Dubash. His back had been turned to her, and the cap had contributed to hiding his identity. They had come to know where Sakshi was, that she was well and happy. And that had to suffice.

CHAPTER 25

SAKSHI

I CANNOT FIND WORDS TO DESCRIBE HOW I FELT ONCE SCOTTY and I were settled at the Farm. I loved the small bungalow. It had just one large bedroom with attached bathroom. A previous foreign tenant had installed a hot water heater, which was a great convenience. The living room occupied the whole front section of the house. Originally intended to be part dining room, I converted that half into a studio for myself. Scotty and I didn't need a formal dining room. We ate in the kitchen.

It was enjoyable doing the place up. Already furnished, freshly painted, it took on a lived-in look with the pretty inexpensive flowered curtains I put up.

Late one evening, I borrowed Aunt Gulnar's little Volkswagen, and drove to the Chitradhar home. Sneha and I were so happy to meet again. We fell into each other's arms. I could not stay long, of course, but while I was there, we talked non-stop. Akash beamed at us. Next evening Aftab drove me in the van to collect my crate of canvases.

We stopped to buy all the paraphernalia I needed for serious painting. I was now ready to set up my easel.

Taking time off from my book illustrations and covers, I made pen-and-ink drawings of the Dubashes. They were delighted, even awed by those simple likenesses. Uncle Sohrab said humorously that he himself couldn't draw a straight line. The drawings were framed and hung up in the lounge where they drew appreciative remarks from visitors. I decided to do an oil portrait of Aunt Gulnar.

She was a little shy about it, but the enthusiasm of husband and son overrode that. Scotty and I made frequent trips to the big house where he was whisked away by the servants. He had become everyone's pet, and that included the stable-hands, and he was in danger of being thoroughly spoilt if I didn't keep a firm eye on the situation. Scotty taken care of, I did a number of preliminary sketches. Married to Sohrab Dubash she might be, but Aunt Gulnar was no horse-woman. She could ride, of course, but it wasn't a passion with her the way it was for Mama and myself. So instead of depicting her on a horse, I used the garden as a background. She was a gardening buff, and the place bloomed with vivid color. She had *malis* to help, but the inspiration, planning and supervision were hers. Her entries won prizes at flower shows, roses being her specialty. I had her seated in a white cane chair surrounded by the brilliance of her blooms. By her side, a small table held a trug from which flowers spilled in glorious profusion, and a pair of shears. I spent much effort in capturing the exact likeness of the sweet kind face.

Uncle Sohrab was enchanted by the portrait. It was given pride of place in the sitting room. Guests expressed profound admiration. I was happy. It was a small gesture in return for all the kindness bestowed on Scotty and me. As a direct outcome, however, I was approached to do other portrait studies, particularly of children. I had to be selective, of course, but the financial gains were quite considerable. The Dubashes had told me to charge whatever fee I thought I should, for these were wealthy people. And so by word of mouth I began to make a name for myself. My only concern was that news of my whereabouts might reach the Samarthas—one Samartha especially. But then, I thought to myself, why would he be bothered? He was happily married now to the woman whom he had rejected me for. Lex had no part left to play in his life. I no longer signed my portraits with my full name, merely an SJ scrawled in the corner.

And I was happy enough. I rode and trained the horses assigned to me. Timings had been adjusted to suit me. Very early mornings while Scotty was still sleeping, and then afternoons when a girl I had employed cared for him. As he grew older, he was brought to watch the horses. He loved doing that. One day, when I had finished my session on the track, I had him handed up to me. He made no protest when I perched him on the saddle in front of me, securely held, and Summer Lightning moved off. Scotty sat still as a mouse. The last thing I wanted was to frighten him. I need not have worried. He was so exhilarated that we had a hard time getting him off. He burst into loud yells of protest.

Uncle Sohrab was amused. "What did you expect from Adrian's grandson, Sakshi? Scotty gets it from all sides, doesn't he? He's going to be an outstanding horseman."

After that, not a day passed without Scotty wangling a ride. I came to know my son was an opportunist. He used his blandishments on Aftab whenever he came up from Bombay by holding up his arms entreatingly. Aftab would laugh and swing him up. The tall man and the small figure in yellow overalls with bunnies embroidered on the front, cap on head, would canter off. Sometimes, it was Uncle Sohrab who caught sight of the big gray eyes fixed on him hopefully, and Scotty would get another ride. So, just as I had, the youngest Samartha rode almost before he walked. I could not help thinking of Mama, Cy and GeeGee, imagining what pleasure they would derive from indulging Scotty in his favorite pastime.

It was inevitable that I would participate in horse shows. Summer Lightning and I were so attuned to each other that we won time and again. Which excited Uncle Sohrab tremendously. I was glad not just for my mount and myself, but because I felt that by achieving these successes, I was in part paying back for the kindness and generosity he had poured upon me. Sometimes when I thought about it, I wondered if I would still be living with Binty, leading a quiet existence, if Aftab had not taken a wrong turn and stopped to ask directions.

As a matter of fact, Binty came down to visit me twice a month. She enjoyed being back in Pune, looking up old hospital friends, and shopping. Most of all, it was Scotty whom she looked upon as her own grandson and couldn't resist. With Binty around, I could get a few extra things done—make considerable progress on the. painting in hand, go out on my newly acquired second-hand scooter to shop or visit the Chitradhars. I was taking risks, of course, but then how long could I stay hidden?

Then came the heartwarming encounter with Mama and GeeGee, he almost unrecognizable now that he towered over me, but still my pal. I was emotionally overcome when Mama and I embraced. She was too, I saw. We covered so much ground in that half an hour together.

The news about Papa delighted me most. How good to know that he was almost back to normal, and blessedly free from pain. And my dear Cy was coming back soon. So much spoken, so much left unsaid. They had not mentioned one subject, nor had I. I had not tried to conceal my Dubash connections. Foolish to try when the announcer had clearly mentioned the owner of my horse, and the program stated it in black and white. I knew I had startled them both when I spoke of having a child. Mama had recovered in time. It had been sad to part with them. Very probably, we would meet again at such gatherings. In parting, I had to make that last request. Mama had understood.

I could not get the Samarthas out of my mind all that day. With the greatest of difficulty, I had pushed them all these days into a recess of my mind. Now they were uppermost. Realization came that I had been deceiving myself all along. They did not belong to the past where I had relegated them. They were still my family. For the first time, I began to feel a twinge of guilt about concealing Scotty's iden-tity from them. In my early efforts to cut myself away completely, I had not given a thought to his grandparents and uncles. But what would be the ramifications of such a revelation? I would have to give the matter intense thought. The fragility of my detachment was brought sharply to me very soon.

I had given Scotty his supper, and then cuddled him in a big old chair for some time. I had some music playing, which he loved, and showed him pictures from a book. He was too young for stories, but he stared at the pictures with great interest, and had his special favorites. Then he snuggled down in my arms, letting the music lull him to a drowsy state. I might be a single parent, but my child wasn't going to feel insecure or unloved. I put Scotty in his cot, and lingered over it, thinking as I did often that he grew more like his grandfather every day.

He looked like a cherub—which he certainly wasn't—cheeks flushed and rosy in sleep, long lashes concealing the gray eyes. Reluctantly, I moved away.

Having been in a disturbed condition all day, I felt no interest in cooking myself a meal. Uncle Sohrab had passed on a color TV set from his house, saying it was getting on in years, and anyway, this was a good excuse to replace it with the latest model. Usually I switched it on as I ate, watching the programs that interested me, and ignoring the rest. But after I cleaned up, I preferred to listen to taped music, opting for classics by my favorite composers. There were times, of course, when the strains of a particular piece were too poignant for me, and I changed to something livelier.

I flipped on the TV, and then fetching some fresh bread slices and a cup of tea, I sat back to eat my simple supper.

The English news bulletin ended with the weather report, and a current affairs program came on. It was to be a panel discussion on a recent industrial policy decision. Not of my interest, I thought, and decided to turn it off for some music instead. Half-full cup still in my hand, I got up and stretched out my hand to the switch. The anchorman had just concluded his preliminary outlines of the subject under discussion, and begun to introduce the panelists. And then it happened. He was introducing a man faultlessly attired in a perfectly tailored suit, the tie in quiet good taste. But it was the face off which I could not take my eyes. My hand had frozen in mid-air, the cup of tea forgotten in the other. Somehow I sank down on the rug in front of the set, my eyes glued to the screen. The camera had passed on, of course. Hungrily, I waited for it to return. When it did, I drank in the sight. Why, I thought in wonder, how different he looks. The beard and hair made a difference certainly, but there was something more indefinable. But, oh, how devastatingly handsome! He was speaking now, the all too familiar voice with its underlying accent making statements with total confidence. I did not take in one word, not turning my eyes from the moving lips, the long narrow hands gesturing for emphasis. Involuntarily, I put out a hand and tried to touch them.

The glass felt cold to my fingertips. The discussion ended, of course. The camera focused once again on the anchorman as he made his concluding remarks, and thanked the panelists. It swung back to the participants. The whole scene faded out. I stared unbelievingly at the screen, which now showed a bright young announcer. No, how could they do this! A comedy came on. It was not to be borne. I turned off the set automatically. I felt dampness on my chest. The tea had spilled on it. The wet patch was spreading. I stared at it unseeingly. Then it hit me. Jai was gone, and I would never see him again. I wasn't conscious of the flood of tears poring down my cheeks.

Utterly bereft, I flung myself on the floor, and wept.

Much later, the chill of the tiles penetrated through my clothes. I stirred and sat up. Brushed my hair out of my eyes. Gathered up the cup. Took my dishes to the kitchen. Went and had a warm shower, slipped on my terry-cloth robe. Then I went back and sat in the squashy old leather chair.

Nothing in me had changed, I thought in bitter grief. If anything, my feelings for Jai had deepened. What I felt for him, I could not feel for any other man. That was why the men who had come my way in recent months—guests of the Dubashes, or those who came to the Farm for the purpose of buying horses—had left me unmoved. Some of them had shown every sign of wanting to know me better, but I had never reciprocated. It was still Jai who lived in my heart. But he wasn't my husband now. Another woman claimed him as that. I was no one in his life. If I allowed myself to drown in emotional storms just as I had done moments ago, it would only mean bitterness and unhappiness for me. I had so much to be thankful for. Scotty, most of all. Kind friends. No financial worries. I was doing things I loved.

One thought buzzed in my brain. What if something happened to me? I wasn't being morbid, but I had to face it, even if the possibility was remote. But hadn't that applied to Daddy, that laughing giant of a man, in ruddy good health, cruelly snatched away in the prime of life? I had to think of Scotty, his future. I couldn't possibly let Jai know. He and Ila could well have a child of their own by now. The last thing I would want was to have my son brought up in the same house where Ila was.

The Dubashes would never abandon Scotty. But was it fair to impose on them? After all, they were not kinfolk.

Then it came to me. Cy was returning one of these days. I must get in touch with him. Talk to him. He would help me to see the picture better. Help me to decide.

CHAPTER 26

JAI

THE PELTING RAIN MADE DRIVING DIFFICULT. CYCLONIC conditions off the Andhra coast had affected the weather in our state, bringing this unseasonal downpour in its wake. I peered through the darkness. The windshield wipers clicked rhythmically. I smiled wryly to myself.

What had possessed me to leave the warmth and comfort of my own house and venture forth? True, I had matters to discuss with Papa. More than that, I had felt suddenly, overwhelmingly, the need to be with my family this evening. There was a party I had been invited to tonight, but somehow, such get-togethers spelt boredom to me. Pointless chatter, Women gushing over each other, hypocritical compliments, too much to eat, and certainly too much to drink. What I really longed for was peace and quiet. The serene company of my mother. An early morning gallop to clear the cobwebs from my mind.

Now that Papa was mobile again, less of the burden fell on my shoulders. With Cy back soon, there would be three of us to share it. Lately, I hadn't been able to help thinking how little I had achieved in my life. Thirty-four years, and what had I done? Such thinking had prompted me to sponsor, under the Samartha Group aegis, a playground on some land the Group owned. It had proved to be immensely popular with the slum children for whom it was intended. Coaches had been provided to train the older children in various sports. Now I was studying plans for the building of a modest-sized gymnasium for indoor sports. The Group had also undertaken a massive tree-planting project in the same slum. It had not been left merely at the planting stage. It had been an appeal to the women, which had provided the essential back-up support. The idea of having trees to provide shade and beauty to their surroundings had struck the right note. The cows and goats, which frequently did the greatest damage being in their charge, they controlled them strictly from straying into those areas. The women also kept a stern eye on small boys who might be tempted to vandalize the young saplings. Papa had given his full blessing on these ventures. Though he studied my face as I outlined plans, he made no sardonic comments.

Waman beamed at me as I dashed from car to ivied portico. I brushed the droplets from my hair and shoulders, nodding to his question about whether I would stay for dinner. Before going off to alert the kitchen, he told me that my parents were in the small sitting room. I could hear voices and smiled to think how surprised they would be to see me. A name caught my attention, and I came to a dead standstill, transfixed.

"How I would have loved to ride Summer Lightning!" my mother was saying. "Sakshi's done a marvelous job of training him."

My father's deeper voice questioned, "How does she squeeze in so many things?"

"She seems to manage beautifully. The Dubashes are lovely people. They must have been very understanding about schedules and timings."

"It makes me feel happy that she's doing the things she loves best. Painting. Riding."

"And the Dubash Stud Farm has the choicest horses. It must be a pleasure to train the ones under her care."

My mother almost dropped her glass when she saw me standing grimfaced in the doorway. Papa followed her gaze.

"You don't have to pretend and try to cover up. I heard some of that conversation." I surveyed both of them. I was seething inside, but if I lost my temper, it would serve no purpose. I controlled it with an effort.

"So you've found Lex, and have chosen to keep that fact from me!"

"At her express request, Jai."

"Don't stand there like an avenging angel, son. Good to see you. Raining heavily, hmmm? Must have been difficult to drive. Get yourself a drink."

I poured myself one, but refused to be deflected.

"So I'm a pariah. If Lex doesn't wish to see me, I can understand. Am I permitted though to ask how you found her?" I kept my tone polite, no easy attempt.

"Quite by accident, Jai. Someone spotted her and told me. Your father and I pursued the clue. Then I met her in person, again quite accidentally."

"So Papa's in this too. Does Lex seem to be well?"

"Oh, yes."

"She has a job?"

"In a manner of speaking."

I stared at Mama. "You're just throwing these crumbs of information at me! Do you think that's being fair? You know well enough how frantically I've searched for Lex since the day she left. That I've never given up the search. And now that you've found her, you give me these answers which tell me precisely nothing!" I put my glass down with some force.

"Jai, I shan't betray her trust in me. Not even for you. It can't have been easy for Sakshi, but she seems to have come out of the monumental crisis splendidly. Carved out a whole new way of life for herself. You talk about my being unfair to you. But what about her? Do you expect me to be so cruel as to destroy her hard-won peace?"

Her words were like blows to me. Worse was to follow. Papa cleared his throat. "There's one thing you should know, Jai. Your mother will be angry with me for betraying a secret, but I feel you ought to know. It may influence your wanting to find Sakshi. There is a child." His keen gaze could not have missed the shocking impact of that sentence on me. "Roza hasn't seen it, but it exists. Sakshi was very frank and open about it. Even before that, she had been spotted with a baby." He waited as I reached blindly for my glass, and put it to my lips. "It may not have occurred to you that every sign points to a new man in her life. A beautiful girl like that—friendless, rejected—" I made a protesting sound "—would turn for help and comfort to someone, wouldn't she? That's how it seems to me. Sakshi accepted your announcement about wanting to close the chapter of your marriage without a single protest. She could have played havoc. Demanded an exorbitant settlement. Given the press a chance to have a field day. Instead of which she slipped away quietly so that you would have no obstacles in your path. If we care for her happiness, it would be best to leave her well alone. She will never lack for admirers. This man—what else can we call him but her lover—" I winced "—perhaps she will want to marry him. And there is the fact of the child. You can't overlook it, Jai."

I had gone to stand by the window. I could see little in the darkness, but tiny rivulets of rain trickled down the glass panes like tears.

My mother said gently, "I give you my word, Jai, she's well and very happy. Very busy, but pleasantly so. And financially stable. I did ask that much—if she needed anything."

I turned around slowly. "You say you didn't see the child?" She shook her head. "Nor the man?"

She hesitated. "I saw someone—who might have been the—the person"

"What makes you say that?"

She threw a look at Papa, who said bluntly, "The man was young. Good-looking. Sakshi won a contest and he lifted her off her feet and kissed her enthusiastically."

My mother shot him a warning look. Papa was rubbing salt into an extremely raw wound. She added, "She seemed to want to keep that part of her life totally private. And I did not probe. She was so glad to see me. Lovelier, if that's possible. Motherhood has only enhanced her beauty."

She broke off as dinner was announced. As we made our way to the dining room, Papa said, "You have news about the Hindustan Kingston merger? You can tell me after dinner."

My report on the merger was delivered in brief. I was too heart-sick to be totally immersed in it. Papa's eyes were upon me as I spoke tersely. Then he sat back and stretched his leg on the footrest. Although there was no pain, the leg was still a little stiff. But he had come a long, long way from the days when pain had been a constant companion.

"Jai." And when I looked up, surprised at his gentle tone, "I know what you're going through, son."

"Do you?" I said bitterly. "You must be glad—even gloat-ing—that I'm being punished with a vengeance. All of you, my brother included, have treated me like a murderer. I guess I am one. I murdered my marriage. Destroyed everything that was beautiful and meaningful in my life."

"I'm not glad, son. You're wrong about that. You know, Jai, I have been guilty myself in this affair. That puzzles you? In the long months of my convalescence, I've had ample time to think. One's perceptions alter in a situation like that. I realized how much has been expected of you since you were very young, because you were Jai Samartha, the C. P., as I know very well you're called. You really weren't given much chance to be young—carefree—or free. There was always this weight pressing you down: You had some respite while you were at Columbia, at Harvard—though there again, it was imperative you get good grades—which you did. And I think you enjoyed your job in the States tremendously. And then I had to go and get involved in an accident. The mantle fell upon your shoulders entirely. And you coped. Marvelously so, given your youth and lack of experience. Yes, I was there in an advisory capacity, but my contribution was infinitesimal. I watched you grow from strength to strength, and I could see you were a Samartha born and bred."

I didn't interrupt. Never before had Papa spoken to me so.

"And yet I was robbing you of your youth. I was killing something in you. As your grasp on the running of the Group grew surer, you were also becoming more unemotional, colder."

"The I.M., Ila told me. I had been nicknamed the Ice Machine." That had been in those last moments of her visit when she turned vituperative.

The distaste on his face was as much for the name as for the reminder of the woman he detested.

"Is that what they call you?" He shook his head. "And your mother and I were seriously concerned about this metamorphosis in you. It grieved her more than she could say. Although the accident was not my fault, its repercussions had a permanent effect on you. And then quite suddenly, you came home and told us you'd met the girl you were going to marry. And that was a further worry. Would she be able to withstand living with a husband who wouldn't be cruel, but certainly wouldn't be capable of showing her affection? We were immensely relieved to meet Sakshi—warm, natural, unaffected. Every one of us reacted the same way to her. If anyone could cope with you, it was this beautiful girl. But she was full of self-doubts. And more than that, she sensed that cold core in you. She came to consult me here in this room. Do you know what she said? 'But he doesn't really care about me. I don't think he believes in love. But to me, love is all-important between two people who are going to spend a lifetime together. My parents had it in abundance. My mother couldn't bear to live after Daddy was gone. Can a marriage set up so cold-bloodedly be a marriage in the true sense of the word?' I answered as well as well as I could, Jai. That was when I told you to court her. Win her over. Which I presume you did successfully."

A knock at the door came almost simultaneously with the ringing of the telephone. The first signaled the arrival of Waman with the coffee tray. The second was a call from Kawamura in Tokyo.

I wandered over to the globe, which stood on its own pedestal. My finger rotated it slowly, my eyes making note of the places I had traveled to. They went practically around the sphere. Wasn't there a saying: "What is a man profited, if he shall gain the whole world, and lose his own soul?" I didn't know who had said it, or where I had heard it, but it applied to me. I had tried to gain the world at least within the environs of the Samartha Group. If the soul referred to the center of one's being, then I had lost mine. Lex had taken it when she went away.

My finger traced the painted surface of the North American continent. My second home. New York where Lex had clasped her hands at the sight of the Statue of Liberty. Boston and Cambridge where she had been wistful over those who had the fortune to study at Harvard. Connecticut at the farm of my friends, Mary Anne and Greg Sealey. Lex asking mischievously if the horses there would know there were aliens on their backs. Suddenly shy when Greg observed that she and the spray of apple blossoms she had held to her cheek had the same delicate beauty.

I had not realized the Tokyo call was over.

Papa said, "You used to do exactly that when you were a little boy." Startled out of my reverie, I let my hand drop. "We did so many things together in those days. Do you remember climbing Pratapgadh? You were very young, but manfully did your best in spite of your short legs."

"I remember. Shall I pour the coffee?"

"Do." After a moment, "Jai." I looked up from my task. "You will be going on a search for Sakshi, I feel certain. It's not in your nature to give up. And I can't stop you. But I beg you not to jeopardize her newfound happiness, or hurt her."

As if I would harm a hair of her head. Why did my parents persist in assuming I would hurt Lex? In that respect, they still thought very poorly of me. Well, I would heed their words. It was up to me to repudiate their image of me as a cold unfeeling brute. When I rose to leave, Papa told me how pleased he was about the slum project. I nodded and left to find Mama. She was in her den. The fund-raising drive for the Children's Wing kept her very busy, though she had a very able secretary. Now she dropped her pen, and came around the desk.

"Jai, you're not leaving? I didn't disturb you because I thought you two were talking business."

I told her I was leaving for Bombay early. As a Samartha wife, long used to schedules and deadlines, she made no demur. "When will we see you again, dear? Not too long a gap this time. Take care of yourself. You work too hard. You must take time to relax."

"I do. I've started playing volleyball with the boys as often as I can. They have a fine team. Get a kick out of my being there. And I enjoy it. Keeps me fit."

"But you've lost weight, haven't you?"

"All mothers say that," I told her, smiling.

"Jai?" And when I looked at her, she put up a hand and laid it gently against my bearded jaw. "I'm sorry for the things I said earlier. I know I hurt you."

"It's okay. I guess they needed to be said." I put my hand over hers. Suddenly, she reached up and put her arms around my neck. We stood quietly, savoring the closeness, yet conscious also of the many undercurrents in our lives. At least, my parents still cared for me.

She loosened her hold. I saw her eyes had filled with tears.

"Mama," I said gently, and stooped to kiss her.

"Do you know," she said in wonder, the tears spilling over, "that you haven't kissed me since you were a small boy?"

"Haven't I? Then I must remedy that." I bent to kiss her cheek again. "I have to go now. I'll try to make it next weekend. I'm longing for a good gallop." I gave her a last hug and went out into the rain, leaving her looking after me.

CHAPTER 27

WHEN I WENT HOME THAT NIGHT, I DID SOMETHING I HAD avoided doing for more than two years. I entered the master bedroom. It was immaculately clean. Evidently, Thelma tended it lovingly. Instead of the musty atmosphere expected in a room so long unused, it had a freshness, which denoted regular airing. Still, I opened a window and let in the cool damp air. I slid open the wardrobe doors. The clothes hung in precise order exactly as they always had been. I put out my hand and touched a drift of pale green chiffon, ran my hand over the textures—silk and satin, cotton and velvet, all with their distinctive smoothness. A faint fragrance from the sachets of sandalwood powder tucked in the shelf recesses pervaded the interior. I picked up a high-heeled silver sandal. It belonged to a slim narrow foot. I could remember it clearly, the nails a lovely oval shape, painted a pearly pink. At the bureau, I took up an atomizer. When I pressed the nozzle, a fine mist of delicate elusive fragrance filled the air. As I laid it down, I saw the man reflected in the mirror. He wasn't the same one I had seen that long ago night when I had been here last. This man wore a beard, very well groomed, of course, that went well with the longer hairstyle, the hair curling down now to the shirt collar, left thickly waving on top, the sideburns longer. Gone was the neater more severe cut.

The changes in the face went deeper than a mere new styling of hair. It bore the marks of experience, not always pleasant, it seemed. The eyes looked out without their habitual hauteur, but as those of a more sensitive feeling person. The mouth, firm as ever, appeared less severe. Not a mouth, which smiled easily though.

From the drawer I took out the inlaid box. I had picked up the little bagpiper myself in London. I balanced him on one hand. He looked very gay. One could almost hear the skirl of his bagpipes as he marched along with lively step. How much pleasure he had brought. A delightful souvenir from Fiona's land.

And finally, I went to the bed. I lay down, stretching my tired limbs, feeling myself sink into its comfort. All around me was the quiet of the night. Rom gave a short bark, but thought it not worth pursuing. A bird twittered briefly in one of the trees that were growing tall and sturdy. After the rain, the air had become fresh and moist. It poured into the room. The house wrapped me in its welcoming embrace. I was glad now to be in Iona. It was home as Samartha House and Kaheksha were not in quite the same way. But it lacked something—the sound of voices, one voice especially, the echo of laughter, the tap of heels, all of which it had once. There never had been any question of disposing of Iona. It wasn't mine to sell anyway. It was Lex's. It breathed of her presence.

Every picture on the walls, every curtain that billowed in the breeze, every stick of furniture had been lovingly, eagerly, chosen by her. I rolled over and buried my head in the green and gold fabric of the bedspread. The Dubash Stud Farm. I knew exactly where it was. Not a geographical locality I frequented, it being in a quite different direction from the Bombay-Pune National Highway, which I traversed. I never did have time to drive around aimlessly, or for the sheer pleasure of it. Had Lex been there all the time?

When Mama called Sohrab Dubash the night after Lex disappeared, he had professed to have not seen her for ages. Had he been telling the truth, or covering up for the daughter of his old friend?

Yet Dubash was known for his integrity. Would he have spoken an untruth, and to Mama at that? Who could know the answer?

I had found out about Lex by accident. My joy and relief had been sharply checked because of the other details my parents had outlined. Was it simply conjecture on their part? No, that was wishful thinking on my part.

There was a child. Undeniable proof of another man in Lex's life. I buried my face deeper in the bedspread. The knife twisted so that I felt it in my gut. Was this how Lex felt when I had spoken to her that night? Lex with another man. A lover. Living with him. Conceiving his child. Tall and good-looking—young, Mama had said. He must have given her everything she needed most at that time—protection, security—love. I had given her the first two, but withheld the third. No use to say that I hadn't known it was in me to give. A half-forgotten line of poetry came to me: "I have been faithful to thee, Cynara! in my fashion."

Well, I had no intention of hurting Lex any more.

I had already inflicted grievous hurt. Nothing I could do now could match that cruelty. My parents need not have any qualms. Need not tell me repeatedly to leave her alone. I would seek her out to ask her forgiveness. And see her with my eyes one last time. Then I would go out of her life, as she would want me to.

Should Lex ask for a divorce, I would give it to her. I would never marry again. It wasn't in me to make a woman happy. I had ruined one life. That was enough. If heirs to the Samartha line were to be provided, my brothers must do the needful. Jai Samartha would not. In ancient India, I thought, men in my state would have become ascetics, wanderers. *Prayaschit* was the Sanskrit word. Penance.

If I didn't have so much responsibility upon my shoulders, I might have gone away. Perhaps after Cy acquired some expertise, learnt the ropes, I could do it. I'd get away.Go to America. Ask Greg to give me something to do around the place. Help with the horses, just about the only thing I was capable of in that set-up.

I rolled off the bed and folded back the bedspread. There were fresh sheets and lace-edged pillowcases on it. Thelma was an incurable optimist. I threw off my clothes and got in. At some point, I fell asleep.

It was still dark when I drove through the silent streets. Occasionally, a truck lumbered past, and the heavy motorbikes of milkmen laden with cans zipped along. The information I had been given was that Lex was out at first light each morning with the horses. If I was too early, it hardly mattered. Waiting for a short while when I had waited for more than two years was nothing.

The Stud Farm was enclosed all around, as my headlights revealed. I parked the car off the main road under a clump of trees, and locked it. On foot, I went along till I found ground that was a little higher. I levered myself up with my hands, and clambered over. The stables were easy to locate, for lights were on there, the sound of movement, a voice. A couple of giant banyan trees spread their branches by the track fence. I was wearing a dark shirt, jeans and boots. No one could spot me in the shadow cast by the trees.

I did not have long to wait. Boots crunching on the ground told me someone was approaching. A figure passed by, and went on to the stables. The slender shape was clearly outlined in the light that streamed out. I heard a cheerful greeting being exchanged with someone who might be a stable hand. A horse whickered. A slight male figure led out a horse. The boy was chuckling. "Feels jealous when you pet Summer Lightning." A fresh young voice, so well remembered, said, "I don't know why she should. She gets as much attention."

Horse and rider began a slow canter around the training track. The boy perched on the railing. Every time they passed him, he called out a remark, not always eliciting an answer. The horse picked up speed. It was much lighter now so that one could see clearly. The slim figure sat with complete ease as they began to jump the hurdles.

They soared over effortlessly. At the highest one, my heartbeat accelerated, but it was cleared beautifully. Only Lex of all women of my acquaintance had that incomparable style. It was incredibly graceful. Even Mama didn't have it. The boy on the fence was applauding enthusiastically. My own palms tingled, but I didn't dare make a move.

CHAPTER 28

SAKSHI

FOR ME, IT BEGAN LIKE ANY OTHER DAY—RISING IN THE HOUR before dawn, washing and dressing, tying my hair back, donning my boots, and slipping out of the bungalow after a quick check of my son. Although it meant cutting short my night's sleep, it was really the most convenient of arrangements, while Scotty still slept. It also left many hours of the day for other pursuits until afternoon when I had my second session on the track, this time with Solitaire. Rajan greeted me cheerily, saddled Summer Lightning. He had whickered in welcome when I arrived. I paused to pat him as Rajan dealt with a last buckle. Solitaire nudged me from behind. It irked her if I didn't greet her first.

I felt the familiar movement of the horse under me as we went through the gate. Having warmed up, Summer Lightning began to go through his paces. As we sailed over the first hurdle, I experienced a *frisson*, for I felt eyes upon me. Rajan, of course, was watching from the fence.

A quick glance around told me no one else was around. In my new state of heightened awareness, I felt distinctly uneasy. It was exactly the sensation I experienced when Jai was near—which was patently absurd. Why was I thinking of him so much that it interfered with my concentration? It was the TV program that had surely put me in this extra-sensitive state. I reprimanded myself sternly, and applied myself to Summer Lightning again.

I was walking back to the bungalow when a shadow moved out from under one of the banyans. My heart leapt in my throat. I didn't have time to feel frightened. "Lex?" I came to a dead standstill. No one in the whole wide world called me that. "Don't be afraid, Lex. It's Jai."

I couldn't trust my senses. Jai? Here? I turned very slowly. He was actually there, standing a few feet away, his face in shadow.

"You mustn't think Mama told me where you were. She's been guarding your whereabouts with her life. I discovered them quite by accident."

Words came to me at last. I said slowly, "Why—have you come, Jai?" A thought struck me. "Is there—some signature you need?"

"No. I came to see you."

"But—why?"

"Because I have so many things I wish to say." I made a startled movement. He said quickly, "I promise I have not come to harass you in any way."

"But—what is there left for you to say?"

"If you let me, I'll tell you."

I was silent. I did not know what I felt. Immense joy at meeting my beloved again, grave doubts about it. I said at last, "I don't know—if I want to hear." It was true. Hearing about him and Ila would only serve to crush my spirit.

"I don't blame you for feeling that way. It's no more than I deserve. But—Lex, I beg of you."

I asked stonily, "Is your wife with you? Does she know you're here?"

He left the question unanswered. "Do you have time now?"

"No. My son—will be up soon. I'll have to go."

He showed no reaction to the mention of Scotty. So he had known I had a child. Of course. If Jai went after a thing, he left no stone unturned. Whatever his source of information, it could not have failed to report Scotty's existence.

"Then tomorrow at this time?"

"Why, Jai?" I did not know from where the words came. "Can the Samartha Group spare its VIP of VIPs for something so unimportant?" I was instantly ashamed. "I'm sorry. I shouldn't have said that."

"It's okay."

The sky had lightened considerably by now. His face was no longer in shadow. I could not stare as I wanted to, but I was able to register in fleeting glances that he was indeed dressed most casually, that he looked leaner, but fit, that the beard and longer hair only served to enhance his magnetic looks. I became aware that I was equally under scrutiny. I didn't know how I looked. I had lost my ribbon, and my hair tumbled over my shoulders. I was wearing a checked shirt and a much-worn pair of jeans, attire almost identical to his.

"Lex?"

I felt torn at the thought of letting him go. What choice did I have? What choice did I ever have? I made up my mind quickly. Jai was not the type to give up. That much I knew only too well.

"I'll be here. Tomorrow morning. Earlier than today."

"Thank you. I'm very grateful." Gravely, he stepped aside for me to go.

Mind in a daze, I walked away swiftly.

I have no way to describe the continued turmoil in my heart that persisted all that day and night. I went through my daily routine without really knowing what I was doing. When Jai had spoken those words asking me for a divorce, so that he could marry another woman, J had taken my own decision about what to do next. That had continued after Scotty was born when I worked out a way to bring in an income. Even coming to the Stud Farm had ultimately been up to me to decide. Now somehow I felt insecure, as if all control was slipping out of my hands. Desperately, I told myself I must think of Scotty before all else. When I thought back, I related the feeling to my meeting with Mama and GeeGee. It had disturbed my carefully built-up stoicism, born and nurtured out of anguish and loneliness. The ultimate in self-revelation had come when I saw Jai on TV. It had crystallized the whole state of my emotions towards him. No, I didn't hate him, as perhaps I should. No, I didn't really hold him guilty of ruining my life. After all, it was common enough for a man who had fallen for another woman to seek release from his marriage. Nothing criminal about it. He was entitled to end his marriage if he so desired. In the social strata the Samarthas moved in, second and third divorces had been known to take place. Jai had made one of his rare errors in judgment when he thought I would be the right wife for him. As he would in business, he had acted speedily to rectify that error.

It was my misfortune that last night had brought home the searing truth—that my love for him was as strong, as undying as it had ever been.

But what did Jai want to talk about? I thought of and discarded many possibilities. Was it the house he wished to sell—or perhaps transfer to Ila's name? The document I had sent Rusi—perhaps it was not legally acceptable for the purpose. Was my signature required to clinch the deal? It gave me a pang to think of my home passing on into other possession. Whether in Panchgani or here, I'd always had this picture in my mind of Iona just as I remembered it with Thelma and Gonsalves, Rom and Reem.

Whichever hypothetical question I had dreamed up, I would know the answer soon enough.

Jai was waiting under the banyans. Silently, we walked beyond them away from the stables where Rajan still slept, to the railing that enclosed the track. Walking by Jai, so close to his physical self, I was bewildered by the treacherous tide of feeling that swept over me, the urgent desire to reach out and touch him. The chemistry, at least for me, was stronger than ever, and I was afraid of it.

We leaned over the railing. The track was barely visible, but some illumination from the stables enabled me to make out the dim outlines of his face.

"I can't tell you how much I appreciate this, Lex," he said, breaking the silence. "You lost some precious sleep because of it. Will you be riding later?"

"Not this morning. I'll be putting in extra time this afternoon."

He took a deep breath. "Then I mustn't waste time. Lex, I came here to beg your forgiveness—only now, knowing what I did was unforgivable, I shan't ask you that. Especially since I haven't forgiven myself. My express purpose is to tell you how sorry I am for the hurt I inflicted, for the anguish I surely caused. When I came home that evening, found you'd gone, I couldn't believe it. Why didn't you wait, Lex? I had so much to explain."

"When you asked me for a divorce—told me why—that was fully self-explanatory."

"No! How could it be? And you took nothing…nothing! As if you wished to have nothing more to do with me…as if you wished to discard every last vestige of our life together."

I turned my head towards him in astonishment. "But what is the implication of a divorce, Jai? Isn't that precisely what you wanted? A severing of all ties?"

"Not quite true. It doesn't have to be like that."

"Do you mean that two people part amicably, keep in touch, perhaps stay on visiting terms?" I asked incredulously. "It's not like you to be so idealistic, Jai. You're the ever-practical one. It's naive to think such a cozy relationship could be established. Off with wife No. 1, on with wife No.2—and we're all jolly good pals?"

"Lex, I haven't the least intention of arguing over it. Tell me, why didn't you take the things I'd given you? The jewelry—the clothes—money?"

"They were given to your wife. Since I was no longer required to be that, keeping them had no meaning. There was no sense in it."

"But what did you do without funds?"

"I was born thrifty. I managed. I worked. And I found friends."

"You left no clues. Not one. You wrote to Mama, but for me, you did not leave even an oral message. We searched everywhere. My parents were as frantic as I was."

The faintest rosy flush tinged the horizon. I had straightened up. I could see his face better now. Jai had turned so that his back was to the railing, and was facing me. His eyes studied me constantly, whereas I was unable to emulate him, much as I would have liked to.

"Why were you so frantic, Jai? I had taken nothing that belonged to you. I was willing to give you a divorce. I had told you that. And to underline the fact that I wanted nothing from you, I thought it best to go out of your life completely."

"Lex." Something in his tone forced me to lift my eyes to him. "When you went, I realized I had lost the most precious thing in my life."

Nothing could have stunned me more.

"Jai," I whispered, "what do you say?"

"You are the only woman who meant everything to me. After you went away…life lost all meaning for me."

I could not believe it. Words burst from my lips.

"You can't mean that! Not when you had another woman to take my place!"

"That's what I believed. I came to my senses in no time at all. And you were gone. I had no way of knowing where." The pain in him was almost tangible. "I went through hell. I couldn't get one sentence of yours out of mind. Do you remember it? You said, 'So it has come', as if you were expecting that I'd do this to you. It implied you had never trusted me. It spoke very poorly for my constancy. You see, Lex, except for this brief madness with Ila, I had never looked at another woman after I met you. How could I when you filled my life so utterly?" I was sure I was dreaming. These words could not be coming from Jai. "For me, the last nail in my coffin was the little package you sent Rusi with your rings. It was a final severance from me—from our marriage."

"But," I said in bewilderment, "how could I keep the rings? They symbolized our marriage. By then you had another wife."

"I have no other wife. Only you."

My hand went out to grip the railing. My legs threatened to give way.

"I didn't institute divorce proceedings. We are legally still man and wife."

"That can't be true!" The words came out in a whisper.

"It is true. Contact Rusi and ask him."

"But—but why?"

"Because more than anything in the world, I love you, Lex."

It was too much for me to take. I turned away.

When I could speak, I said unsteadily, "Jai Samartha doesn't believe in love. He told me so in no uncertain terms."

"Jai Samartha was a darned fool—the world's greatest Know It All. He needed to be jolted out of his smug complacency with a swift kick where it would hurt most!" In a low voice, "Lex, you were happy with me, weren't you?"

After a long moment, I said, "Yes."

"They were wonderful years, weren't they? I've relived them time and again." I opened my lips to speak and closed them again. "I have no right to ask you this, but do you care for the man who is your child's father?"

"Very much."

"I see," after a pause, "Do you still see him?"

"No."

"Doesn't he visit the child?"

"No."

"How come?"

I groped for an answer. I had to be careful. I was skating on very thin ice here. "I—didn't want—to complicate his life with Scotty's existence."

"You call the little one Scotty? In honor of Fiona, I take it?" I nodded. A smile touched his mouth briefly. Defiantly, I added, "He's named Adrian Anton Jerome."

"I like it. Is Anton his father's name?"

"No."

"Was he good to you?"

Suddenly I wanted to weep. I controlled myself. "Very good," I said in a low voice.

We could see each other now for the golden rays of the rising sun were arrowing towards us. I couldn't keep my eyes from wandering over him. I knew Jai was looking at me in the same way.

I made an attempt to cover up the impact of his appearance on me by speaking lightly. "With the beard, you look more like a model than ever, Jai."

"So do you look like a model. More beautiful than all my dreams." The words silenced me. "Lex?" I searched his face. "Is there…even half a chance…that you'll come back to me? I swear by all that's holy, I'll spend the rest of my life making up."

Wonderingly, I studied his face. "Even though there's been another man in my life?"

"Even then," he said steadily, gaze unswerving.

"And Scotty?"

"If you permitted, I'd be proud to adopt him legally as my son."

"You'd do that, Jai, knowing he was another man's child?"

"Yes, because he's yours too."

I was trembling within me. It would be the easiest thing in the world to give in.

"It wouldn't work," I said at last, "any more than it did before."

"Why do you say that?" He spoke urgently. "Barring one single situation, we were as close as any two people could be. Deny it if you can!"

"Jai, I never belonged to your world. That was proved when you rejected me for Ila."

"What are you saying, Lex! Why, you fitted in beautifully! I was always so proud of you—of your looks, anyway—I was the envy of every male around—and the way you related to people! Drawing out the shy ones. You were the perfect hostess. My friends thought I was the most fortunate man in the world to have won the Komal Girl. And I don't need to tell you what my family feels about you."

"It's Jai I'm thinking about, not other people. When I'd had time to think—after I went away—I pinpointed my failing. Your work, your problems, what you were trying to achieve—you kept them away me because you felt I was inadequate—an illiterate in those matters. A wife should have an understanding—even an elementary one—of her husband's work. It hurt me so much when you told me nothing. You flew to Japan so often, had people come out from there. I entertained them for you, took their wives out shopping. And there it ended. I would read in the papers about my husband setting up this collaboration, how it was coming along. And that was my failure, my inadequacy." I could see he was shocked.

"Lex, I didn't do it deliberately. I assumed—wrongly as I realize now—that you couldn't possibly be interested. Mama never was. Not many wives are. And it isn't expected of a wife to be so."

"No," I said sadly, "that was not your expectation."

"You have to get it out of your head that it was your failure or inadequacy. That's absurd. You measured up splendidly in every way."

I laughed without mirth. "Yes, as a hostess I probably did. Don't you see, Jai, what attracted you to Ila? She was the perfect woman for you—fully on your wavelength, efficient to the fingertips, speaking the same language. And there'll be other Ilas. I couldn't bear to go through it all again, Jai. I'm happy as I am. You must lead your kind of life. I don't fit into it."

For the first time, he reached out and held me by the shoulders. "Lex." Was that desperation in his voice? "What must I do to convince you?"

I shook my head. I felt drained. "I must go. Scotty will be up."

"How can I give you up, Lex?"

"You must," I said simply. "It's the only way."

His hands dropped away.

"Goodbye, Jai." I looked at his face one last time. "God bless."

My heart was a stone in my breast. I tried to smile, but failed. Before I turned away, I saw his fists clench slowly, I felt his eyes on me as I walked away. Those steps were the hardest ones I had ever taken.

CHAPTER 29

JAI

BY MONDAY NOON, I KNEW IT WAS NO USE. I CALLED PAPA who was also in Bombay to say I was going away for two days. I left it to him to hold the fort. He was back in full form, achieving more in his four days in the office than most men did in six. Papa did not ask where I was going, and I did not volunteer any information.

I had rung Gonsalves about my arrival. When I reached Iona, Rom and Reem were all over me, practically wagging their tails off. As instructed, Thelma had prepared a cold meal for me. Mama was astonished when on the phone I told her I was here in Pune, and rather alarmed. I reassured her. She would be waiting for me, she said. I showered quickly, but did not eat. That could wait.

"Jai." She came to the door to receive me. Her eyes searched my face. Then she took me by the hand and led me to Papa's den. It was strange to be there without that commanding presence. She sat down on the big leather settee, my hand still in hers. And waited.

"Mama, I saw Lex." She said nothing, but her hand tightened on mine. I went on to tell her. She was very quiet.

"What do you hope to do?" she asked at last.

"I don't know. Is there anything to be done at all?" I must have sounded as hopeless as I felt. "One thing I know for sure. I must walk with care. She mustn't feel pressurized at all. On no account must she reach the point where she has to do the disappearing act again."

"It seems to me, her conviction that she doesn't belong is the biggest obstacle. It goes deep. She had doubts from the start. Your rejection—I'm sorry—" for I had winced, "—was the final proof. That conviction will have to be removed for all time. Jai, how did she react when you offered to adopt the child?"

"Unable to credit her ears. Asked incredulously if I was willing to accept another man's child. I said I was because it was hers as well."

"Oh, Jai." She touched my sleeve. "Did she—tell you more about him?"

"Only that she calls him Scotty."

"In honor of her grandmother?"

"Uh huh. I guess it tickled her sense of humor. It's a cute little name though, isn't it? His full name is Adrian Anton Jerome." I shook my head. "You're wrong if you think Anton is his father's name," to the question in her eyes.

"She told you that?"

"Uh huh."

"But, Jai," she exclaimed, "she seems to have opened up quite a bit if she told you so much! You didn't see the little one, did you? I thought not. I wish I could see him," she said wistfully. "He is Sakshi's child even if he's not my grandson."

"I wonder if he has her eyes."

"Not according to her. Not supposed to be either like her or his father. A different mould, she said."

Suddenly, I could no longer continue my nonchalant pose. I leaned forward and buried my head in my hands. "Mama, I think she's still in love with this other guy." My voice was unsteady. "I can't bear the thought of her with him. What am I going to do? I think what she said—about not coming back to me—was final—yes, irrevocable."

The hand the touch of which was familiar to me since birth stroked my hair gently. "It will be all right, Jai. It will be all right."

"I couldn't stay on in Bombay. I had to talk to you. But also because Lex is here," I said wretchedly. "Like a moonstruck boy. Jai Samartha who claimed love was dreamed up by the poets' imagination! My chickens have come to roost with a vengeance. I realize now I fell in love with her that first evening. In my lordly fashion, I dismissed it as a powerful physical attraction for a very beautiful girl. She was different from any girl I'd met—and I'd met plenty. Yet I'd never felt the least desire to marry a single one of them. A couple of hours in this one's company, and I knew she was the one I wanted as a wife." My head went back into my hands. "My God, I was presumptuous! Going about the whole thing so cold-bloodedly as if it were a takeover bid. The I. M. in person."

"Perhaps. But though you didn't realize it, you became more human after you were married."

I lifted my head to look at her. "Did I?"

"Yes. I was so glad to see it. It was Sakshi's doing, of course. That sense of fun, of humor. The delight she took in the sheer joy of living. Sometimes I wondered how, having come through so much tragedy, she had refused to succumb to a gloomy outlook on life."

"Did I ever tell you about the time we were walking down the main street in Mahableshwar? No? Well, we'd made a few small purchases. Lex loved to choose the fruit and vegetables herself—bargained enthusiastically with the vendors. I never saw what difference a few rupees would make to us, but she always said mischievously, 'Shhh. I have to let Fiona have her way sometimes.' We were on our way to the car park when I found Lex wasn't there! That was another habit of hers. To stop if anything caught her eye. It could be a display in a shop window, a snake charmer, even a film poster. Often quite exasperating!"

"I can believe it would be so for you," Mama said smiling.

"And I'm sure stopping to see a snake charmer was well below your dignity."

"Sure was. I re-traced my footsteps, and found her standing in front of one of those restaurants. You know, the ones where they have those outdoor tables and chairs. A man was presiding over a charcoal brazier with one of those enormous iron things—what do they call them—woks—for deep-frying? And like a little wistful child, my wife was watching the hot *bhajiyas* coming out."

Mama laughed aloud. "This is priceless! What happened next?"

"I'm afraid I was very irritated. Impatiently, I grasped her arm. 'Lex, what on earth are you doing! Come on!' And she said, not taking her eyes off the golden brown piles, 'Jai, do you think—?' I was horrified at the very thought. 'No, I don't think—at all! If you're in the mood to eat *bhajiyas*, Thelma will fix you some. For heaven's sake, woman!' I lost the battle, of course. Those green eyes looking me in the face reproachfully—more than I could withstand. Imploringly, 'Jai, they never taste the same!' What could I do? I waited for a batch to come out of the boiling oil—no germs there, I convinced myself. And then the idiot of a fellow wrapped the whole mess in a dubiously clean scrap of newspaper, God knows how ancient! I could have killed him!" Mama was laughing so much, she had a coughing fit. "Lex cradled that package as if it contained the Tsar's Crown Jewels, and carried it to the car. Once home, she couldn't wait to get a plate and empty out the contents. Gonsalves looked at the greasy paper in horror, lifted it with his fingertips and marched to the kitchen in outraged silence. In the meantime, Lex had started eating with relish. She offered me the plate. They smelt delicious—those *bhajiyas*. I think she guessed I was half tempted. I refused." I didn't tell Mama that Lex with her red mouth smeared with traces of oil had been too much to resist. I had put out my tongue to spear a crumb or two as she bent over me with the plate, and I had pulled her down on my lap, and kissed her thoroughly. "Well, finally, I ate a couple. I had to admit they were delicious. Lex crowed with satisfaction."

We sat quietly for some time.

"You've changed a lot since Sakshi left, Jai."

"Have I? How do you mean?"

"You've become—what's the right word—more compassionate. You care about people now. I think it shows most in your concern for the slum children. It's more than just a philanthropic project. I'm told you get there about twice a week. And that you really play volley-ball as if you enjoy *it*."

"Oh, I sure do." I looked at her sweet face. "From all that you say, I must have been an obnoxious creature. No wonder Lex resisted marrying me for so long."

"Not obnoxious at all, Jai. But as if you'd put up an impenetrable wall around yourself which no one could get through. A man fully in control of himself."

If only my mother knew. That self-control was just a veneer. When I was alone with Lex, all of it fell away. I was just a man, ardent, passionate, worshipping my wife's beauty, shaken by the storm so that I lost my bearings completely. Chemistry between two people, I had assumed coolly. "Lord, what fools these mortals be."

I was warmed by the session with Mama, but deep in my heart the conviction grew stronger every minute that the situation was irretrievable. Lex would never come back to me. It had never fallen to my lot to know such failure. I was plumbing the depths of hopeless despair. In my lexicon, the word defeat had not been included. Always after cool consideration of a problem, I had come up with the solution. Now there was not a glimmer of one.

CHAPTER 30

SAKSHI

ON A SUNNY AFTERNOON, FOUR DAYS AFTER THAT DAWN meeting with Jai, I was leaning over the railings of the training track, having finished my stint with Solitaire, watching two young horses being exercised. Scotty was at the Dubash house, no doubt surrounded by admiring members of the domestic staff. It had been a miserable time for me. The nights had been far worse than the days, for I lay awake for hours, my thoughts going around in circles, hearing again the deep voice speaking, re-living the scene over and over again. Such peace of mind that I had achieved, and which had been so hard-won, had gone.

There was the utterly incredible claim that Jai loved me. Impossible to relate it to him. And he had offered to adopt Scotty. Asked me to go back to him. I had refused and Jai had gone away. I knew now I had cut myself away from him for all time, for Jai was too proud to humble himself again before me. That he had done so once was extraordinary. There was a heavy, dull feeling in my heart, which would not be dispelled.

When someone came to stand by me, I was so lost in my musings, at first I paid little attention. It was when out of the corner of my eye I glimpsed an unfamiliar windcheater that I lifted my head, and met a pair of brown eyes smiling warmly at me.

"Cy! Oh, Cy!" and went into his arms, so glad to see him that I was moved to tears.

"Hey!" he said softly, "is that the way to greet your old partner?"

"I'm sorry!" I gulped, and mopped up. "Cy, why are you here and not in America?" still sniffing.

"Because, my sweet Sakshi, even in God's own country, they have vacations, you know. I've been making it home twice a year. Just got back two days ago. Here for a month."

I was still clutching his sleeve. "You've broadened out a lot, Cy. All that vitaminized food! And looking rather handsome, partner." It was true. In a very different way from Jai, the Parsi strain very apparent, Cy was very good-looking indeed.

"And you're still the most beautiful girl I know. I mean it," he said, not bantering now. "Sakshi, where can we sit a bit? Do you have time now?"

"I'll always make time for Cyrus the Great Here." I led him to a small pavilion where we settled on the steps.

We talked easily, he about America, answering my eager questions. He loved it there, he said. His whole vision had altered amazingly. Yes, he was coming back. About six months. Sad in a way, but he was needed here. And had every intention of not getting so bogged down in the Group that he couldn't get away every two years or so. Now it was GeeGee's turn to go. Interestingly, his young brother had surprised them all by becoming a very good student. He had refused to follow his siblings, and go in for a Master's in Business. His one interest was in Computer Science, and he was graduating shortly, then off to M.I.T. The information was astonishing. GeeGee, my little brother all grown up and leaving for America. Did Cy have a girl friend? One girl friend? What was I thinking about, he exclaimed in mock horror. There was a whole line of them!

"Cy, how did you know where to find me?"

For a moment he did not answer. Then, "Jai told me," he said quietly.

The earlier light-hearted mood evaporated suddenly.

"But even if he hadn't, I would have found out from my parents."

I did not query how they knew.

"He's changed a lot, my big brother," Cy went on reflectively. "Almost to the point of being absolutely unrecognizable." I said nothing, but sat with my shoulders hunched. "Jai and I—never bosom pals. The age gap, for one. His position as the eldest son for another. But my admiration for him—unquestioned—has bordered on hero worship." I sat very quietly, concentrating fiercely on Cy's words. "With ample justification, I must add. But in a certain sense, Jai has seemed remote, far removed from GeeGee and me. All the more surprising to come home the last two times on these brief holidays, and find the guy was human after all. He actually talked with me, all about the States, my eventual return."

The sun was casting long shadows now. For once, I did not give a thought to Scotty's whereabouts. A crow cawed raucously on a nearby branch.

"But it was last night that he really opened up to me for the first time in our lives. Has this crazy idea of taking off once I'm back and settled." He could not have missed my startled movement, but gave no sign of having noticed. He seemed to be musing aloud rather than talking to me directly. "Oh, not the Himalayas or anything like that. Further afield. To the U.S. Won't have anything to do with business, he vows. Something quite different. But didn't specify. God knows I can never fill Jai's shoes. I think Papa will go out of his mind. Not that the parents have an inkling. No, Jai is close to breaking point."

I sat motionless, trying to assimilate what Cy was saying. Jai going away? Out of India? Not forever surely? He couldn't do that when he was needed so badly! Papa was back in almost full swing, but Jai had been a Colossus. What would happen if he went away? "Mama says the slum project has lifted his spirits considerably. Given him a new interest in life." He saw the question in my eyes, and explained patiently. "Jai dreamed up this scheme—a playground for children, coaching in various games included. Chose a particular slum after consulting social workers and welfare people. The Group sort of adopted the whole area. Tree planting in a very big way. Most enthusiastic response from the women for the latter. In time, it's going to be an oasis. But what I really can't get over is that Jai goes as often as he can to play volleyball." I looked at him in complete astonishment. He shook his own head in wonder. "The boys adore him, especially when after a victory against some other team, he takes them for a celebration party at a nearby open-air cafeteria—you know, one of those rickety shed-like structures with a couple of beaten-up tables and benches out in the open? Feeds them to the gills. Wipes out the entire stock of food. They call him 'Jai Saab'. Can you imagine the suave Jai Samartha doing that?" I couldn't, any more than Cy.

I was able to keep silent no longer. "This going away—is it pressure of work? Or just having carried too much of the load too long?"

Cy considered. "Neither, I'd say. It's losing you—the way it all happened—hurting you so badly—driving you to someone else—that's eating him. It's not guesswork on my part, Sakshi. It's what he told me last night. I guess you made your position very clear. He said you were in love with another man. All adding up to too much. That's why he wants to get away as far as he can."

All at once, it was too much for me. Bowed over my knees, I buried my face in my hands and wept. I felt Cy's hand on my back, patting me gently. "There, there, sweet girl. You've been splendid throughout. I didn't mean to upset you. Perhaps I shouldn't have told you."

By degrees, he calmed me, lent me his handkerchief to mop up with and blow my nose.

"I must look a sight," I said shakily.

"You always look a vision."

"Liar," I said smiling through my tears.

"Sakshi, you love Jai, don't you?"

I couldn't deny it. "I do. I do, Cy. And it's killing me!"

"But why won't you go back to Jai? Is it the child?"

"Cy, how can I? If it happens again, I shall die! I shan't be able to take the rejection again."

"That's crazy, Sakshi! Why, the man is so besotted with you, he can't eat or think straight!" He glanced at his watch and groaned. "Good heavens, will you *look* at the time? And the guests must be arriving at this very moment! Old friends of Papa," he explained. "Invited by Mama. Yours truly booked to play charming host." He unfolded his long body, and gave me a hand up.

"I'll come back in a few days time, okay? As soon as I get back from Bombay."

"When you do, I have something important to discuss with you, Cy. I need your advice." I walked with him to where he had parked the car. "In fact, I wasn't expecting you to be back in India so soon. I'd planned to get in touch with you as soon as you returned."

"At your service, ma'am. Ever."

I reached up to hug him. "Dear Cy."

"Make that 'dearest Cy'. By the way, are you sure there isn't another Sakshi somewhere? A cousin maybe? I'd marry her like a shot! GeeGee and I still haven't forgiven Jai for whisking you away from under our noses. We had both decided to marry you."

I was still laughing as he slid into the driver's seat. He lifted a hand in salute, gave me a grin, and drove off.

CHAPTER 31

A SEVERE BOUT OF FLU LAID AUNT GULNAR LOW. ONCE OUT of bed, she was so listless that the doctor suggested a brief holiday out of Pune. A worried Uncle Sohrab decided to take her up to Mahableshwar for a week. I was seriously alarmed when he said he was leaving me in over-all charge. His staff was extremely well trained, he reminded me, but things run better with someone to keep an eye on the Farm. In any case, he was only 75 miles away, he went on reassuringly, and could be summoned any time. Still dubious, I agreed.

Scotty and I watched as luggage was loaded early next morning. A couple of servants had left the day before for Mahableshwar to have all in readiness.

"Cah," said my son, pointing to the big roomy van in anticipation of a ride.

"Not today," I told him.

"Cah," he insisted.

"I wish he were coming with us," Aunt Gulnar said.

"You'll never get a moment's rest if he is," I said firmly.

"You can both come if you wish," Uncle Sohrab joked. "Plenty of room in the luggage section."

I smiled at his kindly face, and hugged them both.

"Off you go, and have a wonderful holiday. Come back with rosy cheeks, Aunt Gulnar."

Scotty had not given up hope. He stared in outrage as the van began to move away without him, opening his mouth to roar a protest. Hastily I said, "Let's find a horse, Scotty."

"Och?" he enquired, still not taking his eyes off the fast moving van, but distracted enough. I pacified him with a quick trip to the stables before carrying him off for breakfast.

Breakfast done, I wiped his hands and the egg off his mouth with a damp cloth, untied his bib, and lifted him down from what used to be Aftab's high chair. As soon as I set him on the floor, he toddled off towards the front door.

"Out," he told me.

"Wait for Ritu. She'll take you later."

"Out," he repeated, so exactly like his father in his refusal to give up. He reached and failed to do more than touch the doorknob.

"No, Scotty."

"No?" he echoed, looking at me over his shoulder.

I couldn't bear it. I swooped down on him and swung him off his feet, burying my face in his plump little neck. He smelt of baby powder, and the faintest lingering reminder of his breakfast egg. Soap and water were definitely indicated, I thought, and kissed his round rosy cheek.

Short arms going round my neck promptly rewarded me. A resoundingly loud damp kiss was bestowed on my face. Thank God for Scotty, I thought. What will I do without him? In the darkest moments, the fact of his existence compensates for all my loneliness.

Scotty wriggled free. I distracted him with a wind-up toy Aftab had given him, kept away and brought out only for special occasions. It kept him absorbed till Ritu came to take him on his outing. I busied myself at my easel, wanting to finish the work in hand. But while hand and eye coordinated mechanically to put in the final touches, my thoughts strayed.

Jai has not attempted to contact me again. Why should he when I had sent him away in no uncertain terms? I can't get over the fact that I'm still his wife. What made him change his mind? What happened between him and Ila? He said he loves me. Can it be true? I shall never know now. Incredible that he didn't start divorce proceedings. Was it because I delayed sending Rusi the letter for seven months? But I had to. I refused to take risks with my son's legitimacy. He wasn't to blame in any way whatsoever for what his parents did. And he's all Samartha. Anyone can see it. Not a sign of the Jeromes or Antons, for all that he's named after my people.

And my dear Cy, How I enjoyed meeting him again. The one person with whom I can relax completely. When he comes again, I'll have to bring out my most guarded secret. I must. And he will tell me what I should do.

Jai. I'm truly afraid to be with him. I can't be sure of not betraying how I feel. The chemistry is there, alive, powerful. I love the way his hair curls on his neck. So much nicer than his old severe style. And the beard. It makes him look like every woman's dream. Mine anyway. Yes, we were wonderfully happy. Till he shattered all our happiness. One moment it was whole and intact, the next in splinters around me.

I stood back to look at the easel. It was done. And I was glad. A sense of weariness came over me. I tidied up, put away my brushes and palette. I heard the door behind me open and close. Something tugged at the leg of my pants. I picked Scotty up and hugged him. The chubby arms went around my neck. It was hard to know who enjoyed these impromptu cuddles more. A smiling Ritu went off till four when she would return.

The woman I employed part time had left the kitchen spotless. Thanks to her ministrations, the bungalow always looked sparkling clean. I began preparing Scotty's lunch, leaving him happily driving plastic nails with a plastic hammer through his plastic workbench. Deeply absorbed, my mind bustling with a hundred thoughts, I worked mechanically. When the crash came, loud and shocking in the stillness, I was jolted out of my reverie as by an electric shock of magnitude. In a second, heart in my throat, I was in the sitting room. Scotty lay motionless on the floor, body limp as that of a rag doll. The heavy bronze sculpture of a horse, which had belonged to Daddy, lay on its side near him, telling the story. An anguished cry burst from me as I bent swiftly over the still form of my child. He was breathing, but a huge lump was forming on his head. I called his name over and over again, somehow found the strength to bring a wet cloth to wipe the little face. Scotty's eyes remained closed.

"Oh God!" The words came out in a sobbing moan.

I had to get help, find someone even though it was the lunch hour, and everyone must be off-duty.

I ran to the door and flung it open, only to crash into a tall man whose hand was lifted as if to knock. "Lex!" he said sharply. "What is it?"

In a gasping whisper, not even surprised to see him, I said, "It's Scotty! He's hurt himself. He won't open his eyes! Jai, help me!"

CHAPTER 32

JAI

WHATEVER I HAD EXPECTED IN THE WAY OF RECEPTION FROM LEX, I was unprepared for this distraught girl who could barely speak coherently. Her last words went straight to my heart.

I went in swiftly, bent over the little form, my eye taking in the bronze horse and the overturned chair in one sweeping glance. My mind worked clearly and quickly.

"I don't like to move him, but we must. We have to get him to a doctor, Lex. Get a blanket."

Within three minutes I was carrying my lightweight blanket-wrapped burden to where I had parked the car. I laid the child carefully on the wide back seat. Lex climbed in. "Keep his head steady," I told her, and raced around to slide under the wheel.

She sat with her hands tightly clasped, not weeping, wide eyes staring blankly. When I came back, she looked at me in wordless anguish, as if ready to hear the worst.

I sat down by her, and took her cold hands into my warm ones.

"They're studying the X-rays. We'll know soon."

She clung to my hands "Is he still—unconscious?"

"Yes."

"Jai," whispering, "is my baby…going to die?"

"Lex, of course he isn't!"

A nurse came to summon me. "I'll be right back," I promised.

Dr Rudra—I presumed it was he—looked up from his desk. His eye went over me curiously, but indicating a chair, he only said, "Sit down, Mr Jaroom." Lex had gasped out the little one's name to the receptionist, and no doubt this garbled version lay on the papers in front of the Doctor. "Mr Jaroom, I'd like you to see the X-rays." He touched a switch. I stared at the screen. "As you see, no internal injuries absolutely. An extremely lucky little chap. The statue must have glanced off. No doubt, he'll have the grandfather of a headache, but that's all."

"Is he still unconscious?"

"Not deeply so. Stirring a little. The nurse will call us the minute he comes to."

As if on cue, a white-capped head popped around the door.

"Doctor Saab?"

"Get the child's mother, Mr Jaroom. It will reassure him—and her."

And so it was that when Scotty opened his eyes, he looked puzzled at the strange faces around the bed until he caught sight of Lex's and said, "Ma-ma?" She fell on her knees by him, and took both his hands. "I'm here, darling," she said shakily, eyes bright with unshed tears. "Ma-ma, 'urt," he complained, lifting a small hand to the lump on his head.

The Doctor looked pleased, and even the nurse was smiling fondly.

"Nothing much wrong with this young man that a night's rest will not take care of. I think we'll leave them for a little reunion. Mr Jaroom?" signaling to me to join him again. We walked back into his consulting room.

It had been the sheerest good luck that this exclusive private nursing home had been a scant mile from the Stud Farm. I had recognized the name on the board and braked at once, Dr Rudra was an eminent neuro-surgeon, and one read about him in the local papers frequently. Indeed, he inspired confidence instantly. Scotty was in the best of hands.

We were seated again when Dr Rudra told me, "The child will be up and running about in no time, but I think he should be kept under observation overnight. Let me hasten to add there is no cause for concern. Just a precaution."

"Just as you say, Doctor."

He surveyed me with some curiosity as if he was puzzled, and trying to place me. "Do you live in Pune? Will this inconvenience you?"

"Yes, we are residents. Even if we weren't, it would not matter."

"That is all right then. Your wife is a foreigner?"

"Not really. Her grandmother was Scottish."

"Ah," as if light had dawned. "By the way, what is her blood group?"

"B Positive."

"Then yours must be AB. It's fortunate you are here."

"Yes, mine is AB Positive. Why do you ask?"

"I wasn't sure if surgery was involved. In case we needed to give a blood transfusion, you would have been requested to donate blood. Our blood bank might not have some of these fairly uncommon types. Contacting one of our regular donors takes time."

I was silent.

"It's always easier to have a blood donor on the spot."

"Are blood groups hereditary?"

"Yes. Now the little boy has inherited your group, you in turn from someone in your family, and so it goes."

"I see," I said quietly. For the next few moments, whatever Dr Rudra said was a blank to me. My mind was whirling with the most startling possibilities. He spoke on pleasantly, but I did not register the words.

"…lump, you know. Headache…sedation…a good night's rest."

Slowly I came back to reality.

"Another reason why he should be kept in overnight."

"Yes. Yes, of course. Then my wife will be needed?"

"Oh, I think not. The child will sleep. Besides, I think Mrs Jaroom looks as if she is badly in need of rest herself." He smiled. "Tomorrow the little boy will be up and running. I think his parents will need all their energy to keep up with him."

I returned his smile wryly. "I suggest a word to that effect from the Doctor himself will be essential. Nothing I say will be as effective. And she is exhausted."

Dr Rudra laughed. "I can be very convincing."

Lex protested, of course, though she looked ready to collapse. Her arguments were dealt with firmly. Scotty lay looking at me incuriously, his eyelids already drooping.

Lex bent to kiss him and he opened his eyes briefly. Then he slipped into sleep.

It was a silent Lex whom I drove home. I did not know where the hours had gone. When we emerged from the nursing home, it was late evening.

This time I parked the car behind the bungalow. If Lex noticed, she made no demur. A few lights shone from the big house, but otherwise all was quiet and dark. The bungalow was shrouded in darkness, but the door being unlocked, it yielded to my touch. Sheer instinct made me locate the switches. When the lights came on, they illuminated Lex's unutterably weary stance.

"Go and have a hot bath, Lex." The green eyes in the pale face looked at me uncomprehendingly. I fought the impulse to take her in my arms and comfort her. "You'll feel better after a bath and some food," I told her gently. My words must have made some sense, for she began to move towards a door.

When she had gone, I took a deep breath and looked around me. The simple furniture, the framed water colors on the walls, the flowered curtains, all added up to an exceedingly cozy pleasant place. Lex's good taste was evident everywhere. The gleaming floor tiles, the lack of dust anywhere spoke of care, but here and there, there was unmistakable evidence that a child dwelt under this roof. A pair of very small shoes with a sock trailing out of one of them. A squeaky rubber toy. A plastic carpenter's bench. I walked to the overturned chair and picked it up. Restored the bronze horse to the table where it surely belonged.

In the small compact kitchen, it was evident preparation for a child's meal had been under way. Scrounging around, I discovered some packets of soup with an English brand name, eggs and fresh bread. While the soup was simmering on the burner, I sliced bread and buttered it, set a tray with plate, bowl, cutlery and water glass, added a paper napkin. Not since I. had left the States had I done these domestic chores. I was glad to see I had lost none of my practiced ease as I scrambled eggs and served them on the warmed plate.

Tray in hand, I knocked on the half-open door. There was no answer. Pushing the door fully open with an elbow, I went in. Lex was sitting on the window ledge staring out into the darkness, for by now the day was over. I set the tray down and went to her.

"Lex?" The face she lifted to me was scrubbed and shining as that of a child, wet uncombed hair trailing over the terry-cloth bathrobe she was wearing. "Come," I said gently. When she did not move, I took her hand and helped her off the ledge before leading her to a chair.

Pulling up another, I fed her like a little child. I could see she was hardly aware of what was happening, but obediently the red lips parted to swallow first the spoonfuls of hot soup, and then the bread and eggs. The food seemed to revive her somewhat, for when I laid down the fork, and said, "Good girl. Coffee? Tea?" she shook her head. What she needed most was the oblivion of sleep, but I did not care for the wet hair, which surely would wet the pillow. Fortunately, I spotted a hair dryer on the dressing table. I plugged it in, and in five minutes, the deed was done.

I stood back and surveyed her gravely. "Bed for you. I'll sleep in the other room on the sofa. Call me if you need anything." I picked up the tray when I heard her speak for the first time. It was a bare murmur, but clear enough. "Jai...thank you." Quietly, I went out.

Some time later, having had a light meal myself and cleared up, I thought of something I had to do. Not far from the Stud Farm, I had seen a public telephone booth on the corner where the road turned. I walked swiftly, slipped under the fence, avoiding the main gates where no doubt a watchman would stop me. I thought wryly how adept I was becoming at sneaking in and out of barriers like a seasoned thief. I thought too that someone should point out to Sohrab Dubash that his security system left much to be desired. Not a situation tolerated in the Samartha Group. In fact, the evening I had met Lex, I had been doing a quick check myself on the efficacy of the security set-up.

There was little traffic now. I made my call, listened to the nurse on duty give reassuring news, and made my way back in the same manner to Lex's house.

I let myself in soundlessly, tiptoed into the bedroom, and bent over my wife. She must have been too tired to remove her robe, and had fallen into deep slumber. I fought the temptation to touch the silken mass of hair strewn on the pillow, the rose petal skin. This way lay danger. Yet if only I could slip in beside her, hold her so that she knew I was here if she needed me. Resolutely, I straightened up. As I did so, my eye fell on a familiar object though I had not seen it for two years and more. It was the framed color shot of Lex and myself, dubbed "The Two Models" by us. I gazed at it for a long moment before I put out a hand to switch off the bedside lamp.

Very quietly, making as little noise as possible, I showered quickly in the bathroom, feeling some of the tension leaving me under the flow of water. I did not bother to dress again fully, carried my shirt and shoes, leaving the bathroom door half ajar so that the light from there would provide some illumination in case Lex woke up in the night.

I went around switching off lights in kitchen and living rooms. I had discovered the sofa was impossible. It should have been longer than six feet to accommodate a man of my height. It was certainly not that. The floor rug was the only alternative. I hung my shirt carefully over the back of a chair, and placed my shoes in readiness under it. Filching a cushion from a chair, I stretched out at last.

Sleep eluded me. For one, I never slept this early. It was just ten, I saw from the dial on my watch. For another, I needed desperately to have time to think, to sort out the jumbled events of this extraordinary afternoon.

Several things stood out sharply. The shocked feeling of recognition when the child had opened his eyes, revealing their gray color, which I had been familiar with since my infancy. Incredible. Indeed, my whole first impression—utterly stunning—the skin tones and burnished hair notwithstanding, was that I was looking at a replica in baby form of my father. The startling reference to blood groups that had come from the Doctor. And finally, my own unexpected reaction to the little boy. I'd never had much to do with small children except the Sealeys' lively brood. When my brothers arrived, I had paid scant attention to them, being little more than a child myself. But today, lifting the small form in my arms, holding it close, then at last the tremendous feeling of relief when he recovered consciousness—I had not experienced any of it before.

So Lex had concealed the truth from me. She had not wanted me to know Scotty was my son, I thought, bitterness eating into me. Had she known about the baby the night I asked for a divorce? If so, it was too terrible to contemplate. Memory stirred. Lex greeting me so radiantly, saying she had wonderful news. And the celebration dinner had not been in honor of my return alone, but for a far more exciting reason. No wonder then that unable to bear the sight of me, she had gone away, leaving no trace. Mama said Lex had not volunteered to let her see the child. It was hardly surprising. Mama would have been the first to spot the resemblance, and Lex knew it. But if the matter of Scotty's paternity was revealed at last, the burning question that gave me no peace was about the other man in Lex's life, the young man who had kissed her at the horse show. She must have met him soon after she left Iona. Had turned to him for succor, and received in no small measure all the support she needed. He had earned her undying gratitude, almost certainly her love, so that she would not contemplate returning to me.

Today she had turned to me in her extremity because no one else had been around. Otherwise, I was the last person she trusted. No doubt about why that was so. She had believed that if I knew Scotty was my son, I would take him away from her. It gave me the most wracking pain to think of it. That she was so sure I was capable of such a cruel act. She had said friends came to her aid. Friends. Not her husband. I thought of Mama and Papa. What wouldn't they have done for their beloved Sakshi if she had turned to them for help? Smuggled her away, kept her hidden if she so requested them. But Lex had not wanted to put them in a position where their loyalties would be stretched to the limit.

It was Cy who had made me come here. It seemed that our roles had been reversed, he delivering a lecture, and I listening meekly.

"What's the matter with you anyway, Jai?" he had demanded. "I thought you were known as a man of quick decision-making par excellence. You've met Sakshi. You know where she is. So why on earth are you here, dithering over the whole thing?"

"She sent me away, Cy. In no uncertain terms. Said she couldn't go through it again."

My brother had snorted. "All that experience with women, Jai, and you swallowed that whole? Man, you should have put all your powers of persuasion to use till she was convinced! I don't recognize this Jai Samartha who gives up so easily."

"Even if I grovel, she'll throw me out again."

"So grovel and be thrown out. Again and again till she says yes out of sheer exhaustion and exasperation."

I could not help smiling. But a tiny spark of hope had been lit. The more I thought, the more my mind was strengthened by Cy's advice, so that today, unable to take the continuing uncertainty, I had taken the car and driven to the Dubash Stud Farm.

One small mystery remained unsolved. Why, if Lex loved another man, had not the smallest desire to return to me, did she keep the photograph of the two of us on her bedside table? Too heartsick to seek for an answer, deeply insecure, I rolled over on my stomach, burying my face on my arm, trying to will myself to sleep.

CHAPTER 33

SAKSHI

I FOUGHT MY WAY OUT OF MY DREAM. IT WAS QUITE HOR-RIBLE.

Scotty was calling me. "I'm coming. I'm coming," I kept telling him, but I could not see him anywhere. The mist wrapped itself around me like wet cotton wool, suffocating me. With a major effort, I came out of it, trembling, my heart thudding in my breast. From the dim light that came from the bathroom, I realized I wasn't in a mist, but in my own bedroom, and that it had been a dream. The relief was enormous, but following its footsteps came the dread reminder. Scotty wasn't in his cot, but in hospital. He had hurt his head. Such a feeling of desolation swept over me that I could not bear another moment in the bed. I sat up. And remembered one more thing. Jai. Incredibly, he was here. What had he said? It came to me now. That he'd be sleeping on the sofa.

I swung my legs over to the floor. It felt cold to the soles of my feet. Barefoot, I stumbled into the living room.

The curtains had not been drawn there. In the faint starlight, which came from the window, I saw the sofa was unoccupied. I put up my hand and pressed it to my mouth in anguish. I wanted to weep aloud. Jai wasn't here. He must have gone. My eye fell on the long shape on the, floor. Of course. The sofa could not possibly have accommodated him. An overwhelming wave of relief washed over me, causing my legs to almost give way.

Jai was lying on his stomach, face hidden in the crook of his arm. I fell on my knees beside him, aching for him to awaken. Once I could have reached out and touched him, and he would have opened his eyes, and pulled me into his arms. Now I dared not take such a bold step.

But I had to talk to him—ask him if he thought Scotty was all right. I needed that reassurance desperately. I had lost so many beloved people—my parents—my grandmother—in a different way, my husband—that I had to know if my son was safe.

I whispered his name. He stirred and rolled over onto his back. I called again, and instantly he was awake. He came up on one elbow.

"Lex?" Then more urgently, "What's the matter?"

"Jai." The name came out in a gasping whisper. "Jai—Scotty?"

He sat up at once. "Scotty's fast asleep. I called the Nursing Home. He's absolutely fine, they told me."

"Oh." A sob tore through me. I began to shake uncontrollably from reaction. "Jai—I'm-so afraid."

Strong arms, so familiar to me, wrapped themselves around me. I did not know why I was weeping all of a sudden. Was it for my child? Or for myself, for all that I had lost? I felt the hand on my back, the cheek against my hair, the deep voice so beloved saying in a soft murmur, "It's all right, Lex. My sweet girl. So brave and wonderful. You're not alone now, Lex. I'm here for as long as you need me." It seemed to me I could have no tears left. Sobs still wracked me, but I was a little calmer.

I became conscious of the warm smoothly muscled shoulder, bare under my cheek, the clean masculine fragrance of soap-washed skin.

"Better now?" I nodded without lifting my head. "Want a hot drink?" I shook my head mutely. I was afraid lest I lose this precious closeness. "Then lie here and rest." Still holding me, he lowered himself to the rug again. "How did it happen?" he asked casually. "Obviously, you weren't in the same room as Scotty."

Painfully, voice not quite steady, an occasional sob still escaping me, I tried to put the story together.

When I had finished, Jai said, "Children are tough little creatures. I can speak for the male of the species. When I look back now, and think of the scrapes we three got into, I marvel Mama kept her sanity." I could tell he was smiling. "Absolute horrors!"

"Were you—very naughty?"

"We sure were. I never meant to lead the others astray, but Cy had to do whatever I did, and GeeGee couldn't bear to be left behind. Climbing trees that were too tall for Cy's short legs, and quite impossible for GeeGee's. Inevitably, there were falls, bruises and wounded small boys. If Cy and I put our heads together over some devious scheme, GeeGee had to be a pest, hampering us. And later, he was the one who screamed the loudest. I was always sent for by Papa to explain. When something happened, it was always a case of *cherchez Jai*. I recall one time—" and went on to describe one or two of the hairier escapades of the young Samarthas.

I listened with all attention. If Jai was trying to deflect my mind from Scotty, he was succeeding very well.

A chuckle escaped me. "Oh, Jai! Truly? Poor Mama!" We were lying face to face with not a foot between us, chatting easily without constraint, as if the years had not separated us, as if my life had not been shattered into tiny pieces because of this man's action. Yet too much had happened to throw it off so lightly. I had to get some answers.

Jai was caught by surprise when without warning, I asked, "Jai? Why didn't you marry Ila? I assumed the divorce was an accomplished fact, and that you had married her ages ago."

After a long pause, he responded. "It took me less than twenty-four hours to know what a terrible mistake I had made. When I realized you had vanished without a trace, leaving no word for me—just the jewelry and check books, I think I went a little mad. It was clear enough you wanted to have nothing more to do with me—were cutting yourself away totally."

"But surely—Ila was still there. And you intended to marry her."

"Yes, she was there. Very much so. And once I did think I wanted to marry her. I can't explain it even to myself, Lex. Don't think I haven't tried. It wasn't even an overwhelming sexual attraction. After all, she'd been rattling around the place for eons, and I hadn't felt a thing. Call it a temporary madness or not, my behavior was unforgivable."

"When—when did you break off with her?"

"Within days after you left." We lay silently, each one thinking back over those days." There wasn't a single avenue I didn't explore to find yon. I tried the police, a private investigator, anything I could think of."

I was astonished. "Truly, Jai?"

"Truly. When your letter came to Rusi with those damning words, giving your unconditional consent to a divorce, I examined the envelope repeatedly to find even the smallest clue to your whereabouts. At least she's still in the country, I told myself, and not in Scotland."

"That would have been my next resort if Binty had not been there. But somehow I was loath to leave India, or to become a nuisance to the Camerons."

"They would have taken you in gladly. If it wasn't for the letter postmarked Bombay, I would have tried Dougal, perhaps flown to Scotland myself." His tone altered. "Lex, who is Binty? Can you tell me now where you went?"

After a moment I began to tell him. He was stunned. "You were in Panchgani all the terrible time?" he asked incredulously. "As close as that? Why, I passed through en route to Mahableshwar at least thrice!" A sound of deep pain escaped him. "Was that where you met this man—the one who you said was kind to you—who you still care for?"

"No." I hesitated only for a moment. "I—I knew him earlier."

"Was he the same one who kissed you after you won that contest?"

I was struck dumb. What on earth did he mean?

I thought back carefully. Jai must mean the horse show Mama and GeeGee had attended. Come to think of it, Aftab had kissed me, exuberant as he was over my winning the first prize.

"Was he, Lex?"

I shook myself. "No. Not at all. That was Aftab Dubash. We are childhood friends. He's like a brother to me."

"Some brother! And you're on kissing terms with him?"

"Only on occasion," I said demurely, suppressing a sudden desire to laugh. Did I detect the faintest touch of resentment there—almost akin to jealousy?

"This—this man. Do you still meet him?"

"Oh, Jai, I'd rather not go into that."

"Because you think I'll track him down—have a confrontation with him?"

"Would you do that?" I asked wonderingly.

"Have I any moral right to do it? But yes, I'd like nothing better."

"Why, Jai?"

"Because I'm insanely jealous of him, that's why! Lex-I—" I couldn't believe it was Jai who spoke so passionately. It was a side of him he had never revealed to me before. What had it cost him to utter those words? Jai who was always so controlled? I put out a hand to touch his mouth. It was caught instantly and held to his lips.

"Does—does Scotty remind you of anyone, Jai?"

After a moment, he said, "When he opened his eyes I was sure I was dreaming. He's the mirror image of Papa,"

"Oh," I said gasping, "you guessed!"

He came up on an elbow. "I thought at first I was imagining the resemblance—but it's unmistakable, isn't it?" He bent closer. "Lex, I must know. That night—when you said you had a wonderful surprise—were you going to tell me about the baby?"

I couldn't speak. I was too choked up. But I nodded. He groaned deep in his throat. "I'm the lowliest worm—not fit to live!"

"You couldn't have known, Jai." I touched his face. "That's why I wanted to hold off divorce proceedings—till the baby was born—so that he would be legitimate."

"God!" The expletive burst from his lips. "Then he was born in Panchgani?"

"Yes." There was no point now in concealing the truth. I told him the whole story. At the end, "When Scotty was being born—Binty said—I'd cried out your name."

Jai was motionless. I felt something warm and wet falling on my face. With a shock, I recognized it for what it was. I moved then. I put my arms around his neck, and held him close. "Jai, Jai, you mustn't! You mustn't shed tears for me!" I couldn't bear it. My proud Jai crying for me! I hadn't known he was capable of it. Was this the man Prem had described as having an icicle instead of a heart? I cradled his head to my breast as if he was Scotty coming to me for comfort after a fall. Jai's face was hidden in the hollow of my neck, his whole frame shaken. All I could do was to hold him, smoothing the thick dark hair. Perhaps, as it had been for me earlier, the release was necessary. We had both bottled up our feelings so much too long. After a long time, I sensed he was calmer. He lay still, neither moving nor speaking. I knew then that any initiative now had to come from me. Jai would not make the first move.

My hand was resting on his cheek. I tried to speak lightly. "I always thought beards must feel like steel wool. I'm quite surprised. Yours is rather soft." Still no movement from him. "Do you know, I've always wondered what it would be like to be kissed by a bearded man?"

He said huskily, "Would you—like to find out now?"

"Uh huh," I told him solemnly.

All thoughts of teasing, all consciousness of everything except this one man left me. I knew only the warm reality that was Jai, his closeness, and his feverish kisses.

"Oh God, Lex," he was whispering, his hands moving over me as if he could not believe it was true.

"Jai, I let you think there was someone else. There never has been anyone. It's always been you—only you."

He became still, as if taking the words in, and then crushed me convulsively in his arms. "It's been—a desert without you," he said brokenly. "Lex, Lex."

We were both lost as the tide carried us away relentlessly, shaking us to the very center of our beings until, at last, we were cast up on the shore, spent, still clasped in each other's arms, falling into oblivion.

A long time later, I lifted my head from his shoulder. "Jai?"

"Hmmm?"

I stroked the soft beard. "Is it true—that you want to go away—to America?"

"Who told you that?"

"Cy."

"I have thought of it, yes. When you told me there was no chance of a reconciliation, I felt I had sunk to my lowest depths. All these days, I had clutched at the hope of finding you, begging you to come back to me after asking your forgiveness. When that hope was gone, all I wanted was to get away." I felt his hand caressing my hair. He went on quietly, "You're all that is good and beautiful in my life. You were as fresh as a fragrant flower, so sweet, innocent and lovely. I fell in love with you that evening when you crashed into me by the elevator. Stubborn fool that I was, I didn't recognize it as such. I gave in to my impulse to follow and track you down, acknowledging the strong magnetic pull I felt. And the pragmatic aspects—I wanted you to be the mother of my children because I admired the qualities you possessed. With such crazy preconceived ideas in my head, I never admitted I'd fallen fathoms deep. After you left, I was practically ostracized by the family. GeeGee came right out and called me a monster, a murderer. I couldn't blame them. I hated myself. But it hurt me deeply when Papa said I'd been very wrong to get you involved with me—that you'd been so happy, doing well at Orion—mentioned the success of the Komal campaign. Said you'd have met someone else—who would have cherished you, as you deserved. Did I not cherish you, Lex? Do you feel I didn't?" He put a hand under my chin and made me look at him. "Tell me, Lex."

I was shocked. "Of course you did! Far more than I had ever expected—far more than I deserved. You gave me everything—poured it on me. You withheld one part of yourself from me—but I'd accepted that. Those were the happiest days of my life. You mustn't let what Papa said upset you ever."

"I let you down when you needed me most. I can't get that out of my head. You were having my child—that was when my presence was so essential to give you every support. Oh, Lex." He buried his face against my breast. "I should have been there—right by my wife's side. I've missed the whole wonderful experience. The joyful anticipation of our child, my son's birth, the first year of his life—and I wasn't there," he said in anguish.

"It's all right. It's all right, Jai." I cradled his bead. "We'll have more children." He lifted his head at that, looked deeply into my eyes, and kissed me tenderly. "And next time I want a small replica of Jai."

"No, he will have to wait, I want to put in my first claim. I vote for a wee Lex with green eyes and copper curls."

I was overcome suddenly by happiness, "I'll do my best. And may we call her Fiona?"

"Make that Fiona Roza, and I'm sold." He laughed aloud, a lovely spontaneous sound, and I laughed with him, "Lex, if I can get away sometime, will you come with me to the States? I don't know when, or for how long it will be possible—but will you?"

"I'll come with you to the ends of the earth, Jai." A spasm almost of pain crossed his face, but it vanished quickly. Quietly we held each other, looking into our future together.

The End

0-595-23921-8

CPSIA information can be obtained at www.ICGtesting.com
Printed in the USA
239309LV00004B/120/A